"Can we go meet the beautiful princess, Daddy?"

Mac didn't immediately respond to Megan's request. He was too busy staring at the woman Megan wanted to meet. *Pretty as a princess* didn't do her justice. Spectacular. Cover-model material. Hell, she'd probably graced every major magazine in the country.

"Come on, Daddy. Let's go before she disappears." Megan tugged at his hand.

"Okay, honey, lead the way."

He couldn't help smiling as he followed his beautiful, delightful daughter through the crowd to the ring of bodies grouped around the woman who—even at a glance—seemed out of place on Sentinel Pass's Main Street. Mac didn't know why his heart rate started to speed up as he neared.

"Hi. Hi," Megan chirped, hopping up and down with her hand in the air.

The woman turned Mac's way and suddenly she was looking straight into his eyes. His heart, which wasn't acting normal to begin with, lurched sideways in his chest, making his throat close up. Suddenly he lost all ability to speak…from just one look.

Dear Reader,

Whether you're new to Sentinel Pass or an old friend returning for this fourth book in my series, I think you'll enjoy Mac's story. He's a go-to guy, the rock who feels most comfortable underground, where he's spent most of his life mining. Forgive the cliché, but he has a heart of gold. A heart that was nearly destroyed when his wife left him and his town turned against him. He's still trying to find his footing as a single parent, and he's certainly not looking for love, but...call it fate. Call it *swoo*. You can't call it a coincidence when you fall in love with the worst possible person in the world for you. A make-believe princess with a made-up life story and too many secrets.

I adored Mac from the first moment he appeared in *Baby by Contract*. You gotta love a guy who wants only the best for his family. I didn't expect to like, much less love Morgana Carlyle, Cooper Lindstrom's second ex-wife. But even the best actress can let little bits of her real self show, and I was intrigued. I hope you will be, too.

I owe a very special thanks to Malte and Allix— the almost-five-year-olds—who were a bountiful resource for Mac's daughter, Megan. Let there be elephants.

To become a member-at-large of the Wine, Women and Words Book Club—and for the inside scoop on all things Sentinel Pass—visit my Web site at www.debrasalonen.com.

Debra Salonen

PICTURE-PERFECT MOM
Debra Salonen

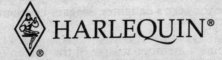

HARLEQUIN®

TORONTO • NEW YORK • LONDON
AMSTERDAM • PARIS • SYDNEY • HAMBURG
STOCKHOLM • ATHENS • TOKYO • MILAN • MADRID
PRAGUE • WARSAW • BUDAPEST • AUCKLAND

Recycling programs
for this product may
not exist in your area.

ISBN-13: 978-0-373-71564-0
ISBN-10:   0-373-71564-1

PICTURE-PERFECT MOM

www.eHarlequin.com

Printed in U.S.A.

ABOUT THE AUTHOR

Debra comes from a long line of storytellers. At slumber parties her mother would enthrall Deb's girlfriends with stories of growing up on the prairie near Pierre, South Dakota. (For you *Jeopardy!* purists, that's pronounced Peer.) One goose-bump-inducing story involved unearthing the casket of a pioneer woman in an unmarked grave. Deb had no problem picturing her mother sitting in the dark, guarding the poor woman's remains while Grandpa Bagby rode back to town for the sheriff. It was a better story than the one involving rattlesnakes.... Nobody got any sleep on the nights she told *that* story.

Books by Debra Salonen

*Texas Hold 'Em
**Spotlight on Sentinel Pass

Daisy B. Robson
May 16, 1913–May 12, 2008
"Those were the days…"

CHAPTER ONE

"SO, WE HAVE A DEAL?"

Mac McGannon nodded, although he wasn't completely sure what he'd just agreed to. Something about excavating for a swimming pool at Mrs. Smith's old house. A swimming pool in Sentinel Pass, South Dakota? That made even less sense than seeing a glamorous movie star chatting with locals on the street of his small Black Hills town.

He forced his gaze to leave the woman he'd been staring at for the past ten heart-stopping seconds and looked at Jack Something-or-other. Kat Petroski's R.U.B. That's what everyone in town was calling him—an acronym for Rich, Urban Biker. In all fairness, Jack seemed like a decent guy with a lot on the ball. And Mac's sister, Libby, was convinced this guy was Kat's time-traveling soul mate. The embodiment of all things *swoo*.

Mac doubted that. He was pretty damn sure Kat's made-up word for the intangible connection between a certain man and a certain woman was pure fantasy. He'd bought into the myth once...and lost nearly everything he held dear because of it. Although he had gained one precious little gift. Megan. His daughter.

"Um...sure. Give me a call when you're ready to go," he told Jack.

The two shook hands, then Jack left, grinning as if he'd just won the lottery.

Poor jerk, Mac thought, looking around for his daughter. Not that Kat wasn't a great gal. If the two of them found a way to be happy together, Mac was all for it. But Misty had taught him that no amount of love in the world can ensure a lifetime of happiness. It didn't work that way.

"Daddy," a small, sweet voice chirped.

Mac turned at the sound and opened his arms to the four—almost five—year-old racing toward him. "Hey, sweetness, I was just looking for you. Where have you been? With your aunt Lib?"

Megan's head of shoulder-length auburn curls nodded affirmatively, causing a pink barrette that he didn't recognize to slip down. She'd inherited Misty's thick gorgeous hair, but her mother had never been happy with her color. Misty had been a blonde when they married but indigo-black at the end. He'd never understood that. Hell, he'd never understood her.

"Auntie bought me candy. The kind that's not good for you," his daughter boasted.

"Hey," a familiar voice complained. "That was supposed to be our secret." Mac knew when his sister was teasing, and so did Megan. Her aunt's complaint only made the twinkle in Megan's eyes more pronounced.

"I'm handing her off to you, MacDuff." His sister had a habit of calling him nicknames he didn't like or appreciate. This was a new one. Libby ignored his scowl. "Cooper's showing signs of exploding into a frenetic ball of craziness if I don't go rescue him. He wants so badly for the locals to accept his people he's hovering like an overprotective parent on the first day of school."

Mac had to smile at the analogy. Libby not only loved her husband, she understood Cooper Lindstrom better than the bad-boy-of-Hollywood knew himself. Mac envied that connection.

He'd had that kind of close bond once. Or maybe he only thought he had, but he could remember a time when Lib had envied him—not the other way around. Now, he was alone, and she was the one thriving in a happy, mutually fulfilling relationship. "Go. Do your matchmaking thing. Megan and I will be right here."

"That's what you think, McDipwad."

His eyes opened wide and he looked at his daughter. "Did you hear what she called me?"

Megan giggled impishly. "She's mad at you because you were talking to Kat's boyfriend instead of mangling with the strangers."

"Mingling," he corrected, giving her a kiss on the nose. "Fine." He set her down and offered his hand. "Let's mangle."

"Can we go meet the beautiful princess, Daddy? I think she might be Snow White."

Libby laughed and shook her head. "Snow White had black hair. The lady you're talking about has my color hair. The hair colorist actually took a clipping of mine to match it, isn't that funny?"

Mac didn't say anything. As far as he was concerned the entire concept of filming a TV show in Sentinel Pass was whacko. He'd managed to get along with Cooper and Shane Reynard, Coop's friend who was also the producer or director or whatever of the show. But this horde of new people who had descended for a week of on-site taping was nothing short of bizarre.

"Okay, reddish-brown," Megan said, tugging on his hand. "She's still as pretty as a princess. Let's go meet her."

Mac knew who Megan meant. The woman he'd been staring at when he should have been paying attention to Jack—a prospective customer. *Pretty as a princess* didn't do her justice. Spectacular. Cover-model material. Hell, she'd probably graced every major magazine in the country. He wouldn't know. He was a miner who usually had his head underground.

"Good idea, Megan," Libby said. "Go rescue her from Marva and Elana Grace." To Mac, she qualified her statement. "Elana's harmless, but once Marva discovered there was money to be made in the gossip trade, she really started living up to her nickname."

Mac frowned. Marva "The Mouth" Ploughman had been one of Sentinel Pass's loudest voices questioning whether or not Mac might have caused his wife's fatal car accident. He had a tough time being civil to her, but he genuinely liked Elana, who ran The Tidbiscuit, the town's only year-round coffee shop.

"Okay, girlie-girl, let's go. We can be social. Does anybody know her name?"

"She's Libby, Daddy."

"Huh?"

"In the show," his sister qualified. "She's playing my character. I'm not sure I like the fact that they kept my and Cooper's first names for the main characters, but they did. She's Libby, but her real name is Morgana Carlyle. She's Coop's second ex-wife."

Mac felt his jaw drop. He looked at the stunning woman wearing the wide-brim hat and fashionable sundress. A mix of Jackie O and JLo.

Libby gave him a little shove. "If you're thinking what I think you're thinking, I'm going to smack you over the head with the talking stick next time you burst into our book club meeting."

He shook his head. "She's pretty, but nobody can hold a candle to you, Lib. Not in Coop's eyes, at least. And that's all that matters, right?"

Her concerned look softened and in her smile he read sympathy. She gave him a quick hug. "You're such a good-hearted person, Mac. Remember how envious I was of you and Misty when you first got married? I'd moan and fret about whether or not Mr. Right would ever wander into my life." She looked skyward as if imploring some divine entity to airbrush the edges of her memory. "Now look at us. Coop is everything I could have dreamed—and more. And Misty is gone. One might think some spiteful deity doesn't want us both to be happy at the same time, but don't believe it, Mac. You're going to love again. I know it."

He wished he shared her confidence, but before he could reply his daughter tugged on his hand. "Come on, Daddy. Let's go before she disappears."

"Don't worry, Megan. Morgana's here all week," Libby told them.

Morgana. Another M-name. Mac had argued with his wife until he was blue in the face to name Megan something else. Anything else, as long as it didn't start with an *M*. But Misty had been adamant. Of course, at the time he'd been unable to deny her anything. So, they became the alliterative family with the return address that read M3MG.

"Okay, honey, lead the way."

He couldn't help smiling as he followed his beautiful, brilliant, delightful daughter through the crowd. He acknowledged several familiar faces with a nod and a smile, but his thoughts were on Megan. She had a willful streak that he knew came from him. Stubborn and single-minded—just like Dad, Libby liked to say. And lately, Megan's focus was consumed by her desire to own a dog.

"But, Daddy, you promised."

"But, Daddy, we need one."

"But, Daddy, every little girl should have a puppy. Great-gran said so."

Mac was almost positive his grandmother had said no such thing, but he couldn't prove it. Gran hadn't been herself for a long time. But Mary McGannon, the woman who'd raised him and Libby after their parents died, had never denied him any of the animals in the eclectic menagerie of his youth.

Maybe, he thought, grasping for a small grain of hope, having all these new people in town would provide enough of a diversion that he could stall a bit longer. Although it might be unfair to his daughter, he wasn't ready for a dog. Pets required an emotional commitment he simply didn't have the heart for.

But try telling that to a four-year-old.

"Meggie…hold up," he called as she plowed through the outer ring of bodies grouped around the woman who—even at a glance—seemed out of place on Sentinel Pass's Main Street. Mac didn't know why his heart rate started to speed up as he neared the crowd. He knew most of the people. The men, anyway. And Elana and Marva. Half a dozen other people—part of the production crew or a body-guard detail, he had no idea—stood nearby.

To make sure she wasn't crushed, he decided when he was close enough to see her from head to toe. The woman was toothpick-thin. He knew that was the fashion, but his gut instinct was to take her home and fatten her up a little.

"Hi. Hi," Megan chirped, hopping up and down with her hand in the air as Mac caught up with her.

The woman turned toward them, her head tilting slightly so the brim of her hat dipped down, blocking Mac's line of sight to her face. "Hello, there. My name's Morgana. What's yours?"

Megan stepped closer. "I'm Megan. You're my auntie. Sorta."

The woman's chin popped up and suddenly she was looking straight into Mac's eyes. His heart, which wasn't acting normal to begin with, lurched sideways in his chest, making his throat close up. His explanation was lost as he stared into her rich golden-brown eyes—color he'd mine forever if he ran across it in a vein of rock.

"She's Libby McGannon…I mean, Libby Lindstrom's niece," Elana Grace said, putting a hand on Megan's head. "Isn't she a beauty? Spitting image of her mama, who's gone now. Poor thing. This is her daddy, Mac McGannon."

"Libby's brother? The miner?" Morgana's face lit up with what Mac would have sworn was honest delight. "I love your character in the show. Dark and tortured. Zane is doing a fabulous job with the role. Have you met Zane? Wonderful actor. He's the one who turned me on to product endorsements. This wholesome small-town postmaster thing really won over my cosmetics company. They think Libby is going to appeal to Middle America like you won't believe."

Even if Mac had been able to speak, he had no idea how to reply to something like that. So, he did what he usually did when faced with awkward situations. He kept his mouth closed.

"You own a cosmetics company?"

The question came from the woman who owned the town's only restaurant. Morgan had been introduced to her shortly before the handsome miner and his daughter joined them. From her peripheral vision, she could see the rapt attention of the restaurant owner's friend, who was all but taking notes. Morgan's paparazzi radar kicked in. She knew anything she said would be repeated—probably inaccurately—in some tabloid the next day.

Although it would probably prove a waste of breath, she tried to set the record straight. "I recently signed with FreshFace, a new, green and sustainable division of…" She whispered the name of the company, knowing that being given insider information would make her listeners remember it better. "The products use all natural ingredients. The pomegranate vinegar hair rinse is amazing, but my personal favorite is the carrot cake scrub. Yum."

The child looked at her father and made a face. In truth, Morgan felt the same way. The samples she'd been given weren't all that great. But the money the company was paying her to promote the stuff was worth every smile she had to fake.

She looked at the little girl's father again. The guy was big-screen handsome in a down-to-earth way. The lean, sharp angles of his jaw and cheekbones made him look sort of dangerous and haughty. His thick masculine eyebrows had obviously never heard of wax. Oddly enough, that rustic realness was what she found most appealing about him.

A throwback to my roots?

She pushed the thought away. Just being back in the middle of the country was bad enough. She didn't need to start remembering. She'd erased every tie to that inglorious beginning for a reason. And it was more imperative now than ever that her past remain a secret. After all, her current corporate bigwigs had picked her specifically because of what they believed was her poor-little-rich-girl backstory. If they had wanted a dirt-poor-orphaned-farm-girl, they would have picked someone else.

"My mommy made carrot cake for m' birthday. When I was four," she said pointedly. "I'm almost five now. Right, Daddy?"

The child had to tug on her father's hand to get him to respond. His gaze hadn't left Morgan. She was used to men staring at her. In fact, she counted on that kind of response. Normally, she was so inured to ogling and leers she felt nothing. But this man's stare was different. It was as though he was looking beneath her perfect makeup and designer dress to her chemical composition. She couldn't repress a shiver.

Which he caught. She could tell because his eyes opened slightly wider.

"What, honey? Oh. Your cake. It was good. But your mom didn't bake it."

"Yes, she did," the little girl insisted. "She said it was her mommy's receipt."

"Recipe," Morgana and the man said at the same time.

Morgan felt herself blush. Good lord. She didn't go around correcting children. She didn't have a motherly bone in her body.

Megan pouted. "Yeah. That."

Mac's eyes, which were the same shade of dark chocolate—Morgan's one vice—returned to her for the briefest of seconds. She wondered if he'd read her thoughts.

Then he lowered himself to one knee beside his daughter and pulled her gently to face him. When he leaned his head to touch hers, Morgan got a clear view of their profiles. She saw a family resemblance despite what that Elana woman had said about Megan looking like her mother. Megan's upturned nose was different and reminded Morgan of someone, but she couldn't think of a name. Probably a child star she'd acted with over the past dozen or so years of her career.

"Megan, love, your mommy liked to grow things in her garden but when it came to eating the stuff…well…she preferred things that came from the store. Don't ask me why. Mommy bought the cake you're talking about from a lady in Rapid City. It was special for her special little girl. And it was very yummy."

Morgan could tell that Megan was satisfied by her father's explanation. "Oh. Okay. Can I go play with Jordie? His mommy went on the motorcycle and Miss Char was watching him, but she's back now." She started to take off, but he caught her arm in a gentle way. She stopped, but her impatience was clearly visible in her knitted brow. "Jenna's there, too, Daddy, and she has her dog. His name is Luca," she said to Morgan. "We're going to get a dog soon. Aren't we, Daddy?"

Her father's groan was barely audible but Morgan heard it—and had to bite her lip to keep from smiling.

"Not one that big. Luca could eat you for lunch. Stick by Jordie. At least he doesn't bite." He planted a tender little peck on her forehead then patted her bottom as she turned to dash off. "Remember…if you can't see me, I can't see you. That's the rule."

She skipped off a few feet then stopped to look back. "You're very beautiful, princess. Bye."

The comment sent a funny thrill through Morgan. She'd been called beautiful thousands of times, but this compliment was so genuine it touched her heart. She blinked back the unexpected moisture in her eyes. "Thank you," she called after her newest fan.

Once she had her emotions under control, she looked at Mac and said, "Your daughter is lovely. And you don't have to worry about Luca. Shane's brought him to the set several times and he has the manners of an old-world butler. Polite and regal."

His expression turned skeptical, but there was a hint of resignation in the set of his jaw. He might not *want* a dog, but he was going to have one. The thought crossed her mind that this might be the definition of a real dad—doing for your child the last thing in the world you want to do.

"Is Jordie Megan's boyfriend?" she asked, changing the subject.

"Good God, I hope not," he said with feeling. "Elana Grace, you know what's going on in this town better than anyone. Is Megan seeing Jordie Petroski behind my back?"

His tone was light, but Morgan heard a faint hint of bitterness. She wondered…but the older woman's answer caught her attention. "No, Mac, I think you're safe for a few years. Jordie's more interested in arrowheads from what I hear. If he's in love with anyone, it's Char Jones."

Mac's grin made the lines at his eyes crinkle in a totally real and sexy way. "Isn't she a little old for him?"

Elana Grace looked at her friend and shrugged her thin, slightly stooped shoulders. "You know men. No accounting for taste."

Mac's smile disappeared. He inhaled sharply and straightened as if someone had poked him. Even Zane couldn't have portrayed repressed hurt more convincingly. Mac nodded to the three of them and said, "I'd better go check on the grilling."

"As in…interrogation?" Morgan quipped, hoping to lighten the moment so he'd stick around.

He pointed to the emblem on his shirt pocket. "Volunteer firefighter. Presently inactive." His frown told her this wasn't by choice. "Cooper hired us to cater lunch. I may not be able to train with the guys or go on calls because I don't have a wife at home to watch my kid, but I know my way around a grill." He gave Morgan a tight, polite smile then left.

The gossip lady—Morgan's label for her—made a tsking sound. "He took that personal, Elana."

Her friend looked distressed. "I didn't mean it that way. His wife wasn't a bad person, but she was never right for him. You could see that from the first day he brought her home. Another one of his poor, broken things. Mac tried his best to fix her, but in the end…"

Morgana caught herself leaning closer to catch the woman's words.

"Yep," the gossip lady said, her too-pink lips pulled to one side in a look of disgust. "She used him and left him. Some men can't see beyond the pretty trappings. Hopefully, Mac learned his lesson with Misty."

Misty?

Morgan lost the feeling in her fingers momentarily and her purse slipped to the ground. Grass stains on her Kenneth Cole bag were the least of her problems, she thought as she gracefully dipped to pick up the few personal items that had spilled. Lipstick. Cell phone. PDA. Driver's license.

She ignored the hubbub around her as the crew members Shane had asked to look after her rushed to her aid.

It's okay. Everything is fine. There have to be hundreds—thousands—of women named Misty. No way in frigging hell could Mac McGannon's wife—late wife—be my Misty. No. Not possible.

Even the older women tried to help. They were kind. Sweet. Genuine people. Exactly the opposite of her. She was an actor. A made-up person who played other made-up people for a living. A marginal living that was finally starting to pay off. As long as she remembered who she was…and who she wasn't.

CHAPTER TWO

"She's the one, Daddy. I know in my heart she was meant to be ours."

Mac dropped to a squat beside his daughter and watched her squeeze her tiny little hand inside a gap of the animal shelter's chain-link fencing to touch the scruffy, white-blond coat of the pen's lone occupant.

All the other concrete and metal holding pens had two or more dogs. He wondered what made this animal special—or dangerous. "Don't put your hand in there, Megan. It might bite."

"No, she won't, Daddy. She loves me. Can't you tell?"

Me? Mac was the last person to ask. He'd gone in blind and wound up blindsided by love. Only for Megan would he risk opening up his poor battered heart again. And he knew himself well enough to admit he couldn't adopt a pet and not become emotionally attached.

"How do you know it's a she?" he asked, not curious enough to put his head near the dusty concrete floor to look at the dog's underside. There was a typed card in a plastic holder on the door of the cage, but he'd left his reading glasses in the truck. The funky plastic-frame glasses were a symbol of how old and worn-out he'd felt lately. They weren't prescription. What single father could afford the time or money to see an eye doctor? He'd picked up an over-the-counter pair at Walgreens and they worked okay...when he remembered to put them in his pocket.

"I just do," Megan said equitably. "Isn't she beautiful, Daddy?"

Beautiful? Scruffy, matted and in need of a bath was his opinion, which he kept to himself.

At that moment the exterior door to the shelter opened and a young woman walked in. The name tag on her colorful lab coat said Sondra. In letters big enough for Mac to read.

"Hi. You work here, right? What can you tell us about this dog?"

"Her name is Morgana," Megan said, looking up. The dog, whose mouth was at least twice as big as Megan's hand, began licking the little girl's fingers.

Megan laughed in a way Mac remembered hearing but couldn't pinpoint the last time he'd heard the sound. Going on a year or better, he thought bitterly. About the time her mother decided she didn't want to be married to a tightwad, mostly broke miner anymore.

"Really?" the woman exclaimed. "I didn't know that. I asked her her name when the animal control officer brought her in, but she wouldn't say. How clever of you to listen so closely."

Mac removed Megan's hand from the cage. "No, sweetheart," he said firmly. He might have lost control over every other aspect of his life, but he wasn't going to lose this battle twice. "Morgana is a nice name, but we have enough M-names in the family. Think of something else."

Morgana *was* a nice name. But it was also tied to a real person. A heart-stoppingly gorgeous woman he hadn't stopped thinking about in the two days since Cooper's All-Sentinel Pass party. Mac didn't need another beautiful—very temporary—woman complicating his life. And he damn well wasn't going to adopt a dog with that name.

"How 'bout Bella? That starts with a…buh, buh, *B,*" she said, mimicking the phonic letter sound of her favorite computer game.

"That's a very pretty name," the young staffer said. "I'm sorry I don't know Bella's history, but I can try to find out, if you don't mind waiting."

"We don't need to wait, Daddy. Bella will tell me everything once she gets to know me better."

I wouldn't count on that. She's a female, after all.

"Well, it pays to find out these things ahead of time, Miss M," he said, trying to mask his bone-deep cynicism. He could blame Misty for that, but why bother? She was gone and he had to move on—hopefully without carrying too much toxic baggage. For Megan's sake, if not his own. To the lab tech, he said, "Thanks. I'd appreciate anything you can tell us."

"Is this your first?" the pretty young woman asked. Her tone was kind, and possibly even interested in a man-woman way. Or was that wishful thinking?

"Um…Megan's first," he said, his mind scrambling over some very unfamiliar terrain. He couldn't remember the last time he'd felt like anything other than a single dad trying to keep his head above water. He honestly couldn't be sure what kinds of signals he might be getting. Or giving off. "Her mother was allergic."

Smart move. Bring up the dead wife. That's a surefire way to flirt with a pretty girl.

She smiled and left.

Libby liked to say Mac had inherited a uniquely McGannon look from their father. She called it the "maroon gloom." "Comes from working in a mine," she'd tried to explain to Misty. "Rocks don't care what you're thinking so it's easy to shut down emotionally when you're underground."

He couldn't argue that their childhood hadn't been the most bucolic, but he'd never felt particularly gloomy—until last November when his wife announced she was leaving him for another man.

He looked at his daughter as she spoke in a soft whisper to the dog. A part of him, he had to admit, was relieved that Megan's ten-month campaign for a puppy was over. He only had himself to blame. He'd casually agreed to the idea of a pet as a way to compensate for the loss of her mother, but no hamster, fish-filled aquarium or parakeet had been enough.

"Wally's gone, Daddy. I think he died. I haven't heard him making noise in the wall behind my bed for weeks," she'd told him that morning.

Wally—the small tan-and-white rodent whose original name he'd forgotten—had somehow escaped from his high-tech plastic condo in Megan's bedroom and moved into a vacant mouse hole. Mac wished he could have worked up more angst over the loss, but he was actually relieved.

"He's gone to heaven to be with Mommy. That's why I need a dog, Daddy. Dogs don't get lost as easy."

The gone-to-heaven-to-be-with-Mommy card had been the pay shot. Not that Megan knew what that was. She wasn't a master of manipulation like Misty. She was a lonely little girl who needed a dog. And he was the jerk standing in the way of her happiness.

He wasn't sure if Misty actually used those words the

day she told him goodbye but it was possible. Some of her words he'd never forget.

"All you do is work, Mac. If you're not in a truck, you're at the mine. Well, guess what? I need more than that. I'm leaving and I'm taking Meggie with me."

That was the point in the conversation where "all hell broke loose," as one of his neighbors so self-righteously put it when the police started investigating. Misty had carried their fight out of the house to the front lawn. For all of Sentinel Pass to either witness or hear about the next day.

Mac had stood his ground and refused to let Megan get in the car with her. Not once since that day did he regret losing his cool, despite the suspicion it threw his way. He'd physically yanked the sobbing child out of Misty's arms and had refused to listen to Megan's pleas to go with her mommy. He understood why Megan wanted to go—she was certainly closer to her stay-at-home mother than her workaholic father. But where Megan was concerned, Mac's line in the sand never wavered. And he thanked God every day since that he'd had the backbone to fight for his daughter.

Misty had slammed the car door and tore out of the driveway without a backward glance. That early-winter evening was the last time Mac saw her. Luckily, dental records and DNA had provided the means to identify her body after a hiker discovered a wrecked and burned-out car at the bottom of a gully not ten miles from Sentinel Pass.

"Honey girl," Mac said, focusing his attention back on the present, "I know I said you could pick out our dog, but *with* my help, remember? We talked about not going over a certain size. We don't want one that is going to get as big as Jenna and Shane's dog, right?"

Megan looked up, her eyes wide with surprise. "Why

not, Daddy? Luca is a dreamboat. Maybe he and Bella could get married and have puppies someday."

Dreamboat? Where did she get words like that? he wondered. "Nope. Sorry, kiddo. That's not going to happen. The rules for buying a rescue dog include one about agreeing to have the animal neutered."

"New-tered? Is that better than oldered?"

He worked to keep from smiling. "Neutered means they can't have babies."

"That's mean."

He shrugged. "It's the rule."

Sondra returned at that moment, a clipboard in hand. She obviously assumed this transaction was a done deal. "Okay. Here's what we know. It's not a lot, but—"

"You're mean," Megan said, her bottom lip quivering as she faced the surprised lab tech.

"P-pardon?"

"I told her all the animals that leave this shelter are spayed or neutered. She thinks that's cruel. I don't share that opinion, by the way."

"Oh," Sondra exclaimed. She immediately dropped to one knee and launched into a long, mostly-over-Megan's-head speech about responsible pet ownership. Mac didn't know if the young woman's passion or her message won Megan over, but he could tell his daughter now accepted the fact that her dog wasn't going to procreate.

Megan reached into the pen again and petted the dog's wide, squarish crown. "It's okay, Bella. You can still come live with us, even if you can't have puppies."

"If," Mac stressed, "we find out… Oh, never mind. You started to tell us about this one?" he asked the tech.

"The card says Lab–Border Collie mix. I have no idea

if that's a guess or the former owner knew for sure. I can tell you that she's up to date on her shots, she's been wormed and appears to be very healthy."

Mac was too tired to argue. He knew from the parenting magazines he'd forced himself to read each month that Megan was still processing her mother's death. Megan's most recent explanation for her mother's absence was: "Mommy's helping Jesus plow his garden in Heaven." An image planted and fertilized, no doubt, by Megan's daycare provider, Barb Kellen.

Mac could only hope Misty was plowing by hand. On the edge of Hell. Without a hat.

Bitter? He thought sardonically. *Not me.*

But it was hard not to harbor resentment toward a woman who'd left him for another man, stolen his inheritance and totaled a car she'd begged him to buy less than six months earlier.

At least his finances were starting to stabilize. With the infusion of money from his brother-in-law, Mac had been able to quit his job at the gravel pit and devote more time to updating his equipment and doing some freelance backhoe jobs. And clean up the Little Poke, where some of this week's filming was taking place.

The future was looking up. He and Coop were still hashing out the plans, but Mac hoped to turn the place into a paying operation again—even if it wasn't a working mine. He'd made a promise to his grandmother when he took over the mine that he'd keep it in the family. He was still honoring that promise—just not in the way it was intended. Unfortunately, mining was only lucrative for wealthy conglomerates, not for a single father with too many family obligations. Gran would understand…if she were still herself.

"So…" he said, coming to grips with the fact that they were going home with this shaggy mutt. "How 'bout we swing by Gran's and introduce her to Bella?"

Megan clapped with joy, which spooked the dog. The animal barked a soft, muffled woof and hunkered down as if expecting to be kicked. The soft spot in Mac's heart that had made him collect wounded things ever since he was a kid opened wide enough for a new addition to his collection. He'd only had a couple of failures over the years. A hawk that nearly took off his finger—he'd been glad to let that one go—and Misty, of course. His biggest failure of all. Despite all the love and patience he'd tried to give her, she'd never come around.

"You can't fix them all," Gran had told him after the hawk incident. "Watch that scar on your finger. It will grow thicker and tougher than the skin around it. Some animals—and people—have scars you can't see, and believe me, there are some that never get better. Ever."

She'd been right, of course.

He looked at his watch. He had to swing by the real-estate agent's office and pick up the plans Jack Treadwell had faxed. Kat's dentist from Denver wasn't wasting any time planning his move. Other than that, Mac was free to help Bella assimilate into the family. A process that normally wouldn't be complete without Gran's approval.

"Okay, Miss M," he said soberly. "You're sure this is the right dog?"

Megan clapped ecstatically and threw herself into his arms. "Thank you, Daddy. You're the best daddy ever. Bella and I both love you. Don't we, Bella?"

He looked at the scruffy, far-from-pedigreed dog that

was studying him with serious brown eyes. He was pretty sure Bella had her doubts—and the feeling was mutual—but there was no denying Megan's instant connection with the animal. Who was he to question the authenticity of love at first sight simply because it didn't work out for him?

"I guess we have ourselves a dog."

"YOU DON'T GET IT, do you?" Morgan said to her costar, making an effort to remember that he was Cooper-the-actor, not Cooper-her-ex-husband. "You don't belong here."

Coop looked wounded. He was really good at looking wounded. His expression made women go, "Ohh…poor boy. Let me open up my heart, my wallet, my bank account and take care of you."

"You're wrong about that, Libby. You want me to be just a nondimensional cardboard character, but I'm not. I'm more— What?" He groaned, obviously sensing her unintentional response to his gaffe. "She's giving me that look, Shane."

"I am not." But she was. She couldn't help it. Morgan had always been able to sense when Coop's mind wasn't on his work. She didn't know where his brain was at the moment, but they'd been struggling with this scene for three takes, so it was apparent to everyone he was preoccupied.

"Cut," Shane's voice called. "It's one-dimensional, Coop."

Cooper's naturally full lips pouted. Coop was a good kisser. Morgan had liked that part of their sexual relationship the best when they'd been married. Not that he wasn't an okay lover, but she liked foreplay—the cuddling, kissing, petting, wooing—better than actual sex. William, her agent, called her a good beginner, a fair middler and a terrible ender. He was referring to her life in general, not sex, since theirs was a wholly professional relationship. Some in the business believed William was gay, but Morgan knew otherwise. He was particular. She liked that about him. She didn't like his poking his nose into the non-professional parts of her life.

"Darn," Coop said. "I always get that mixed up." He rolled his eyes at Morgan, then looked pleadingly at Shane. "Can we take a break? I want to call Lib and see how Gran is doing."

Shane, who was standing twenty feet away under an umbrella that had been erected to keep the director and main cameraman in the shade, checked his watch, then nodded. "Half an hour, people. That's thirty minutes for those of you who don't know how to tell time." He was looking at Coop when he added the last.

Morgan sucked in her upper lip to keep from smiling. She knew Cooper wasn't dumb. But at times he came across scattered and a little simple. His mother had always been able to keep him in line with a sharp look and a lifted eyebrow. Morgan had hated that look when she'd been Lena Lindstrom's daughter-in-law.

Good riddance had been Morgan's first thought when she heard the old battle-ax was gone. *Maybe now Coop will have a real life.*

And it appeared she'd been both right and prophetic. Shortly after Lena passed away, Cooper had followed his instincts to the Black Hills, where he'd found both a story and the love of his life. Morgan knew she wasn't going to be that lucky. She'd visited the Hills once as a young child. She'd never expected to return, and, honestly, couldn't wait to get back to L.A. to start work on the new ad campaign. The sooner that money was in the bank, the sooner she could breathe easy and look for an acting project to be her "breakout" piece.

As William often reminded her, shelf life in Hollywood wasn't much longer than Starbucks' scones. Morgan knew she needed to make her move soon if she was going to segue to the large screen. Unless, of course, *Sentinel Passtime* became a hit. She could live with that, too. In her book, money was better than fame. With fame came questions she never wanted to answer.

"Morgana," a female voice called.

Morgan looked around until she located a pretty brunette cuddled up tight in Cooper's arms. Morgan wondered why she felt not one twinge of jealousy. She'd only been married to Coop for nine months, but that was an eternity in Hollywood time.

"Oh, hi, Libby," Morgan said, putting down the stack of fake mail she'd been holding in the scene. Morgan and Libby had met several times since filming began. Libby had generously offered to let Morgan stay in the little cottage that had once belonged to her grandmother. "How's your grandmother?"

Libby's brown eyes filled with tears. "She isn't eating. I want to take her to the doctor, but Cal—who I guess you'd call her common-law husband—has Gran's durable power of attorney and he doesn't agree. And he's the one author-ized to make health decisions on her behalf. If my brother had a cell phone, I'd call him about fighting this in court, but he doesn't, and he probably wouldn't do that anyway."

Morgan had no idea what to say. The last time she'd been involved in life-and-death matters she'd been a child and had had no say—one way or the other.

Libby took a halting breath and rested her cheek against

Cooper's shoulder. "Mac would say Cal is right. Gran never wanted anyone sticking needles and tubes and stuff into her when it was her time. But I can't help thinking she just needs some…I don't know what. There must be something."

"I wish I could offer you some suggestions, Libby. My father is a lawyer, but he specializes in tort law." A lie. But one she'd said so often she almost believed it.

"And Morgana hasn't talked to her parents in what—fifteen years?" Coop said, making a Cooperesque quantum leap of topic. "For all you know, they could be dead, right?"

Morgan took note of the way Libby flinched at Cooper's blunt question. She'd try to remember to use that body language sometime if the right situation came up in the script. As far as she knew, Shane and Jenna hadn't written in anyone's untimely demise, but Libby's response bespoke an innate and deeply abiding empathy that Morgan could use.

"Cooper, as I've told you many times in the past, you're so far past obtuse you're practically a circle."

His handsome, perfectly shaped eyebrows flickered in hurt and surprise. Actually, she'd never said that to him in the past, but the ploy got him off the topic of her imaginary parents.

Libby patted her husband's cheek tenderly. "She's kidding. And you both need to get back to work. I just popped in for a quick hug of support before I head back to Gran's."

Morgan started to leave but Libby stopped her. "Did Coop remember to ask you to dinner? Mac left a message on my phone that he and Megan are going to drop by Gran's to show off Megan's new puppy, so I'll invite them, too."

Morgana shook her head. "No. He never mentioned it. Thank you so much for asking, but I couldn't possibly impose."

Libby looked at Cooper.

"Morgie…"

Morgan gave her usual exaggerated sigh. "You know I hate being called that." Because it reminded her of her childhood and a person who called her that day and night.

"Morgie, I need you."

"Morgie, tuck me in."

"Morgie, why did Mommy and Daddy die?"

"I know," Coop replied. "But it's also the name that gets your attention. So? Can you come to Libby's hou—" His wife elbowed him. "I mean, our house for dinner? Or, rather, *supper,* as they say around here."

Morgan knew supper. It had taken years and years of voice coaches and linguists to get her to drop her midwestern accent and phraseology. "I'd planned on going over my lines. We're filming our hike scene tomorrow. Remember?"

Cooper looked at his wife tenderly. "How can I forget? It's the moment I knew for sure she loved me."

Libby threw back her head and laughed. The sound was infectious and Morgan felt heads turning. She realized at that moment that Libby truly was beautiful. She wasn't surprised that Cooper had fallen for her—just that he took the time to notice. Maybe that's what getting lost in the hills was all about and why Shane felt compelled to use the location.

Libby was still grinning when she reached out and touched her hand to Morgan's arm. "Please come. If I can't feed Gran, I've got to feed somebody. And I've been feeling so neglectful with you in the guest cottage and Cooper and I in the main house. I'm not usually such a lousy hostess, but it's been…well, hectic."

The actress in Morgan recognized that she was being offered a chance to watch and learn from the woman she'd been hired to portray. That tipped the scales. She wasn't particularly practiced at family get-togethers, but she'd suffered through worse for her art.

"You're very kind. I'd be delighted to join you tonight. What may I bring?" Good breeding meant good manners, one of Morgan's acting coaches once told her. She'd never forgotten.

"Well…if you have a chance to pick up a bottle of wine, great. If not, don't worry about it. I have sun tea brewing. A delicious herbal blend I ordered online. It's called SummerBrew."

Tea sounded great. Morgan didn't drink, but Morgana owned an extensive wine cellar and knew all the right terms of a vinophile. "I'd be happy to bring wine. There must be a liquor store in town."

Cooper let out a hoot. "Yeah, right. Sentinel Pass's lone bar carries beer only. When I suggested the names of a couple of reds and a midrange chardonnay to the owner, the locals nearly fell off their bar stools laughing."

Libby had that resigned look on her face again, then suddenly she brightened. "I know. Mac can drive you to the Junction. They have a nice selection."

Mac. The miner. The man who refused to get out of her head. Morgan had run through the dialogue they'd shared at the Sentinel Pass party a dozen or more times. She wasn't sure where her fascination with the guy stemmed from—his raw, unpolished masculinity or the questions surrounding his past. Plus there was that small coincidence that his wife shared the same name as someone in her past. Her real past.

This morning between takes, she'd joined a group of locals who had been hired as extras. As subtly as possible, she'd asked a few leading questions. Was Libby's brother seeing anyone? Did he still work in the mine? Where was his late wife from and how did they meet?

Kat, the pretty little blonde who had been giving henna tattoos on the side, had cut short the gossip. "Mac is a good friend who's had a rough time this past year. Enough said."

Maybe if Morgan satisfied her curiosity about his late wife, she'd be able to get him off her mind. "If you're sure it's no bother, I'd love to see a little more of your delightful country," she told Libby. "I believe my last scene is at four. *If*—" she stressed the word for Cooper's benefit "—a certain leading man can keep his mind on his lines."

Coop gave Morgan a look she remembered all too well from their short marriage. It said quite eloquently, "Bite me."

CHAPTER THREE

"THE TROUBLE WITH small towns is they don't play by the rules," Mac complained to his sister.

"What rules?" Libby was sitting on the love seat across from Gran's chair—a well-padded recliner that was supposed to keep the elderly woman's ankles from swelling.

"The one that requires you to get your dog fixed before you take it home. Megan blinked her eyes a few times and sniffled a bit and the pretty young intern caved. I saw it happen right before my eyes."

"She was pretty? How young? You know, Mac, you should start thinking about dating again. You should—"

"Get the damn dog spayed," he said with more force than he'd intended. Too many people had suggested the same thing lately. Cal had even gone so far as to suggest setting Mac up with his granddaughter, who had just separated from her abusive husband.

Mac had declined. He might not still feel that black cloak of mourning weighing him down, but he wasn't in any hurry to risk making the same mistake again.

His grandmother, who had appeared to be napping, started suddenly. Her watery eyes blinked several times until she finally focused on him.

"Sorry, Gran," he said, hating the heat that crept into his cheeks. "I didn't mean to cuss."

His grandmother had the ability to make him feel fifteen. About the age he'd been when his father died and Gran took over raising him and Libby. Gran had been Sentinel Pass's postmaster for most of her life…until Libby took over the job.

He glanced to his right and saw Libby's amused smirk. "Where is this miracle canine? Stuck in the blizzard?"

Mac shook his head, baffled. "What are you talking about? It's over ninety out there. And humid. I think a front is coming in."

"Weren't you the guy who told me it would be a cold day in hell before he bought a dog? Especially a used mutt from the used-mutt hotel."

Mac growled. "What are you—the memory police? I might have said that a few months ago, but a lot has changed since then. Including the fact that you're gone half the time and Megan misses you. If you were still around to take her places and do girlie things, I might not have been bombarded with nonstop pleading for a dog. A man can only take so much whining."

"That's true," Gran said, her voice a softer, less definitive version of itself. "Those were the days."

Libby looked at him a second, then they both turned to their grandmother. Her blue eyes sparkled, but probably more from the light that flooded the enclosed porch than from the wit she'd once been famous for. "What's that, Gran?"

"Those were the days that tried men's souls." This had become one of her favorite sayings.

Libby's eyes filled with tears. In the past couple of weeks, their grandmother's cognitive abilities seemed to flick on and off like a lightbulb with a bad connection.

"You got that right, Gran," Mac said, patting her hand. Someone had painted her nails a bold fuchsia color that appeared at odds with her withered skin.

Within seconds she seemed to lose interest. Her chin dropped and her gaze returned to the little ball of fluff on her lap. Onida. Gran's beloved teacup poodle.

The dog suddenly bounced to life with a high-pitched yip that made Mac jump. Over the loud, frenzied barking, he heard his daughter call, "We're ready, Daddy."

He'd left Megan in the kitchen securing Bella's fancy new collar and leash.

"Help me catch Onida," he ordered Libby. "Quick. Meggie's dog would take one look at Onie and think lunch."

"Oh lord, you really are a soft touch," Libby said, laughing. She tossed aside the book she'd been reading aloud to their grandmother and scrambled to her feet. Her pregnancy was beginning to show. Mac wondered if his sister would get as large as Misty had. In her final two months of pregnancy with Megan, Misty had called herself an elephant on roller skates.

"Wait, Meggie. Not yet. Let Aunt Libby catch—" His warning went ignored.

The door opened and Gran's ancient, pampered ball of fluff met Megan's street-smart, world-weary, possibly mistreated enigma with teeth. For about an eighth of a second neither dog moved, then the much bigger, younger, healthier pup turned tail and split, yanking the leash clean through Megan's fingers.

Megan let out a yelp of pain. Onida croaked pure adrenaline and triumph. Since Megan never remembered to close a door behind her, when they turned to follow Bella, the dog was outside and nowhere to be found.

Mac scooped up the still-barking Onida and walked her inside to deposit on Gran's lap. "Hold tight, Gran." Then he raced outside again.

Giant tears were streaming down Megan's cheeks. "Find her, Daddy. Find Bella."

The daddy part of him turned to mush. "Don't worry, honey. She's around here somewhere. I promise. Don't cry, baby. We'll find her."

He handed her to Libby so he could make better time. He sprinted headlong down the lane, calling, "Bella? Come here, Bella." That's when he noticed a woman walking toward him.

Oh, jeez, not just any woman. The woman from his dreams. The freaking famous actress who had less business walking toward his grandmother's house than she had traipsing through his subconscious. But there she was, moving with barely a trace of hesitation—just like the way Misty used to.

He'd never understood where an ordinary girl from a small town in Nebraska came by that sense of entitlement, but Misty always sallied forth as though the world owed her a favor and she was there to collect.

Morgana walked with poise and purpose. She wasn't Misty, but she seemed to exude the same confidence. A shiver raced up Mac's spine until he reminded himself that that was their only similarity.

Morgana was polished, fashionable in a way only the rich and famous could be. And hot, he finally admitted to himself. Yes, he found her attractive. Except for one thing. Make that two.

First, she was playing his sister. Which in some circles was probably creepy enough to qualify as incest. Not really, but he knew if he so much as gave this woman a second look someone in town would bring it up.

Second, he wasn't in the market for a woman. Especially a beautiful woman. He'd had one and blew it so badly he'd fallen under suspicion of murder. Nope. He wasn't going down that road again. Dreams he could handle, but in real life? No way.

"Oh," she said, looking around, obviously trying to figure out what was going on. "Hi. Again. Libby said you'd be here, but I'm a little early." She pointed at Mac's truck. "Are we taking your truck?"

Mac had no idea what she was talking about, but before he could answer, Libby rushed to his side. "Hi, Morgana. Great timing. You met Megan, right? Her new dog ran away. Do you have your cell phone with you?"

Morgana nodded, but Mac sensed her reluctance to get involved. *Too bad, princess,* he silently sympathized. *Welcome to my world. What Libby wants, Libby organizes.*

"Here's the plan. You and Mac take the truck and scout around the neighborhood. Meggie and I will search closer to the house. Heck, she might have even slipped in the back door, right?"

Mac shook his head. "Doubtful. My sense of Bella is she's been mistreated and would never willingly walk into a stranger's house. I do think she and Megan formed a real bond, though, so if you two walk around softly coaxing her to come out of hiding, she probably will—unless she hasn't stopped running yet." That was his real fear.

Libby gave him a sour look. "Well, let's hope you're wrong, McGloomandDoom. If we find her first, we'll call you. Hopefully, you'll be in a place that gets reception."

"What about the wine?"

"What wine?" Mac asked, trying to keep up.

Libby gave him a frustrated look. "Just go. Quickly. Megan's going to be heartbroken if you don't find that dog."

Morgan was dressed for dinner, not for dog hunting, but she figured any kind of adventure would beat sitting around the tiny cottage behind her ex-husband's wife's house fretting about who amongst her peers was going to win an Emmy award. William had called twice with updates. She wasn't expecting anything, but it still hurt that her name wasn't on anybody's short list. "I'm game. What are we waiting for?"

She wasn't sure at first if he was going to follow her lead or not, but as she reached for the door handle, he beat her to it. "It's a big step."

He wasn't kidding. She hitched her purse strap across one shoulder, planted her demure white eyelet flat on the slightly rusted platform, then grabbed a conveniently placed metal bar to pull herself upward. A warm, solid hand on her rump provided the extra boost she needed. She wasn't a stranger to men's hands on her butt, but there was something different about Mac's touch. She couldn't define it, but an electrical current seemed to branch out from their point of contact. One significant tingle wound up in the wrong place. Sexual urges paired with real-world people like Mac were never a good idea. Nonshowbiz people got their feelings hurt when her make-believe world intruded.

Once she had her emotions under control, she looked at him and flashed a cool, calculated smile. "Thank you for your…help."

The part of her brain that constantly critiqued her performance gave her two thumbs up. Not the least bit flirtatious—even if she did stumble a bit in the delivery.

"No problem."

And damn if he didn't appear to mean it. Either he was the better actor or he honestly hadn't felt the same connection she had. If she didn't know better, she might have assumed he was gay because by all outward indicators the internal short-circuit that lit up her body completely fizzled on his side of the agenda.

She reached out to check her theory, but he adroitly side-stepped her touch. "Door," he said by way of warning, then slammed it closed and marched around the back of the truck.

A smile slowly formed on her lips. She'd never met anyone as self-disciplined as her. In a perverse way, Mac's emotional rigidity not only made him more attractive, but added an unparalleled degree of challenge.

Maybe she could overlook the fact he was a civilian—and her ex-husband's new wife's brother—long enough to get a reaction from him. Nothing more. Her ego demanded a little satisfaction, but she wasn't a fool. She knew her limitations.

CHAPTER FOUR

"ARE YOU SURE you want to do this?"

Mac felt obligated to ask, and in the three or four seconds it took her to answer he was almost positive she was going to say no. Which certainly would have suited him fine. A girl in pretty white shoes and a frothy brown and white dress that reminded him of the airy mixture at the top of a root beer float had no business riding around in his could-use-a-good-cleaning truck.

"Another set of eyes can't hurt, right?"

The question wasn't an answer, but he figured that was the best he was going to get. He'd noticed his new brother-in-law had a hard time making definitive statements, too. Maybe actors were used to having other people think for them. And as long as he believed that he could control the ridiculous reaction he'd felt when he touched her.

To help erase the memory of her womanly form against his palm, he leaned over the steering wheel and gave the key a crank in the ignition. Harder than necessary. He was lucky the key didn't snap off. His truck was old and needed to be replaced but money wasn't the only thing keeping him from shopping for a new one. If you believed his sister, you might think he had a hard time letting go of things. And people.

No matter. The old truck might be challenging to drive,

but he had its quirks down pretty well. And there was a certain comfort in the tried and true. The truck got him where he needed to go and everyone in town recognized it. That worked for him.

"I don't know much about dogs—never owned one, but I've worked with a few. Where do you think—"

"You've never had a pet?"

Her cheeks colored slightly. She looked at him but didn't quite meet his eyes. "I didn't say that. I said I, personally, have never owned a dog. One of my former roommates came with a parrot. Messy. Very messy. We never bonded. The bird or the roommate. I guess I'm not a bird person."

Mac liked birds—especially birds of prey—but he didn't see the point in keeping any living thing in a tiny cage that you had to clean, unless you were nursing it back to health. "Me, neither."

He turned sideways to rest his arm on the back of the seat as he reversed the truck around the semicircle driveway. Once it was facing the road, he said, "The dog we're looking for is a true mutt. Scruffy coat. Sorta blondish in color. Medium size. Ears that flop over. Bright pink collar." He let out a small huff of air. "I should have said that first. How many loose dogs with bright pink collars can there be in Sentinel Pass?"

Her smile was so sweet and understanding he stepped on the gas without depressing the clutch first. The engine coughed and died. Heat filled his cheeks and he tugged on the bill of the new *Sentinel Passtime* ball cap his brother-in-law had given him, as if that might hide his embarrassment.

"I like the hats Cooper had made up," she said, politely ignoring the fact he was acting like a kid with his dream date in the car. "I see them everywhere. And I heard someone was selling one on eBay for a hundred dollars."

The caps were high-quality cotton. Black, with a glittery gold *Sentinel Passtime* logo emblazoned atop a background of mountains with a fuzzy image of Mt. Rushmore in one corner. "Coop does everything with style. The party was a huge success," he told her, driving slowly enough to scan the underbrush.

Gran's house, which actually belonged to Calvin, sat at the edge of a meadow that was linked to town by a well-worn footpath. The native grasses were turning golden-white—about the same color as Bella's coat.

When they reached the first cross street that turned right, he sped up slightly. "She won't go here," he said, nodding toward the house on the corner. "The owner has three dogs that are more wolf than canine."

"Is that legal?"

"I don't know. They've never caused any problems, but I'd never let Megan step foot on the property."

He noticed that she stretched her neck to see more of the place. The perimeter was overgrown with lilac bushes and weeds that blocked her view of the various wrecked or nonoperational junk heaps. Libby's house had accrued a similar collection over the years, but Mac had finally had the last of them towed away a few weeks earlier when she was in California.

"Where would she go? The dog, I mean. Not your daughter."

"I have no idea."

He didn't mean for his tone to sound quite so annoyed, but when he glanced her way he saw her pretty, perfectly shaped eyebrows raised expressively. Rather than admit the truth, that he didn't understand females of any species, he said, "She's still a pup. Not quite a year old. And she came from the animal shelter. If she tries to go back home…well, I don't know where that is."

"Oh, I see. She's an enigma, and that bothers you. You like things black and white, don't you?"

Something in her tone said this was a bad thing, but he wasn't going to lie. "Yeah, I do. I lived with an enigma, as you say, once, and it pretty much sucked. I'll take up-front and truthful any time."

"But it's not the dog's fault you don't understand her. She can't exactly tell you all the details of her past. And yet you judge her."

Mac shook his head, not at all certain what they were talking about. His dog? His late wife? His life?

Fortunately, he was saved from trying to defend himself by the jingle of her cell phone. He recognized the tune but couldn't name it.

She pulled a small, glittery phone out of her purse. After checking the display, she said, "Coop?"

She listened in silence a moment then let out a sigh. "Good. I'll tell him."

Mac pulled over to let the car behind them pass. He saw her put her finger in the opposite ear to be able to hear over the truck's muted roar and quickly killed the engine. She flashed a grateful smile his way then cocked her head to listen to the caller.

He couldn't help but study her profile. Not classically beautiful, perhaps. Her nose was a little short and her cheeks a little thin, but her skin was gorgeous. The same color as Megan's in the winter—warm peach. In the summer, his daughter turned as brown as a toasted almond.

But Megan's little-girl cheeks were round and full. Morgana didn't have an ounce of extra plumpness anywhere on her body. He wondered if that was due partly to how she was brought up. Did rich people really believe that adage that you could never be too rich or too thin? Or had she bought into the skinny-at-any-cost philosophy he'd read about? That spelled eating disorder and that was the last thing he wanted Megan to emulate.

She lowered the phone and looked at him. "Good news."

"She's back?"

"Apparently she never left. Megan found her hiding under a bush around the side of the house."

"Damn." Morgana looked surprised by his response so he told her, "You can be sure that at some point tonight Megan is going to claim that this proves she and the dog have some kind of psychic connection. Not that she'll put it that way, but…she's a very savvy four-year-old."

"Almost five," Morgana corrected. "Your daughter was adamant about that when we met."

He couldn't help but smile. This woman was smart and observant, he'd give her that much. Probably went with the job. What other reason could there be for her to give his daughter any extra attention? "I guess we can go back," he said, starting the truck again.

She turned sharply in her seat. "What about the wine for dinner? Libby said you'd drive me to a place called the Junction. Or something like that."

He'd caught some mention of that but had pushed it out of his mind when the dog went missing. "Wine. Okay. We can do that. But it'll take half an hour. Could you call Coop back and make sure he and Libby bring Megan and the dog home with them?"

She made the call, and also used the time to find out what kind of wine Cooper thought she should bring that evening. Mac didn't know the difference between a cabernet and a chardonnay, but he found listening to her voice extremely pleasurable. Not easy to describe, though, because it changed so quickly and fluidly. Happy was bubbly. Serious was the sound of water over boulders.

"May I ask you a personal question?"

Here it comes. He knew she'd heard about Misty's death. Invariably, at some point, morbid curiosity got the best of everyone. "Okay. I won't promise to answer it, though."

"Fair enough. How come you and Jenna never hooked up?"

He blinked twice, completely thrown by the question. "Jenna Murphy? Shane's Jenna?"

She nodded. "She wasn't Shane's Jenna all the time you two were growing up. From what I heard, she was your sister's best friend. She's smart and pretty and, until a month or so ago, single. I would have thought logic and proximity might have been enough to draw you together."

He laughed. He couldn't help it. "*Logic and proximity?* No wonder you and Coop are divorced. Sorry. I didn't mean that the way it came out, but I can tell you firsthand there's no logic to love. In fact, it's just the opposite."

"You loved your wife a great deal."

A statement, not a question, but he heard an underlying doubt. Not surprising given the circumstances. "When I met Misty, it was like catching a bowling ball, midgut, without being braced for it. Wham. Out of nowhere. I'm at this funky campground and the girl behind the desk is reading *Catch-22.* I saw the title before I saw her, but then she looked up. Pow. That was it."

Her head tilted as if picturing the scene in her mind's eye. "She was beautiful?"

"Yeah, but it wasn't her looks. There was something sad and weary in her eyes. Like she'd seen too much. Which was weird because she was young."

She nodded slightly. "You're a hero. You rescued the fair damsel in distress."

They'd reached the main highway. He stomped on the brake a bit harder than necessary and checked both ways twice rather than look her in the eye. "*Hero* implies a happy ending, right? That lets me out."

He put on the blinker. Changing the subject, he pointed out the large white teepee to their right. "Have you met Char Jones yet? She owns this place. She's one of my sister's book club members."

"Hmm…I'm not sure."

"She has funny hair. You'd remember."

"Oh. Her. Yes, we were introduced. She's…unusual."

He shrugged. "My sister likes different. Look at who she married. Not your average boy-next-door. As you must know since you were married to him, too. How's that working out—the two of you playing opposite each other?"

Morgan hesitated a moment before answering. She wanted to be honest, as he'd been with her, but nonactors sometimes had a hard time understanding the method behind an actor's process. "Believe it or not, our having been married seems to add an interesting dynamic to our on-screen personas. Or so Shane says. I think it's because Coop and I were friends before we married. In hindsight, our decision to elope was probably based on a lot of reasons not related to love or passion. His mother… My agent at the time… Really, it's all history. Not worth talking about. But Coop is such a nice guy I felt bad that I didn't love him enough to stay married."

He didn't say anything, but Morgan could tell he was listening closely. She shifted sideways slightly so she could study him. "We went our separate ways but there weren't any real hard feelings. Except where his mother was concerned. Libby is so lucky the evil witch is dead. Lena was poison to everyone who cared about Coop. Shane's one of the few friends Coop had who could handle her."

"Didn't she pass away shortly before Coop contacted Libby?"

Morgan nodded. "He was a little lost without his mother running the show. Honestly, I expected Libby to be more like Lena. But she's not, thank God. I don't think I could have played her. Too much of a stretch. Now, Tiffany, Coop's first wife…not a problem. She could impersonate Lena like you wouldn't believe. It was uncanny. Of course, she didn't even audition for the role of Libby because…well, she's off doing something else."

A book tour of her mostly made-up tell-all that included intimate details of her new love life. With a woman. Morgan didn't believe any of it, but she also didn't really care.

Neither spoke for a few miles. The silence wasn't uncomfortable, but the more Morgan saw of the landscape, which she'd supposedly never visited before, the more a niggling uneasiness started to grow in her belly. She'd visited the Black Hills as a child. A happy memory she'd tucked deep into a secret place because it didn't jibe with any of the fake memories she'd built to go with her new name and persona.

Looking around the inside of the vehicle, she spotted a booster seat and some children's books in the rear passenger area. Stretching, she managed to reach one. Settling back, she scanned the cover. *"Walter the Farting Dog?"*

Mac sort of ducked his head as his cheeks filled with color and his face scrunched up in an apologetic look that made all of her senses react—pulse racing, nostrils flaring, fingertips tingling. She looked down to see if there was an invisible bowling ball sitting in her lap.

What was it about manly men who turned into little boys at the first mention of bodily functions that got to her? She had no idea.

"Megan and I have been going round and round about a dog for months. I thought maybe this book would help, but turns out she loves Walter. She feels sorry for him. We have an entire library of Walter books. The grosser, the better."

Damn. The rough, tough miner was a pushover for little girls and farting dogs. Morgan could fall for a guy like that. If she let herself. Which she had no intention of allowing to happen.

"Could I borrow this? I want to lend it to Zane. The guy who plays your character. He needs to show a bit more humility."

Mac shrugged. "Sure." He glanced her way. "Hey. That reminds me. Coop said something about buying his ex-wife a poodle. That wasn't you?"

"No. T-Fancy. I mean, Tiffany. I think she still has the dog. Coop said she gave it a four-thousand-dollar leather couch as a chew toy."

"Wow. Four grand? And I thought six bucks for the hard nylon doggie bone we bought at the pet store was a rip-off."

She agreed. Although she'd never say so out loud for fear it might seem out of character.

At a wide spot in the road, they pulled into a gas

station that apparently served as a minimarket, too. Half a dozen pickup trucks—most with gun racks in the back window and in about the same shape as Mac's—were parked outside. With its gray clapboard siding mostly obscured by advertisements for beer and cigarettes, the store hardly looked as though it would have much to offer in the way of wine selections, but looks could be deceiving, Morgan decided.

"My goodness. California wines. Australian. Organic. This is impressive," she admitted a few minutes later.

Mac's broad shoulders lifted and fell. "I remember tasting watered-down wine once a year at Christmas when my parents were alive. After Mom died, we barely even had a tree and presents. Gran tried to revive a few traditions once she took over raising us, but she wasn't much of a drinker."

Morgan's hand trembled slightly as she selected a chardonnay that she'd had before. His memories paralleled hers in an uncanny way. When her parents had been alive, there'd been abundance—not the wealth of her made-up bio, but the kind of plenty that made a child feel safe and loved. When they died, her world became a study in penury and starkness.

"H-how many bottles?" she asked, her throat unnaturally tight.

"You're asking the wrong person. One? Two? Libby won't drink any."

"And Coop and I have to work tomorrow. The hike scene." She took a step to the right and studied the reds a moment. "This pinot should be fine," she said, making her selection.

Mac took both bottles from her and carried them to the counter. His gentlemanly gesture was both sweet and strange. It drove home the fact that she didn't know men like him. Not anymore. *And I wouldn't know what to do with one if I had him.*

Well, aside from the obvious. Which, of course, was out of the question.

CHAPTER FIVE

"Good choice on the wine, Morgie."

Morgan gritted her teeth and gave her ex-husband a look she knew he'd understand. "Thank you. I didn't expect to find such a variety of selections."

"Because you thought everyone around here was a hick."

One bad thing about cultivating the image of a snob was having everyone think you were a snob—even the people who should have known better. She leveled a second critical look at her ex. "No, because the store was so small. It seemed odd to find it devoting so much shelf space to one type of product."

She lifted her glass toward Mac, who was sitting across from her. Originally, she'd been designated to sit on the side with one chair, but Megan had insisted—very nicely but in a tone that invited no argument—that she was sitting beside "the princess."

With unfailing good manners, he refilled her glass, even though she had no intention of drinking it. One glass of anything was her limit. Drunk people said things they shouldn't. She couldn't afford a slip-up, even if there wasn't a horde of paparazzi waiting outside Chez McGannon. Or was that Lindstrom?

"Can I have wine, Daddy?"

Morgan looked at Mac. "Sure," he said. "When you're twenty-one."

Megan gave a most put-upon sigh.

Although she had no intention of commenting, Morgan found herself saying, "In France and Italy, children are given watered-down wine with meals."

Mac looked at her and their gazes held for a second or two. Long enough for Morgan to read his unspoken response. "Mind your own business, lady." Out loud, he said, "If she ever gets adopted by an Italian or a French family, she's welcome to give it a try."

"My mother let me have a sip of whatever she was drinking," Cooper said cheerfully.

"Right up to the day she died, I'd wager," Morgan said, again before she could stop herself. She looked at her wineglass and nudged it a little farther away from her plate. What was wrong with her? She was rarely this contentious unless the part called for it.

Cooper, being Coop, laughed off the slight. "Pun intended? After the scandal sheets ran all those pictures of Mom sitting at a slot machine before she died, how could you miss it? You know, Morgana, she always liked you best."

"Coop, she hated me and Tiffany with equal measures of loathing and envy. Envy because we were young and pretty. Loathing because we had your ear and she was afraid we might talk her golden goose into flying away."

Her frankness earned a look of concern between Mac and Libby, but Coop shrugged it off. "True. You and Tiffany both told me she was robbing me blind, but I didn't believe you. I should have listened."

Morgan knew why he hadn't. Love. The kind that didn't come with a balance sheet. He'd loved his wives that way, too. And Morgan had divorced him because she never felt worthy of that devotion. She had too many secrets she didn't dare share with a man who was so open and transparent. He would have tried his best to remain mum, but she knew that at some point, he'd blab. He was Cooper.

Now a guy like Mac could easily take a secret to his grave. She was sure of that.

"Princess?" a little voice said at her elbow. "Can I come watch you and Uncle Coop work tomorrow? Auntie said you're going to be outside, but I would still have to be real quiet. I can do that."

The little girl's earnestness wormed its way right under Morgan's defenses. "Um...I don't know. Shane is the director. You'd have to ask him." A total cop-out. The adults knew it. But it was the only excuse she could think of.

"Daddy, if Uncle Shane says it's okay can I go to work with Princess Morgana? Pwetty please."

Morgan hid her smile behind the napkin she pressed to her lips. The girl was good. Megan didn't have a childish lisp...except when she wanted something from her daddy.

"I don't know, Miss M. I have to look at a backhoe job in the morning, and Libby is busy with Gran. I was going to let you hang out at Child's Play for a couple of hours."

She wiggled excitedly in her booster chair. "But Miss Barb is going to Sioux Falls for her granddaughter's graduation. Remember? The day care isn't open."

His scowl was rather impressive. Megan didn't appear at all intimidated, but a stranger certainly might have turned tail and run.

"Maybe Megan can stay with me," Libby said. "It depends on what kind of night Gran had."

Megan looked at Morgan as if she were a banana split

she'd just been told she couldn't eat. "O-kay," she said with a sigh.

"Tell you what," Morgan said impulsively. "I'll check the shooting schedule first thing and give you a call," she told Mac. "If Shane doesn't have any objection, she can hang out with me."

She couldn't tell from his eyes what he was thinking, but after a few seconds of silent deliberation, he nodded. "I could probably run her up to the location before I go look at the job. Coop can give you my number."

It wasn't a date or anything, but the knowledge that they were going to see each other the next day made her heart do a silly little dance. Odd. Perplexing.

As she reached for her wine—one more sip—she saw the look Cooper exchanged with his wife. Coop wasn't pleased. Because having a child on the set might delay filming? Or was it because his ex-wife was being friendly toward his brother-in-law?

She didn't know why he'd care, but she wasn't going to let his opinion bother her. She still needed to put her mind to rest where Mac's late wife was concerned. Apparently, the only way to do that was to get close to Mac.

Her hoped-for opportunity to peer through Libby's family photo albums had been a complete bust. Coop had responded to her request with skepticism. "Why? You're not a senti-mental kind of person. You want to see me looking like a lovesick sap, don't you? Well, forget it. What Libby and I have is real. Perfect. The less you know about us the better."

Fine. If he was going to be that way, she'd wrangle an invitation to Mac's home, where there had to be at least one picture of Megan's mother. Morgan had already tried every resource available online, searching for something about one Misty McGannon. The woman's obituary ran in two local papers but the notices only amounted to a few lines broadcasting the time and date of a memorial service. Neither had included a photo. And if she ever wanted to purge this silly notion that her mind seemed fixated on, she had to make sure that Mac's Misty wasn't her Misty, too.

"WHAT GIVES? Is my future business partner getting cold feet?"

Mac had purposely volunteered to clear the table with Libby because he needed to feel her out. Coop had been giving him strange looks all through dinner and Mac didn't have a clue why.

"It's not you. He's upset with me."

"What did you do?"

"I sent you and Morgana to buy wine."

"So?"

"He's afraid you two might…" She brushed back a lock of hair impatiently. "Actually, I'm not sure what he's afraid of, but he doesn't like seeing you together."

"Why? It's not like I'm going to make a move on her."

"No one would blame you if you did. She's gorgeous. And nice. Surprisingly."

That was true. He hadn't expected someone so beautiful to be so patient and kind with Megan. "Yeah, she's pretty. She's also too thin. I've read a whole slew of articles about eating disorders, and as the father of a young girl, I would never get involved with a woman who had body-image issues." His brows wiggled expectantly. "How's that for nonminer lingo?"

"Fabulous, Dr. Phil, but Coop insists Morgana is high-strung, not anorexic."

Mac shrugged. "High-strung equals high-maintenance in my book, and I had enough of that to last a lifetime. Even if she was perfect, I'm not the kind of man who fishes in another guy's pond without permission."

Her horrified look told him he'd made some kind of social blunder.

"What?"

"Women are not game fish, you big dufus. And, even though I abhor that analogy, I'd like to point out that Coop is done fishing. Period."

Mac loved that he could still get her goat. "So, why does he care who I buy wine with?" He grinned. "Like that one better?"

Her snarl told him no. "He cares about Morgana. In an old-friend way. He doesn't want to see her get hurt. Plus, this new endorsement of hers is with a squeaky-clean company that keeps a tight rein on its celebrity spokesperson. I don't know the details, but apparently Morgana needs the money. Something about a lousy former agent and a short dry spell—workwise."

Mac respected Coop's concern on Morgana's behalf. He knew all about taking care of your own. Up till last year, not a soul in town would have questioned his reputation as a champion of the underdog. But things changed with Misty's death. He didn't like the idea of Coop questioning his motives, too. "Well, tell him not to worry. This was the last wine we're going to buy while she's here. Now, I'd better get Megan home. Did I tell you Kat's R.U.B. bought the Smith house?"

"Kat did. She's pretty conflicted at the moment."

"Why? Jack seems like a good guy."

She sighed. "It's complicated."

"No. It's a book club thing, isn't it? You know, Lib, you women are real snobs."

"We are not."

"Four original members. Static. Closed to the public. You're elitists."

"That's not true. We've invited other people. In fact, Jack sat in with us at the last meeting. And I tried to get Gran to come for years, but she claimed her eyesight was going and she didn't want to read anymore." She made an aha sound that never boded well for him. "That reminds me. I want you to read to her when you visit. Keeps her mind active and it'll be something you'll look back on fondly when she's g-gone."

Tear spilled over her eyes before she even got the word out. Mac tossed his towel aside and pulled her into a hug. He murmured the kinds of things he said to Megan when she had a bad dream or remembered something sad about her mother. The fixer in him hated to see the people he loved upset, but he knew that what was happening to his grandmother was outside his control.

"Shh…shh…okay. You had me at *read*. I'll do it. I hope she likes *Walter the Farting Dog* books."

Libby smiled through her tears. "Sorry," she said, wiping her eyes with the back of her hand. "I've never been so emotional. I hope it's pregnancy hormones."

"Misty was the same way," he assured her. Although in all honesty, his late wife had been her happiest while carrying Megan. It was later, when Megan became more independent and Mac was working long hours at two jobs that Misty's emotions spiraled downhill.

He stepped back, keeping one hand on her shoulder. "Are you sure you're okay?"

She nodded. "Healthy as a horse. Speaking of animals, where's the new dog going to sleep?"

Anywhere she wants. "On the back porch."

She laughed as though that was the funniest thing she'd ever heard. "Right. Good luck with that."

He ignored her—even though he knew she was probably right. He'd turned into a real pushover where his daughter was concerned. When Misty had been alive, he'd known his role in the family. Just like his father, Mac had been the breadwinner, the hard rock miner, the strong silent type who could enforce the rules with a pointed stare. Now, he was part mother, too, and that part was in direct conflict with his rigid, miner self. Rules were breaking faster than shale under a sledgehammer.

CHAPTER SIX

"HURRY, DADDY. Hurry. We don't want to miss the Princess and Uncle Coop."

Mac stumbled over an upraised root while his daughter skipped nimbly toward the fifty or so people assembled near the trailhead Mac had been across many times during hunting season. They'd had to park half a mile away and pass through two checkpoints of, in his opinion, overzealous security guards. For once in his life, though, the name McGannon seemed to hold some real power. Because of Libby.

Ironic, he thought. Growing up, he'd been sure that he'd strike the mother lode, find the vein that would make them all rich. Instead, Libby did that simply by putting her heart on the line…and on the Internet.

"Megan. Stop. Right there. Wait."

She paused, but her impatient fidgeting reminded him of Misty when they disagreed about something. He'd never liked arguing with his late wife, but Megan, fortunately, seemed to understand that she couldn't always have her way. Like this morning, when Morgana had to renege on her invitation because the shooting schedule called for a closed set.

"Why, Daddy?" Megan had cried.

"I don't know. Maybe they need it extra quiet," he'd suggested. Or maybe Morgana and Cooper were going to be doing something Shane didn't want the general public to see until he had time to edit it. The thought left Mac with an unpleasant taste in his mouth.

Libby also had been too busy to babysit. She'd called shortly after Morgana to say she was accompanying Cal and Gran to the doctor to discuss Gran's lack of appetite and increased dementia. Mac had asked, half-heartedly, if she needed him to go, but Libby had quickly nixed the idea. "Poor Gran gets flustered easily. We should keep the distractions to a minimum. Why don't you two come see her later, after she's had time to rest."

He'd quickly agreed to the plan. So, with Megan's usual babysitter out of town, he'd had to drag her along to the new job site. *Thank God for Bella,* he'd thought more than once. The dog rarely left Megan's side, which freed him to take the measurements he needed.

He tightened his grip on the dog's leash. He'd wanted to leave the animal in the truck, but Megan had seen that as cruel and unusual punishment.

"Can I walk Bella now, Daddy?"

They were still a distance from the white tents, which, he knew, was where the real action in the taping process took place. Tracks had been laid for the camera that operated on some kind of dolly system. Clusters of people milled about in the shade while others scurried around like ants.

He put a hand on her head. "Sorry, honey, she's not used to so many people. I don't want her to bolt and pull you over. Let's stand here and watch."

She leaned over and hugged the dog, then in a loud whisper said, "Whatever you do, don't bark, Bella. Or howl."

Mac stifled a yawn at the reminder. The howling—a

mournful sound that made the hair on the back of his neck stand on end—had awoken him from a dead sleep about midnight. At first, he'd thought he was hearing a tornado siren or smoke alarm. Adrenaline pumping and firefighter training kicking in, he had the lights on and was starting to dress before he figured out the sound was coming from his garage.

He'd moved the dog to the laundry room. With an extra blanket and a night-light.

He'd just fallen back asleep when the next round of howling began. Naturally, this time it was louder. And it woke up Megan. Too exhausted to argue, he'd opened the laundry room and followed as Bella trotted triumphantly straight to Megan's room.

As he closed his eyes, Mac had been certain he heard his father grumble, "Dogs don't belong in the house." That was easy for the dead to say; they didn't have to get up in the morning.

"With any luck, the howling is a thing of the past," he said.

The no-dog-in-the-house rule seemed like a minor infraction compared to letting a new dog sleep on your child's bed. But, despite his gut reaction to the idea, Mac had had to admit this morning that maybe Bella was the answer to his prayers. His little girl had finally slept through the night without wetting the bed or waking up in pure terror from a nightmare too scary to tell him about.

Unfortunately, Mac's sleep had been anything but restful. He'd had way too many dreams. Most of them involving a beautiful actress.

"Mac," a familiar voice called. "This is a surprise. Is everything okay with Libby? Hi, Megan. Nice dress. Bella, you look very pretty today."

Coop's demeanor seemed as friendly and easygoing as usual. Mac assumed that meant Lib had talked to him about the wine-buying and they were back to being friends again.

"Bella went to the dog beauty parlor while Daddy and I had lunch. Dogs that sleep on your bed need special grooming, Daddy said."

Cooper's snicker made Mac feel like the total push-over he was. "We stopped at Gran's on our way here, but nobody was home. I went inside and tried Lib's cell but she didn't answer. Do you have reception here?"

Cooper shook his head. "No, damn it. Morgana and I even talk about it in the dialog. Comes off funny, but it isn't."

"We're here to see the princess," Megan said, tugging one of the many pockets adorning Coop's hiking pants. Mac couldn't think of a single local who actually wore that kind of gear while out in the woods, but it probably fit some wardrobe person's idea of hiking clothes.

"R'member last night when she said I could come? Sorta." She frowned. "I wore my princess dress, too."

The fancy dress left over from Halloween the year before had seen better days, but Megan loved the pale lilac satin and sparkly bodice—even if Mac had insisted she had to wear sneakers in place of her fake glass slippers.

"I think Morgana has one just like that, although today she's wearing hiking boots and jeans. We just finished our last scene together. She's going over the tape with Shane. I'll let her know you're here."

Mac noticed Coop hadn't invited them to come closer. Before he could decide whether or not he should feel put out, his eye caught sight of a familiar redhead. Jenna Murphy left the group of people she'd been talking with and jogged over to where he and Megan were standing.

"Hi, you two. What are you doing here?"

Jenna and Libby had been best friends so long Mac didn't take offense to the blunt question. "Megan's become a Princess Morgana groupie."

"Oh," Jenna said, bending down to give Megan a hug. "So that makes you her driver."

Mac chuckled. "And the dog's."

Jenna went nose-to-nose with Bella, ruffling a spot behind the dog's ear that appeared to produce pure canine bliss. "I heard about this new addition to the family. Congratulations." She looked at Mac and added, "By the way, Shane's thinking of forming a support group for men who were pulled kicking and screaming against their better judgment into the world of dog ownership. In case you're interested."

Mac shook his head. "You and my sister talk too much. What's new at the Mystery Spot?"

She returned to her feet. "Not much. My manager leaves for college soon. Fortunately, we're only open on weekends after Labor Day. Then the season's over." She pretended to wipe sweat from her brow. "The Mystery Spot survived another year. Dad would be proud, wouldn't he?"

Mac was well aware of Jenna's love-hate relationship with her family's summer business, Sentinel Pass's lone tourist trap. "Lib said your new manager worked out."

"Robyn's fabulous. I'm hoping to make her a full partner next year. Heck, I'd give her the thing, but Shane says we have to wait and see if the show is a success before we burn all our bridges to gainful employment."

Her chuckle held a note of irony that Mac could appreciate. Familial obligations were often more of a millstone than a guarantee of fiscal success in Sentinel Pass. Lately, Mac had found himself questioning what he might have done differently if he hadn't promised his grandmother that he'd keep the Little Poke in the family.

"So, Megan, when are you going to bring Bella over to introduce her to Luca?"

Mac gave Jenna a friendly poke. "That reminds me. I have you to thank for Bella's size. Megan had agreed to a little dog until she met Luca. What kind is he again?"

"Burnese mountain dog. And it could be worse. Shane and I went to a screening of *Marley & Me* last week. Our book club read the book in January and now it's a movie." Her look of wonderment was one of the things he'd always liked best about her. "Anyway, the story reminded me that dogs pick people, not the other way around."

He shook his head. "You've been in California too long."

Before she could defend her point, he became aware of another person approaching.

"Hi," Morgana said, smiling shyly. Not at all as confident as he would have expected a big star to act in a group setting. "Coop told me you were here. Shane's making him redo the scene where he gets caught in some bushes. He's not happy," she added. "Hi, Megan. I love your dress. All you're missing is a tiara."

Megan beamed.

Morgana looked at Jenna and said, "I heard you mention *Marley & Me*. I read that book, and I honestly don't think I would have been able to stick it out through Marley's early years." She glanced in the direction she'd just come from. "Coop and his first wife, Tiffany, had a Marley dog. Different breed but insanely destructive."

"The poodle?" Mac asked.

Before Morgana could answer, Jenna said, "You read? Well, duh. Of course you read scripts. But books? For pleasure? Oh, heck, you know what I mean."

Morgana nodded as if it were a trick question.

"Cool. Our book club is squeezing in a second meeting this month because some of us have to head back to California in the very near future, and I've heard a rumor that some people—" she looked at Mac "—think we've become a bit elitist and cliquish. Would you like to join us?"

Mac let out a grunt of disgust. "The grapevine in this town has the Internet beat for speed."

Morgana looked down as if trying to not laugh. "What book are you reading?"

"Last Dance at Jitterbug Lounge," Jenna answered, her enthusiasm for her new idea obvious. "I have an extra copy you can have."

Morgana held up her hand to exchange a high-five with Megan. "I was hoping you'd say that. I read it on the plane."

"Seriously?"

"Shane recommended it. As another way to get into Libby's character."

Jenna laughed and looked toward the director's tent. "I keep forgetting how observant he is." To Morgana, she said, "Then you'll come? I'm hosting at my house. Wait. I have a great idea. I'll give my extra book to Mac to read and he can host. After all, this was his idea. And I think this would be a good story for him. What do you think?"

Morgana froze, obviously not thrilled to be put on the spot. "I don't know him well enough to say what kind of books he'd like."

Jenna shrugged. "Well, I do. Mac." She tapped her index finger against his chest. "Stay. I think my copy's in my tote. And don't worry about the food. I'll bring that. You and Morgana can provide the wine. I heard you're good at that."

Mac didn't mind reading a book—even on short notice—but her reference to buying wine ticked him off for Morgana's sake. "Hey, who died and made you the director?"

Her eyes went wide. "Good line. I think I can use that. Sounds like something Coop would say." With a little wave of her fingers she walked away.

Mac stared after her a full minute before he realized Morgana was still standing there, looking at him. "Oh, sorry. My sister's friends are all crazy."

Her smile looked amused, but happy, too. "I like them. Kat's part of the group, right? Look at the pretty little tattoo she gave me." She pulled up the hem of her jeans—the exact same kind his sister wore when she went hiking—exposing her ankle. The design was a Celtic symbol of some kind. He liked it, but his reaction was downright ridiculous. He'd seen a hell of a lot more flesh than that on a woman and not gotten turned on. Damn. He was losing it.

"Kat," he muttered as if just remembering something he'd forgotten. He would have preferred to see more of her leg. "I was supposed to call her. About the swimming pool. Damn. Um…excuse me. Come on, Meggie, we have to go."

"Oh, Daddy, do we have to?"

Before he could reply, Morgana said, "Um…I'm done for the day. She could stay with me. I have a driver."

The offer surprised him. He wouldn't have thought she was all that interested in kids. Unless she was using Megan to get closer to him. He dismissed the idea with a shake of his head.

"Okay," she said, quickly covering her initial look of hurt. "She just seemed so interested in visiting the set last night. I thought I could show her around."

"She's four. There's a lot going on. I wouldn't want her to be underfoot."

"I won't, Daddy. I'll stay over foot all the time."

Mac scratched his nose to keep from laughing.

Morgana used the chance to add, "I'll watch her closely. I used to babysit—" She faltered. "I mean, I had a baby-sitter—a nanny, really—who was adamant about making sure I was safe. She followed me everywhere. She was an excellent role model."

She's lying. Mac wasn't sure how he knew that, but he did. He didn't know why she'd lie to him over something as innocuous as a babysitter. It made no sense.

Toward the end of their marriage, Misty had lied about everything. What she ate. Where she went. Who she talked to. Stupid lies that could be proven wrong with a simple phone call.

Mac hated lies. And he sure as hell didn't want his daughter exposed to another person who manipulated the truth to fit her own needs.

He looked at his daughter, and the dog sitting patiently beside her. "Bella." The dog's tail swished back and forth, picking up twigs and leaves. "Megan, what's the one thing we were supposed to do today that we haven't done? Make Bella's appointment with the vet."

His daughter started to pout but he gave her a look he knew she'd understand. "Remember what the lady at the shelter said?"

"No puppies."

"I meant the part about being responsible for your pet's health. Bella's your dog. You have to do right by her."

Megan looked over her shoulder toward the action near the tents. She might have argued the point, but Morgana lightly touched her cheek. "It's okay, sweetheart. You're not missing anything. And your dad is right about Bella. Dogs come with responsibility."

"And fleas. But we got that fixed, huh, Daddy?"

Mac was impressed by how coolly Morgana handled his rebuff. The casual onlooker might never have known she was hurt. But he could tell.

"So," she said brightly, flashing her fake smile. The one the cameras loved. "I'll…see you two later, then. At book club."

Mac gave a light tug on Bella's leash. "Um…what about the wine?"

"I'll have three or four bottles delivered."

And with that he was dismissed. A chill—too early for autumn—closed in around him. Bella let out a soft whine.

Damn, he thought as he watched Morgana walk away. He wasn't sure what had just happened, but it was probably for the best. At least, that's what he told himself.

MORGAN WALKED AWAY fuming. She wanted to hit something. Stomp her feet. Throw a diva fit. She'd slipped out of character for half a second and the way-too-astute Mac McGannon had caught her in a lie. That never happened. Never.

What the hell is wrong with me?

She didn't know, but she was glad he'd turned down her offer to watch Megan. That had been impulsive and reckless. Morgana didn't do children. Hanging out with four-year-olds would do nothing to further her career.

She was off the hook. She should have been relieved. Then why did she feel so disappointed?

"Morgana."

She turned toward the voice. Cooper. "Hi, Coop. All done?"

"I don't know. Shane's reviewing the last take. I saw you talking to Mac."

She cocked her head, trying to define that certain quality in his tone. Jealousy? Possessiveness? No, Coop had never been jealous or possessive when they were married so why would he care who she talked to now? Her hackles went up all the same. "So?"

"So what's going on with you two?"

"Gee, Coop, I don't know. He's a local. I was told to make nice with the locals to promote our acceptance and ensure a smooth production. Didn't you get the memo? Oh, wait…it *was* your memo."

He took a step back. "Whoa. It was a simple question."

She knew she was blowing this out of proportion, but he was a convenient target for everything that was bugging her. "No, it was a judgmental question that implied I was doing something wrong by talking—not flirting or hitting on, but *talking*—to your brother-in-law. Is there something I should know that you're not telling me? Is the gossip right? Did he do in his wife, and any woman who crosses his path is in danger?"

Coop looked aghast and quickly grabbed her arm to pull her farther from any eavesdroppers. "No. Of course not. Mac's a great guy. I feel honored that he's accepted me and calls me his friend. But you and him—he and you—whatever…that's just not a good combination."

Morgan agreed on so many levels it would have made Coop's head hurt to think about them all, but that didn't give him any right to point that out. "Why?"

"Uh…well…um…" he stammered. "You live in L.A. and he lives here."

"Like you and Libby?"

"That's not the same."

The fight went out of her. She sighed and put a hand on Coop's forearm. "I know, Coop. Relax. Nothing is going on. We were just discussing the book club. Apparently, we've all been invited to a one-time special meeting at Mac's house."

"Please tell me Jenna was joking. The book club is for women only."

"They've made an exception." Because she knew him well, she added, "I can lend you my copy of the book, if you need it."

"Does it have a comic version?"

"Not yet."

"Damn. Oh, well, Libby will bring me up to speed."

Morgan was sure of it. And, suddenly, for the dumbest reason of all, she was envious of Cooper. What would it be like to have someone in your life who always, unfailingly, had your back?

Morgan had been a very young child the last time she'd known that kind of peace, and she was afraid she'd never know it again.

CHAPTER SEVEN

MORGAN DUG HER BARE TOES into the soft, wet grass at the edge of the stoop where she was sitting and let out a long, deep sigh. Last night's sleep had been ghastly. The product of too much wine.

She'd tapped into the stash she'd asked her driver to buy for the book club for no other reason than she was alone on a Friday night and she had no one in the world who she was accountable to. So there.

She grimaced. She'd actually said those two words out loud. Like a child Megan's age.

"So there," she muttered. "So there goes some more brain cells."

Then, despite her best efforts and the white noise produced by the expensive sound machine she'd had shipped from home, she'd awoken far earlier than necessary. So, she'd hiked into town to the newly acquired Wi-Fi site at The Tidbiscuit. Tucked in the corner booth, hiding under a *Sentinel Passtime* ball cap, she'd cruised the Internet until her third cup of coffee left her so jittery she had no choice but to jog back to her little cabin.

That felt like hours ago. She'd showered, read the *Rapid City Journal* front to back and started a new book, but the coffee was still coursing through her system. She felt restless and confined. If she'd been home, she would have been shopping on Rodeo Drive.

Not that she was a big spender. Money didn't come easy, and with her true background she'd learned never to take anything for granted. But there was a certain art to shopping, and Morgan had learned how to turn the exercise into a media event.

She sighed and used her big toe to nudge a pebble out of the earth. She and Misty had loved to collect rocks when they were kids. She had no idea why. Or why the memory hit her so clearly.

"Hi, Princess Morgana."

Startled, Morgan looked up.

A princess of another kind was standing a few feet away on the well-worn path between Libby's home and the more modern ranch-style house beyond the hedge. Megan. Not the tomboy she'd first met or the wannabe princess with the well-worn costume dress, but an actual girly-girl with dark shiny hair pulled back and tied with a ribbon. Whoever had tied the bow wasn't terribly skilled, but Megan didn't seem to notice. She was smiling as if she was on the way to the ball.

"You look gorgeous. Where are you going?"

Megan pointed. "To Auntie's house. Then we're going shopping. For her birthday present," she added as if that might be a secret. "Daddy gave me money and I know just what I want to buy her."

Her pride and confidence was so genuine and sweet, Morgan had to blink to keep her tears at bay. Thank goodness she still had her sunglasses on. "That sounds like fun. Is Uncle Cooper going, too?"

She thought she'd seen Coop take off jogging shortly

after she returned from town but he could have slipped back in while she was in the shower.

"No. This is a girls-only day. We're going to have lunch and see a movie, too. G-rated. G is for girls. He's a boy."

"Oh. Right. I knew that."

Morgan looked in the direction that Megan had come from. No sign of Mac. But the sound of a screen door slamming drew her gaze to Libby's house, where Coop's wife was standing, phone to her ear. "She's here. She stopped to say hello to Morgana, who is sitting on the stoop. Gran used to love to sit there, too, remember?"

Libby's voice carried perfectly well. She waved. First, a friendly hello to Morgana, then a quick, hurry-up motion for Megan.

"Bye, Princess," Megan said, skipping away.

The frilly lace top of her left sock was folded under, Morgan noticed. She sprang to her feet and hurried after her. "Wait a second, honey. Let me fix your sock."

Megan stopped. She looked down at her feet. "Oh. Daddy put those on."

"It's just a little thing," Morgan said. She squatted beside her and quickly made the fix. The crisp lace felt stiff and scratchy compared to the soft material of the sock, but the effect was purely little girl. "There. Perfect. You look fabulous."

Megan's smile could have lit up the Hollywood sign for a week. "Thanks. Bye."

Morgan stood and took a deep breath to relieve the tightness in her chest. She didn't know what it was about that child that got to her. If she'd been able to ascertain that they were related, she'd understand it. But, as far as she knew, Megan was just Cooper's new wife's niece. Period.

Morgan stood a moment longer watching as Libby helped Megan into the shiny new car Coop had bought for her as a wedding present. "Aunt Morgan," Morgan said under her breath.

The word combination sounded wrong. Like President Morgan. Ambassador Morgan. But like a song that gets stuck in your head, the melody played on. "Hey, Aunt Morgan, thanks for the great graduation present. Auntie Morgan, I need a loan for college. Aunt Morgan, I'm in love. Aunt Morgan, you'll never guess what…I'm getting married."

A wave of sadness swept over her. Which was crazy, she told herself. This child was *not* her niece. The odds were too outlandish. She refused to believe it. She absolutely, positively would not think about this scenario until— unless—she found out otherwise. And she'd have her chance to see Mac's house in two days. At the book club meeting. Surely, there would be a photo of his late wife somewhere in the open.

The sound of a man clearing his throat made her jump.

"Sorry. I could tell you were deep in thought and I didn't mean to disturb you but…um…they already left, right?"

Morgan's heart still raced—from fear or from him she wasn't sure. Since she couldn't find her voice, she nodded.

"Damn. I have to go to my grandmother's, and Libby thought I should read aloud to her from that book club book. Kill two…um…birds, as they say." His dark complexion seemed to deepen a shade. "Unfortunately, I didn't stick around long enough to get Jenna's copy and I can't remember the title."

"Mine's inside. Do you want to borrow it?"

He hesitated. "Sure. That would save me hunting through Libby's bookshelves."

He followed her to the cottage. "Wait here. I'll be right back." She'd left a bit too much of herself around the tiny place to invite a stranger's eyes. Nothing overt, but clues a discerning person might pick up.

She found her carry-on bag in the micro closet where she'd left it. The book was stuffed in with a couple of scripts she'd been studying. Lucky for Morgan, she had a near photographic memory of written words. Where her work was concerned, she was a quick study. It was the stuff of real life that she found so much more challenging.

"Here you go," she said, holding the trade paperback out to him.

He'd moved into the shade of the building. Not surprising. The day was heating up. She was going to need to find something cool to do today. She had no idea what that might be. Shane had given the entire crew the weekend off. Generous of him since the production company was picking up the cost of lodging and meals. Most crew members were gathering for a picnic at one of the nearby lakes.

"Thanks," Mac said, straightening.

He really was a handsome man, she realized. A little rough around the edges, but that was part of his appeal. Untamed. Edgy. Rough and ready testosterone domesticated by circumstance and obligations.

She'd heard his name mentioned several times in the past few days. Mac McGannon was well thought of in this town. A go-to guy. "Salt of the earth," Elana Grace, the owner of The Tidbiscuit, had said. Whatever that meant. Her aunt and uncle had been called that, too. *Before* Morgan and Misty went to live with them.

"What are you up to today?" he asked conversationally.

"I..." She considered lying. Weren't celebrities supposed to have more demands on their time than they could meet? But her mind went blank. "Nothing."

"By choice?" He seemed surprised. And maybe a little sorry for her.

I should have lied. Told him I was going waterskiing with the younger staff. She'd been invited but had declined because she didn't want to admit that she didn't know how to swim. What blueblood from Long Island wasn't given swim lessons from day one?

"Yes." That was the truth.

"I'm going to run up to the mine after I read to Gran. Would you like to see the Little Poke? I know the film crew is using it in some scenes next week, but it'll probably be a little crazy when everyone is there."

While a part of her was jumping up and down, the actress in her calmly replied, "That sounds interesting. Coop and I have one scene there together. It's an emotionally charged black moment. It might not hurt to get a lay of the land, as they say."

Professional. Not pathetic.

"I don't know if Coop told you, but we're thinking of using the mine as part of a tourist package. Stay at the Little Poke Inn, then dig for gold. Coop thinks both men and women would go for it. I'd like to get a woman's opinion."

The name made her smile. "The Little Poke Inn? I love the double entrendre. Was that your idea or Coop's?"

"Shane's. He and Jenna have been helping develop the concept to take to the bank. Jenna has her experience from running the Mystery Spot on her side. The big question at the moment is whether to convert Lib's house into the B & B or build a place closer to the mine."

They both turned and looked at the unpretentious two-story home. The big front porch gave it a friendly feel. "I haven't seen the mine yet, but my first inclination is to use this place. It has a certain charm, and this cabin would make a great honeymoon cottage," she said, gesturing toward the little bungalow she presently occupied. "Maybe you could even build on the fact that Cooper Lindstrom slept here."

"That's a good idea. Really good. Plus, I think Gran would be pleased by the romantic angle. She lived here after our mom passed away and for a short time before she got together with Calvin. They're not married, you know. Gran loves being able to tell people she lives with a younger man. He's, like, eighty-four," he added.

Her laugh was genuine. She admired people who lived honestly even though she wasn't able to do so herself. "So…when would this tour of the mine take place?"

He thought a moment. "I'm giving Cal a break to run some errands—he doesn't like leaving Gran alone anymore—but he said he'd be back at lunchtime. How does one o'clock sound?"

"That would be fine."

She didn't mean to make her tone so stilted and formal, but she knew that was how it came across by the way he nodded and turned to leave—as if dismissed.

He was a few feet from the hedge when Morgan called out, "Wait. What if I go with you now? To save you a trip back." What? A whopping ten or twelve blocks? "I'm pretty good at reading aloud." She felt her blush intensify. "Comes with the job."

He was too far away for her to read his expression. That was probably a good thing, she decided. He had to be confused. Why would someone like her volunteer to read to an old person? Wasn't she a self-absorbed socialite-slash–TV star? This kind of gesture was out of character.

And why had she volunteered? Morgan decided not to look too closely at her motives. Maybe it came down to boredom. A handy distraction to keep her from worrying about the state of her finances. She hoped that's all it was.

"Okay," he said. "If you're sure."

She wasn't. Not at all. But that didn't keep her from dashing into the house for her purse and sun hat. The latter was probably a foolish thing to take along. A mine was dark, right? But her milky-white skin was part of her trademark, and the cosmetics people probably wouldn't appreciate it if her true heritage—tanned arms and a freckled nose—became part of the package.

"Psst. Mac. I need your help a minute."

Mac looked toward the doorway and spotted Calvin motioning for him. Cal was back already? He glanced at his watch. Good lord. He'd been sitting beside his grandmother for two hours, holding her mostly impassive hand in his while Morgana read aloud.

True, the story had been intriguing, the characters real and flawed, like people in real life. But it was the way she read that made what could have been a torturous task pass in a blink.

And even if his grandmother's attention seemed to come and go, Mac had sensed the peace and contentment she took from Morgana's voice.

He drew Gran's hand to his lips then carefully tucked it in her lap. Her head was tilted back, eyes closed, but Mac wasn't certain she was asleep. He stood slowly, trying not to disturb her. As he turned to leave, he made eye contact with Morgana, whose reading didn't falter for a second. He nodded toward the door and she acknowledged his intention with a regal tilt of her head.

Once he was out of the room, he paused to massage his neck. His throat was so tight you would have thought he was the one doing the reading. But, no, all he'd had to do was sit and listen…and be lured into Morgana's spell. Like that sailor he once read about. Odysseus.

Only, Morgana wasn't a witch or seven-headed monster. She was kind and professional and generous. And he was a pig for thinking totally inappropriate things in his dying grandmother's presence. Thank God Cal was back, he thought, hurrying into the kitchen.

"Hey, Cal. You're back early, aren't you?"

Calvin was sitting at the dinette, staring out the window, obviously too lost in thought to even notice the splendor of the hollyhocks waving in the breeze. "Didn't take as long as I expected. They're delivering a hospital bed in a few minutes."

"A hospital bed?" Gran had seemed weaker today than the last time he saw her. He'd had to lift her from her wheelchair onto the sofa, but…

"I could use your help setting this up. It isn't—" Cal's voice broke. "I didn't think it would come to this, but I can't sleep at night worrying that Mary's going to fall out of bed and I won't hear her. It would kill me to lose her that way. Undig—"

Mac understood. His grandmother was dying. He'd resisted admitting the fact these past couple of months. Her decline had been slow—some might even say graceful—

but most definitely persistent. He wondered if maybe his subconscious had grasped the truth while listening to Morgana read aloud to Gran.

The actress's voice—as clear and lilting and nearly as beautiful as she was—had pulled him into the story of a long-married couple dealing with both changes to their relationship and the impending death of the hero's grandfather. The grandfather—who was about Gran's age—recalled moments from his life between doses of painkillers, but there was a sense that he wasn't going to come out of this decline.

Freed from the task of struggling to read the words aloud, Mac had been able to watch his grandmother's face as Morgana read. The intelligence and wit that were Mary McGannon Tyler's trademarks had vanished, leaving behind a shell of the person they all knew and loved. No wonder Libby had been so distressed lately. He tried to visit his grandmother often, but with a young child and all the demands of being a single parent, his attention had been divided.

Until now.

His heart thudded heavily in his chest. A part of him knew it was only a matter of time. Days. Weeks. Not years, that was for sure.

He walked to where Cal was sitting and bent down to give the older man a one-arm hug. "A bed, huh? Sounds like a good idea. Where are we putting it?"

"In our room," Cal stated as if expecting an argument. "Near the window so she can see the birds. She always loved those damn birds. The noisier and messier the better."

His bluster, Mac knew, was to cover his pain. And his fear, too, Mac suspected. Watching a loved one die had to remind a person of his own mortality—especially when you were in your eighties.

"Show me what needs to be done."

The large master bedroom was an interesting design that incorporated a modest bay area that held two upholstered rockers, a small table and a large lamp. Mac carried one of the chairs to the garage and covered it with a sheet. The end table, lamp and second chair would remain adjacent to the bed that was coming.

He was just starting back to the house when the sound of a truck pulling into the driveway stopped him. He walked around the building and used hand signals to help the driver back up. "Whoa. That's good," he said.

A movement to his left caught his eye. Morgana stood in the doorway watching, Gran's old toy poodle in her arms. The dog was trembling but for once didn't bark. Mac was glad for the help. He and Onida didn't get along all that well. The dog preferred the company of women.

The actual delivery and installation was a simple affair. It seemed apparent that the men doing the setup were extremely familiar with life-and-death situations. One of them gave Calvin a quick but thorough demonstration of the bed's functions, then they left.

"Shall I bring her in now, Cal?"

Cal hesitated a moment then shook his head. "After lunch. Mary likes to rest after lunch. Would never call it a nap. Said naps weren't for average people."

Morgana, who had followed them into the bedroom, gave a soft chuckle. "I had an aunt like that. Might have worked her fingers to the bone all morning but she wouldn't have been caught dead napping."

That gave Mac pause. Was one part of her family less

well-off than her parents? He would have asked, but she got a look on her face that told him she'd said more than she wanted. Or had her mention of the word *dead* embarrassed her? He was willing to give her the benefit of the doubt because she'd helped so much that morning.

"Fresh tomato sandwiches, anyone?" Calvin asked.

Mac hadn't planned on staying to eat, but he heard something in Cal's voice that robbed him of the ability to say no. "Morgana? Do you have time or do we need to get to the mine so you can make your other plans?"

She looked up from petting Onida, who was still quite contentedly cuddled in her arms. For a woman who had never owned a pet, she had a way with animals. "I love homegrown tomatoes. Haven't tasted any in years. It would be a real treat." She leaned over and set Onida down. "Calvin, may I make the bed for Mary while you fix lunch?"

She knows how to make a bed?

"That would be very nice. Thank you. Mac knows where the sheets are. Mary and I will be in the kitchen."

Mac wasn't ready to be alone with Morgana. His emotions felt too…un-him. "Do you need me to get Gran in her wheelchair, Cal?"

"No, thanks. I can manage. She still enjoys watching me cook. I usually puree whatever I'm having and add it to one of her protein drinks."

Because his grandmother had forgotten how to chew. His heart had shrunk two sizes when Libby told him that.

"The sheets?"

Morgana's voice shook him out of his funk. "Right. Hall closet. I can do this, Morgana. You don't need to. Wouldn't want you to break a fingernail."

He wasn't sure why he was intent on pushing her away,

but he figured it had something to do with her seeing him so weak and vulnerable. His emotions were raw. So much had changed in the past year; he wasn't ready to lose his grandmother, too.

She placed a hand on his bare forearm. "These are your sister's hands, remember?"

He looked down. Slim, beautiful fingers devoid of polish or fake nails or anything he might have pictured. Plain hands. No rings, either. But that only served to remind him that she had been married to Cooper. His business partner and brother-in-law.

He reached out to open the closet door, effectively breaking their contact. He liked her touch too much. He had to make sure that didn't happen again. "Single bed," he said, mostly to help maintain his focus. "I wonder where…"

She leaned past him to point to a shelf marked single bed sheets. "Here?"

Her breast brushed against his upper arm. He knew it was a breast without looking. He knew because a fire so intense it almost made him double over ripped through his gut. Okay, his groin. Damn, this was not acceptable.

He grabbed the two sheets without looking to see if he had a flat and fitted pair. Luckily, the bedroom was to his left so he could make his escape without bumping into Morgana.

"Was Gran asleep when you left her?" he asked, hearing her footfall behind him.

"She nodded off shortly before you left but she looked so peaceful, I kept reading until I came to the end of a chapter."

"Thanks. I…um…mean that. I don't read that well. Never have. I can get by with Megan's books but…um…you did a good job. A whole lot better than I could."

"I've had a lot of practice. Even when I was a young girl I liked to read aloud. I'd pretend to be the people in the story and would change my voice to portray different characters. My little sister loved that."

He stopped what he was doing to look at her. "You have a sister?"

Instead of helping him, as she'd offered, she walked to the window and looked outside, keeping her back to him. She didn't answer right away. For a moment, he was certain she wasn't going to, then she said, "I don't know. We haven't spoken since I left home. I can't say for sure if she's alive or dead. Isn't that a horrible thing to have to admit?"

He opened the bottom sheet with a crack. "Shane had a falling-out with his brother, too. For good reason. I'm sure you heard about that."

"Everyone did, thanks to the media. My sister wasn't psychotic or anything. Just a lot younger than me and impressionable. I'm sure our…um…parents poisoned her mind against me after I left home."

He heard something terribly sad in her tone, despite the effort she made to sound resigned. Her haughty Eastern accent had returned, but he didn't buy it. She wasn't an uncaring person. Whatever had driven her away from her family must have been bad—and none of his business.

He quickly finished the bed, adding a couple of pillows he knew were his grandmother's. "There. I'll let Cal finish up. He knows what kind of blankets she prefers. She's always cold—even in summer."

"Dinner's ready," a thin, reedy voice called from the other side of the house.

"Dinner," she repeated softly.

"It's a Midwestern thing," he said, letting her go first. "Breakfast, dinner and supper."

She looked at him for a bare second but he saw something surprising. Grief.

"Yes. I know," she said, hurrying away.

Because she'd studied for the role of his sister? He wanted to believe that, but a disquieting voice said otherwise. He didn't know what that meant. And why did it matter? She was only here for a very short time. He needed to remember that.

CHAPTER EIGHT

"So, THIS IS A GOLD MINE. Where's the gold?"

Morgan immediately liked the place. She couldn't say why. The smell? Musty and faintly metallic. Maybe it was the quiet. A distant sound of water dripping seemed to be the only noise beyond their breathing.

"Much deeper. You'd need different clothes, shoes and a breathing apparatus for that."

"Won't your guests want to go where the gold is?"

He'd given her the requisite hard hat, which was equipped with an individual light, but since they were only a hundred feet or so into the horizontal shaft which had an electrical lighting system in place, they hadn't turned them on.

"My guess is yes. Coop and I have talked about it. He has a pal who runs a racetrack in California, and they make a good living by offering driver-for-a-day packages. He said they bought some used cars, and teach regular people how to race. Then before the big event that night, they run an eight- or ten-lap competition for the first-timers.

"Coop thinks we should do the same kind of thing here. We supply all the clothes, boots, safety equipment, etcetera, then take them down to a shaft with some established color and let them work. What they find, they get to keep."

She could picture it. "That's a great idea. Cooper thought of that?"

The look on his face said he was ready to defend his brother-in-law but when he saw she was joking, he smiled. She really liked his smile. Manly. Elusive. He was a serious guy, but then why wouldn't he be? Single dad. Widower. Trying to eke out a living in a difficult profession.

That was one thing they had in common. She was impressed that he'd been able to roll with the economy and look at the Little Poke in a new way. Many men wouldn't have been that flexible.

"How many days will they be filming here?"

He thought a moment. "Well…I really don't know. I haven't seen the script. I don't know if this is the part where I leave Cooper in the dark or—"

"You what?"

He held up one finger. "Wait here. I'll show you."

She didn't move, but she didn't take her eyes off him, either. She wasn't ready to be left alone in this place, even if she did have a safety light on her head.

He wasn't more than ten feet away when he reached overhead and suddenly there was no light. She blinked twice, three times, but all she could see were the tiny flashes that floated past her eyelids when she closed her eyes. "Oh, my lord. So, this is dark."

She heard him moving toward her, but her senses weren't acute enough to judge distance. She cocked her head and strained to listen. Crunch. Shuffle. A muffled curse.

"Are you okay?"

"Yes. Damn it. I forgot I had Megan here the other day. She likes to stack rocks in little piles. She calls them rock people and gives them names." He hesitated. "I think I just murdered the Slocum family."

Morgan's laugh brought a strange kind of release. In the dark, she was free to giggle at silly comments and joke back. "Oh, dear. Not the Slocums. They were friends of mine. Jessie, Peter and little Lu-Lu."

His deep chuckle sent shivers down her spine. He was close. She could sense his body heat—or thought she could. Was that possible? The sound of his breathing was nearby, but the tunnel created an echo effect. She didn't know for sure what was real and what was imagination.

But she'd never been accused of lacking an imagination. In her mind's eye she pictured him standing mere inches from her. Leaning in to inhale her perfume. Their male and female auras overlapping.

He cleared his throat before asking, "H-how well did you know them? Did you know they had rocks for brains? Anyone who would live in a mine shaft—"

Was he talking about himself, now? Was he trying to talk himself out of doing something he might regret later? Something they both might regret?

"I can't speak for the Slocums, but it's easy to see how this kind of place might grow on you. Never having to see the judgmental looks in people's eyes. No cameras clicking. No reporters trying to nibble off some spare pound of flesh. I think it's very…liberating. You can do anything you want and no one would ever know."

She waited to see what his reaction to her obvious come-on would be. Would the lights flick back on? Would he hightail it and give her time to come to her senses before he rescued her from herself?

"I never thought of it like that before," he said. She'd

already decided that Mac's voice was one she'd never forget. She could recall it perfectly when he wasn't there. There was truth and humility and strength in his tone. And in the dark, all of those things wrapped around her like a security blanket.

She felt safe. Safe enough to reach out and do what she'd wanted to do for days. Even sightless, she found him, unerringly. Her fingers touched the crisp material of his buttoned shirt. An unobtrusive plaid cotton shirt that he wore tucked in. No extra roll around Mac's middle that he had to hide. He was one of the most fit specimens of forty-year-old men she'd ever seen.

"It's possible the Slocums chose to live here because of the view," she said, seeing with her imagination. Her fingers inched upward. She felt his sharp inhale when she reached the open V of his neckline. Bare skin was right beyond the edge of fabric.

"Maybe they're crazy," he said, reaching out to pull her close—as efficiently as a sighted man in daylight.

His lips found hers just as easily and she answered without hesitation. In the light of day she would have stopped, thought, turned and run, but where could she go in the dark? The blackness felt like a cool, silk net suspending them in a cocoon.

The absence of outer stimuli made her more sensitive to specialized stimuli. *Taste.* His tongue slipped between her lips. Wet, slippery, strong, basil. The words actually flashed in her mind. Not something she could ever remember happening when she kissed someone.

Basil. The word lingered and brought with it images she'd have preferred to keep at bay. Cal's garden. The fresh tomatoes. Mac's grandmother's hospital bed where she would probably die. Sooner rather than later. *Will I even be here?*

The question gave her pause. She pulled back and closed her eyes. The reaction, she knew, made no sense.

Mac's arms relaxed their hold but didn't fall away. Neither spoke. Probably because they were both breathing hard. In the dark, that reality was very audible.

"Well, I didn't see that coming."

Morgan laughed. He might not consider himself a great orator, but the man could definitely think on his feet. "The Slocums are probably scandalized."

Their bodies were still touching in certain places and she felt him chuckle, too. That pleasant thumping of belly and chest was really what sealed the deal for her. Humor got her every time.

She'd often been told that she was too serious, high-strung, intense. "Lighten up, Morgie," Cooper had said a thousand times while they were together. Maybe a million. But she couldn't. She didn't know how.

Until now. In the dark. With a man who was all wrong for her. Disturbingly wrong on so many levels. *If...* She gave her head a little shake. *Enough.* The negatives that existed before she and Mac entered this tunnel would still be there—regardless of what happened between them.

The darkness emboldened her, but she wasn't deluding herself. They were both here for a reason. Hopefully the same reason. "Is there any way I could talk you into making love with me?" she asked.

"Here? Now? In front of the Slocums? Little Lu-Lu could be scarred for life."

It wasn't a no, but it wasn't quite the answer she'd expected. "Do you have a better idea?"

His hand made a lazy, scintillating foray up her back. "Well...I have a futon in my office."

She wondered how often he'd made love to his wife on it.

As if reading her thoughts from a page of script, he added, "I don't know how comfortable it is. I bought it in case I ever got snowed in and had to spend the night here, but so far all it's been used for is a place to stack old mining magazines and stuff."

Good, but... "I like the dark. There's a certain anonymity that makes me feel safe. Weird, huh?"

"Makes perfect sense given the paparazzi that follow you around. But my office is actually less crowded. No Slocums."

Her grin—the one he couldn't see—was as liberating as the darkness. She wanted this. Badly. And she believed him. Trusted him. That in itself was huge. She also knew that he was enough of a gentleman not to hold her to this impulse if she reached the daylight and changed her mind. "So...let's go."

He didn't move right away. Instead, he felt around for her hand and brought it to his lips. He kissed each knuckle in a lingering way that made her knees weak and another part of her body, not far from her knees, wet and yearning.

Then he squeezed her fingers supportively, as if reassuring her that she'd made the right decision. A second later, a bright shaft of light cut a swatch into the blackness. She blinked, trying to get her bearings. He tightened his hold on her hand. "Let's take it slow."

"Yes," she said, stumbling slightly. She wrapped her free hand around his arm, too, like a shipwreck victim finding her feet on dry land.

They listed to the left. "Watch out. Don't step on the Slocums."

Tears filled her eyes. She couldn't say why. She wished she could blame her emotional state on the imaginary rock family or, even, Mac's failing grandmother. But, in truth, there was a very good chance she was falling in love with Mac McGannon.

Mac's relief at finding the miniblinds that covered the lone window in his office closed couldn't be overstated. He didn't know exactly what just happened, but he was pretty sure his beautiful guest was *this* close to bolting. A dusty office filled with daylight, which was directly linked to reality, could have made all the difference.

Which might not be a bad thing, a part of his mind said. But it was a very small part.

Kissing Morgana in the dark had transported him to a place he honestly didn't think he'd ever been. He wasn't the kind of guy who used words like *mystical* and *life-altering,* but that kinda felt like what happened. One minute he was joking about Megan's imaginary rock family and the next he was making out with the sweetest-tasting woman he'd ever kissed.

How that could be, he had no idea. They'd eaten the same lunch, but her mouth was so amazingly perfect. Inviting. Delicious. Delectable. Damn, he didn't have enough words.

"This is it," he said, taking her hard hat from her when she removed it.

He said a silent thank-you to his father for planning this back way into the office. The bisecting tunnel had wasted some extra time and money, but it provided fresh air and an escape to safety. Or, in this case, an escape to something entirely different.

Maybe.

He watched her as she looked around. His office was neater than usual because he'd known the film crew was coming. He'd cleaned off the large metal drafting table where the underground schematics usually rested and he'd boxed up the mountains of unread mining magazines that had accumulated since Misty's death. There was never enough time to do what he'd taken for granted in the past.

But the space was still far from pristine. He used the back of his hand to wipe off a layer of dust on his desk chair. "Keeping my house clean is hard enough, let alone this place, too," he said, hoping he didn't sound too whiny. "I'm not complaining. It's just the way it is."

If she heard him, she didn't comment. Her attention seemed pinned to the old photos on the wall. Pictures his grandmother had framed. Sepia prints of his ancestors. All miners. But the one she lingered over was the small portrait resting on his desk, barely visible above a stack of mail.

A shot of him and Megan last spring when Gran's tulips were in full array. Megan was seated on his lap, head back against his chest, laughing at something Libby had said. He'd loved the photo because that had been one of the first real laughs he'd heard since her mother passed away.

"She's really a special child, isn't she?" Morgana asked.

"I think so. She's not a part of this, though. I know that. So, you don't have to worry."

She looked stymied. "Worry about what?"

"That I'd read more into what's going on between us than you'd intended. I know you have a life. A big life. Megan's and mine is very small."

She looked at him but didn't say anything. What could she say? He'd been trying to make it clear that he didn't expect anything beyond what she was comfortable giving. He thought for a faint second that he'd hurt her feelings, but then she smiled prettily. "Did you say something about a futon?"

His heart made a funny roller-coaster motion that left him slightly breathless. Was his tiny world big enough for someone like her? He hoped to God, yes. Because he wanted her more than he'd ever wanted anyone else. Anyone. He didn't want to think about what that meant.

He reached out and reeled her into his arms. Once she was tight against him—a position his body seemed to remember like some kind of imprint—he looked over her shoulder at the futon he'd picked up a year or so ago when he and Misty first started having problems. Or, rather, when their problems became the kind that necessitated a night or two apart.

"Very attractive," she said, following his gaze.

"And rock free. I couldn't make that claim in the shaft."

The humor had returned to her eyes. Her gorgeous honey-gold eyes. He'd never seen that color before. He wondered if she wore contact lenses. He wondered, but not enough to ask. Frankly, he didn't care what was real and what was not. The parts he could feel were warm and genuine and that worked for him.

He ran his hands up and down her beautiful creamy white arms. A bit on the skinny side, but smooth and toned. "You are beautiful everywhere. In the dark. Or the light."

"Thank you."

She reached up and placed her hand along his jaw. He tried to remember if he'd shaved that morning. Yes, he was sure he had because he was going to Gran's.

"I like your face. And the rest of you, too," she added with a girlish bat of her eyelashes. "There's strength of character in this face. I can see why the people of the town look up to you."

"They do? That's news to me. You should have been here last winter when— Never mind. That's nice of you to say. And I sorta know what you mean. I've lived here my whole life, except when I went to trade school. And as a volunteer firefighter, I get called in times of need."

She looked down then up, a teasing grin on her lips. "What kind of need?"

A jolt of heat went straight through him. "Most any kind. I'm always ready and willing to help."

He had a hard time saying that with a straight face. He knew she got his drift because she went up on her toes to kiss him. A lingering kiss that fueled the fire. "I haven't been with a man in a long time. I think that qualifies as need, don't you?"

"Absolutely."

"Do we have to pass some kind of test first?"

He puzzled over her meaning a moment. "What kind?"

"Health and fitness. Practical matters in this day and age."

"Oh. Yeah. I got tested after…um… It seemed like a good idea. There hasn't been anyone since."

"I'm an abstinence kind of girl. Less complicated."

He knew exactly what she meant. When your life was in chaos, the last thing you needed was to add any of the complications associated with sex and dating. "Birth control…" he said. Was there any chance he still had a leftover condom or two from before Megan was born? Would such a thing still be good?

Morgana cut into his thoughts. "I took a shot that's good for three months. There was a guy I was considering dating and I wanted to be prepared, but it turned out he wasn't interested in taking things beyond a professional level."

Why? his mind shouted. *Was he nuts?*

But he knew better than to ask. Look at his messed-up

life. Even people you thought you knew and loved could act in crazy, fickle, unpredictable ways. So maybe that made him and Morgana right for each other. At this moment in time. He knew it would never go beyond this, and he was okay with that. He hoped.

He scooped her up in his arms and carried her to the futon. Her right arm slipped around his neck and she leaned close to nuzzle his ear. Her breath was hot and provocative as she outlined the rim of his ear with her tongue. He had to tighten his grip to avoid dropping her.

Her laugh was playful. "Careful there. We don't want to ruin the moment with a couple of broken bones."

"That won't happen. I promise." It's all he could promise. He had a feeling she understood that and wouldn't ask for more.

He let her legs lower to the floor but she remained pressed against him, as if any separation might ruin the moment. He was worried about that, too, but there were a few practical matters that needed to be handled and he wasn't suave and proficient enough at the art of seduction to do them without her help. "Um…I haven't opened this thing up in a long time. I'm not sure I remember how."

She grinned. "It'll come back to you." Her teasing tone eased the tension. "How can I help?"

He walked to the side closest to the desk. "I think there's a latch you pull to release." She followed his lead. "If we do it at the same time, it's easier."

She was a quick study. With very little effort, the wooden frame slid out and the thick foam mattress covered in a chocolate-brown microfiber material became a bed. She straightened and brushed her hands back and forth, smiling. "Perfect."

It crossed his mind that she was much easier to please than he'd expected a Hollywood star to be. He tossed her a cotton sheet from his bottom desk drawer. "Air conditioner on or off?" he asked, standing by the unit.

"On, please."

He pushed the button then locked the door—just in case—and joined her.

"Now…" He didn't touch her immediately. He wanted to tell her what this meant to him. That she was the first since…in a long time. That he'd loved listening to her read to his grandmother. That her voice had pulled him into a place he'd forgotten existed. A safe, serene place where you didn't feel as if the bottom was falling away from beneath your feet.

He didn't know her beyond this moment and time, and to his profound surprise, he was okay with that. Even after all he'd been through, he'd rather be here—with her—than anyplace else.

But he didn't say any of those things. His jaw locked shut in the way his late wife had hated so much. "You're dumb, Mac. Not stupid. Dumb. As in you never open your mouth and speak about anything other than work or mining or Megan or the fire department. I spend my days with a toddler, Mac. I need to hear multisyllable words. I need conversation."

He'd failed her. He'd given Misty everything he could, but in the end that hadn't been enough.

He wondered what he had that this beautiful woman could possibly want from him and if he'd fail her, too. He almost turned and headed back into the mine, but then Morgana kicked off her shoes and stepped onto the hastily made futon. She held her arms out for balance and laughed in a girlish way that sounded happy and beckoning.

She crooked her finger at him. "Despite all those adages about looking and leaping and thinking before you act, I've found that sometimes it's best to just do whatever it is you're in the process of doing and worry about consequences later. Does that work for you?"

"Yes," he said, unbuttoning his shirt.

She smiled. "A man of few words. After living with Coop, you have no idea how refreshing I find that."

"Actually, I think I do," he said, nodding. "He's my brother-in-law, remember?"

That should have been a deal-breaker right there. Cooper wouldn't be happy with either of them if he knew what they were about to do. But, for the first time in a long time, Mac didn't care what anyone thought. He was sick and tired of pleasing people, carrying the weight of the world on his shoulders, always doing the right thing.

Screw it.

He tossed his shirt over the back of his chair and undid his belt. He'd worn jeans and his old running shoes because the strap on his only pair of sandals had broken when he pulled them on that morning. He didn't bother with the laces, just jimmied them off, then, balancing on first one foot, then the other, pulled off his socks. He left his jeans on.

She hadn't undressed, he noticed, although her gaze never left him. He crossed his arms and waited. "Well?"

She turned so her back was to him. "Zipper."

He smiled at her one-word answer. He wasn't surprised to see his hands tremble as he tried to make his too-large fingers work the small plastic zipper. "This one is worse than Megan's."

Her soft snicker made her shoulders wiggle under his

hands. Her scent, probably some designer perfume that cost more than he made in a month, instantly imprinted itself on his olfactory sense. He'd never smell this fragrance again without thinking of her. This moment. The scary, exhilarating feeling building in his chest.

The zipper finally cooperated, baring her beautiful back. Warm white. Not the typical California bronze he'd come to expect from Cooper, Shane and the rest of the crew. Her skin was pristine. He leaned down and explored the area with his lips and nose.

"You not only smell beautiful, you taste good," he said, trailing the tip of his tongue along her backbone, which was exposed all too clearly.

The thought crossed his mind that if she were his he'd make sure she ate more.

She shivered and turned around. The shoulders of the dress had fallen off so the material barely clung to the top of her breasts. Apparently the dress had a built-in bra. "Nice dress. Forget I complained about the zipper," he said, grinning.

For a small woman, her breasts were voluptuous, straining against the material. He hooked his index finger in the V and slowly tugged it downward. Slowly to savor the moment. Slowly to draw out the suspense. His gut tightened as the fabric fell away.

He couldn't speak so he swallowed and, after drinking in his fill, looked up. "Beautiful."

She smiled and wiggled the rest of the way out of her dress. Her panties were mostly lace. Purple. High cut over her hip bones. Another V, inviting his attention. But first, he needed to touch…and taste.

"Ice cream," he said, palming one breast so he could lick the areola.

She gave a little laugh, but it was sketchy. Broken.

He knew she was feeling this, too.

"Ice cream? You're hungry?"

"For you. Your skin reminds me of vanilla ice cream. My favorite. This—" he encircled the nipple with the tip of his tongue "—is the color of butterscotch. And just as sweet." Then he took the nipple in his mouth and sucked, teasing a bit with his teeth.

"Oh, oh…my…nice."

Her fingers winnowed through his hair and her chest swelled against his mouth. His other hand cupped and toyed with the opposite breast until he was ready to shower his attention on it.

She made low, appreciative sounds that encouraged him to explore. Holding one hand flat against the small of her back, he nuzzled her belly, inhaling the earthy scent of woman. Woman ready for lovemaking.

He ran a finger along the top of the lace, stretching the material to give him a peek. He couldn't help but stare. *They call it a modified Brazilian,* a voice in his head said. One of the guys at the station had explained to the others why the foldout didn't look like their wives.

He almost said, "Wow." But managed to keep the thought to himself. "Every inch of you is beautiful."

She looked at him and laughed. "That's my line." Then she pushed away and stepped back, wobbling on the dense mattress. "I need you out of those jeans first."

"Yeah." He was damn sorry he'd been too modest to unzip his jeans when he'd removed his belt because the pressure was intense. He hadn't felt this horny since he was a teen.

He started to sit, but she stopped him, dropping, instead,

to her knees. She lassoed his belt loops with two fingers and tugged him a step closer. Then, looking up to watch his expression, she undid the metal button and slowly unzipped.

He sucked in his gut. A pinch on a fragile spot might definitely ruin the moment, but she was careful. And his package, as the guys liked to call it, helped by bursting to safety at first chance.

"Sexy undies," she said, giving him room to yank down his jeans and kick them out of the way.

He didn't have to look, but he did. Low-cut. Black with tiny silver zigzags. "I started buying crazy underwear while at trade school. Every other guy on campus wore tighty-whities. My shorts never got lost…or stolen."

"Smart man. And stretched tight like this, the silver lines resemble lightning bolts," she teased. "Very cool."

He couldn't help but smile. Her humor put him at ease without taking away from the moment. He liked that. He liked her. Maybe he more than liked her. He hoped not. Like would do.

"Come here, sparky. Let's make some friction."

He didn't need to be told twice. One knee then the other. Face to face. Belly to belly. Lace to lightning bolts…for a few seconds, then simply skin to skin.

He reached between them to explore the warm, wet recess he couldn't wait to fill.

"Are you—"

"Yes, please. Ready."

She reached for him, too, and guided him to her, lifting up slightly.

He leaned back on his heels, taking her with him.

"Oh, my…oh, yes," she grunted, closing her eyes as she sank around him. She wiggled and shifted her hips in a way that nearly made him lose it. But he doubled his concentration. He wanted to make this good. Memorable. For both of them.

He put his hands on her buttocks and squeezed, at the same time kissing her breasts. She found a rhythm that worked for her and he matched it. He didn't try for finesse. The pleasure was intense enough from the simple friction.

Her hands squeezed his shoulders as she reached that ultimate place. He matched her soft, guttural shout with one of his own a second or two later.

The aftershocks quaked through them, together. As one.

Mac felt a powerful rush of emotion that didn't seem at all appropriate. He had to use every bit of willpower left to keep from weeping.

CHAPTER NINE

"WOULD YOU LIKE something to drink?"

He wasn't sure what the appropriate protocol was for this kind of thing. He'd never had sex with a relative stranger in his office.

"Yes, thank you. That sounds good. And a bathroom."

Grateful for something to do—other than make love again, which was what he wanted—he scooted back, handed her a box of tissues from his desk then yanked on his shorts.

"The restroom is through that door in the locker room. I'll be right back with a soda." He felt her watching him get dressed. There was something so intimate and homey about the moment he decided to skip his shirt. Maybe they would do this again.

He didn't bother with socks but shoved his feet into his shoes. A shop was a dangerous place to walk barefoot. He hesitated, hand on the doorknob. Was there something he should say? Probably, but he didn't know what. A lot of words were racing around in his brain, but trying to pick the right ones was going to take time. He'd think about how to express what he was feeling on his way to get the drinks, and hopefully her feelings wouldn't be too bruised before he got back. "Okay?"

Morgan's heart was so full her chest hurt. She didn't know how or why one quick, mutually pleasurable act of making love should have this profound effect on her, but she was speechless. It seemed Mac was, too. She nodded.

His small, tight smile went straight through her. God, she was a mess. An emotional quagmire. Poor guy. If he actually knew how complete that sexual act had made her feel, he'd be running away to hide in the deepest, darkest shaft in this mine.

Once the door closed behind him, she tidied up, snatched her clothes from the floor and the back of the chair and dashed into the adjoining room. The asphalt tile floor was old and not particularly clean-looking, but she guessed the darkened path was from years of miners coming back from their jobs underground. She didn't begrudge the place a little grit and grime.

She used the restroom, which was clean and antiseptic-smelling, then took a seat on a painted wood bench in the locker room to pull on her undies. She zipped her dress, smiling as she remembered using the old I-need-help-with-my-zipper ploy. Not that Mac needed to be tricked into seducing her. They'd been on the same course since the moment he'd invited her to see the mine. Substitute *etching* for *mine* and you had a classic pickup line, she thought with a smile.

Not that Mac was a player. He was a decent guy who felt the same attraction she felt toward him. Simple. That they'd been lucky enough to grab a few uninterrupted minutes out of time…well, she wasn't going to knock it. Good things did happen. On rare occasions.

As she adjusted the bosom of her dress, her nipples tightened. She closed her eyes and pictured him kissing and fondling her breasts. Mac's hands were big and a little rough. Working hands. His touch sure and firm, as if he could feel beneath every layer of her skin.

Stop, she told herself, forcing her eyes open. No use imbuing the man with superhero qualities when she was only going to be here another few days. She couldn't remember when her flight was, but she knew it was soon.

She slipped on her shoes and took a breath. Time to get her game face— The thought went out of her head when she spotted a five-foot-tall, gunmetal-gray locker straight across the room from her. The name MAC had been stenciled in all capital letters on the door.

A couple of other doors were open, the lockers obviously empty. Mac's was closed but not locked. A locker was where you kept the things you didn't want to share with the rest of the world, right? Pinups. Or photos of loved ones.

Somehow, Morgan had pushed aside the possibility— no, the impossibility—that her Misty and Mac's late wife were even remotely connected other than sharing the same name. But suddenly her earlier doubts, questions and concerns resurfaced, turning her stomach into a ball of acid.

Here was her chance to put her mind at ease, she told herself as she crossed the room.

"There's no way…none. It's absolutely absurd to worry about something so insanely not possible."

Her hand was shaking when she pulled up on the release. The door opened with a noisy creak that made the hair on the back of her neck stand up. She glanced over her shoulder to see if Mac had heard the sound and come running. Luck was with her.

Holding her breath, she opened it wide enough to make

use of the natural light coming from the high windows. She didn't look inside, although some part of her brain registered a set of coveralls hanging from a hook. There could have been fourteen bars of gold sitting there and she wouldn't have seen them because her gaze was pinned to the inside of the door.

Her hand shook as she reached out to touch the eight-by-ten glamour shot of a young woman with long blond hair and pretty brown eyes like Megan's. There wasn't a date on the photo, but she guessed it was taken right out of high school. Maybe even her graduation photo.

Misty.

Morgan would have known her anywhere, even though the last time she saw her sister, Misty was just a young girl.

Morgan ran her fingers over her sister's hair. Not her real color, she was sure. As a child, Misty had loved to have her hair brushed until it crackled with electricity.

The memory hit Morgan so hard she staggered backward a step. She grabbed the door to keep her balance.

Dead. Misty's dead. Tears flooded Morgan's eyes. Her stomach buckled and she swallowed repeatedly to keep from throwing up. Her knees started to feel shaky and her vision swam. She closed the door and lurched to the bench to sit and get her bearings.

Her baby sister was gone. Her aunt and uncle, too, apparently. Someone—maybe the gossip lady—had mentioned something about Misty's family's tragic demise before she and Mac met. How did they die? Other questions crowded in without answers. Memories flashed through her mind. Faces. Misty—the little girl Morgan remembered, not the dead woman in the photo. Aunt Binnie and Uncle Nolan. The farm she'd hated with such passion.

She'd told herself for years that they were all dead to her, so why did the reality of knowing the truth hurt so much?

Maybe because she'd believed, deep down, that some day she'd stumble across the bridge that would take her home. There were so many questions she'd planned to ask her sister. "Did your life improve after I left?" "Did Aunt Binnie learn to smile?" "Did Uncle Nolan sell the cows?"

Nolan was a third-generation farmer but he always swore he'd been born too late. The glory years of farming had passed. His cherished way of life was on the verge of collapse. He'd threatened to sell the herd every time the price of milk dropped.

To this day, Morgan couldn't stomach the taste of milk. She told people she was lactose intolerant, but the cause wasn't physiological. Just emotional. Because from the day her maternal aunt and uncle arrived in Michigan in time for her parents' funeral, Morgan's life turned upside down. On some level she'd always known it wasn't right to blame them for what happened, but to a twelve-year-old girl who had been her parents' golden child, it was easy to get locked in the anger stage of grief.

Against her wishes, Morgan and Misty were moved to the farm outside Valentine, Nebraska. Their family home in Ann Arbor was sold, the proceeds set in trust. Ironically, she hadn't been lying when she called herself a trust-fund baby. But the money hadn't been much, and as she discovered when she turned sixteen, her aunt and uncle had been allowed to access it for the sisters' "care and upkeep."

The hullabaloo that ensued when she accused her aunt and uncle of stealing her and her sister's birthright had turned ugly. Her uncle, never long on patience, had backhanded her, splitting her lip. The sight of blood had always terrified Misty, who screamed so loudly their uncle had stormed out of the house.

That had been the pivotal moment when Morgan knew she couldn't stay. Misty was easy compared to Morgan. Misty and Aunt Binnie got along well. With just one child to support, the girls' inheritance would go further and Misty might actually be able to go to college. If Morgan left, the tension that surrounded her would diminish and Misty could have a normal life. Once free of the constrictions and daily chores that she hated, Morgan would find a way to create a life that made sense to her—even if she had to lie about her roots.

That's what she did. She pulled from bits and pieces that she remembered of her life when her parents were alive, added images she'd picked up while visiting her wealthier friends' families and fleshed out the framework with what she'd learned from her reading.

Daydreams had been her only escape when she'd been forced to do chores that seemed utterly repugnant and brutal to a spoiled city girl. Milking at dawn and dusk. Mucking stalls. Feeding the pigs. Driving the tractor. Picking berries from vines with inch-long thorns.

She'd hated everything about the farm, and in her mind she became Cinderella abused by wicked stepparents. Her aunt and uncle, whom she'd only met once before her parents' accident, certainly fit the roles she'd created for them in her mind. Older—about the age she was now, she realized—and childless, Binnie and Nolan had had no clue about how to care for young, emotionally traumatized girls.

They made mistakes. Like sending Morgan to her room without dinner when she did something wrong or when she failed to complete a task to her uncle's rigid standard. Somehow failure and food had become intricately connected in her mind. Even now, she couldn't eat before a big scene for fear she'd get sick and throw up. People called that an eating disorder, but it was more a life disorder. Parents weren't supposed to die when their kids still needed them.

She swallowed the bad taste in her mouth and tried to use the yogic breathing techniques that helped her clear and center her mind before a scene. But nothing could alleviate the grief that pressed down on her from every angle. The bridge she'd hoped would one day magically appear was gone. Dust.

Every reunion she'd ever imagined would never take place. Now, the only person who could tell her anything about Misty's life was Mac.

She sat up sharply. "Mac," she whispered, her mouth going dry. She couldn't tell him the truth. Not now. Not after what they'd just done. He'd be horrified. He'd not only hate her, he'd hate himself.

She swallowed hard and closed her eyes, making every effort to keep from throwing up.

"I'm Morgana Carlyle," she murmured softly. "Morgan James is dead. Just like everybody she ever loved."

She needed to remember that. For Mac's sake, as much as hers.

But what about Megan's sake? a voice in the back of her mind asked. *Megan. My niece.*

She dropped her head to her hands and slowly rocked back and forth. Her brain felt like it might explode. How could anyone be expected to think straight when she went from the high of making love to finding out her sister was dead—all in under half an hour? She needed time and space to sort this out.

She jumped to her feet. Too quickly. She had to reach out to catch her balance. When her vision cleared, she saw her fingers spread flat across the name on the locker. MAC.

She yanked back her hand as if it were touching a hot griddle and started toward the office. She quickly gathered her things. She was just about to go in search of Mac when she heard a voice she knew all too well coming from outside.

"Don't give me any bullshit, Mac. Cal said she was with you."

"What were you doing at my grandmother's?"

"Checking in on her. For my wife. When Cal mentioned the pretty gal who read so nice, I did the math. One missing Mac and one missing Morgana means something I don't want to think about."

"Then don't. This isn't any of your business, Coop."

"Like hell it isn't. Morgana is—"

"An adult," Morgan said, marching across the cavernous shop. Grease and oil smells reminded her of her uncle's tractor. Bile rose in her throat. *Pretend. Morgana would never stand for someone second-guessing her choices. Pretend.*

"And unattached at the moment," she said haughtily. "So, much as I appreciate your concern on my behalf, Cooper, let's agree that I'm fully able to make my own decisions. Okay?"

Cooper looked from her to Mac and back. "Okay. I just— Well…this isn't like you, Morgie."

"It's Morga— Oh, never mind. Did you drive here?"

He nodded. "I borrowed Shane's car because Libby has ours."

"Give me the keys."

"What?"

"You heard me. I—I have a headache and I want to lie down." She held out her hand, palm open. When he was slow to respond, she made an impatient gesture reminiscent of the kind his mother would have made.

He caved to her wishes, as she knew he would. Coop was a good person and a kind soul. She knew he worried about her. He'd gone out of his way to secure her an audition for the role of Libby, but at the moment she wished they'd never met. If not for Coop, she never would have been in Sentinel Pass. She could have blissfully continued her life, imagining pleasant little fantasies about her sister's life.

"Thanks," she said, her fingers closing around the key fob. Without a backward glance, she started for a different door than the one she'd entered through, praying it would take her outside.

She realized this type of behavior wasn't like her. She wasn't a diva. Divas got more publicity than she wanted and she damn well couldn't afford for any of this to get out. Her new contract depended on her being one thing. What she'd found out today didn't jibe with anything her new employers believed true about her.

She wasn't sure what would happen if they found out her entire image was a carefully crafted lie, but she couldn't picture any good coming of it. Nor did she want to face the humiliation and ridicule of her peers. She'd worked too hard to achieve some tiny modicum of success in this business. The past had to stay in the past.

As she opened the door a voice called out, "Morgana."

Mac. She hadn't forgotten about him, she simply didn't know how to look at him without crying.

You're an actress, she told herself. *You can do this.*

After taking a deep breath, she turned. "Yes?"

He walked toward her. Shirtless. No belt. Bare ankles. Hair tousled. He looked like a pinup of a man who'd just made love. She'd remember this image for the rest of her life.

When she lifted her gaze to his, she read his confusion and hurt. Tears burned at the edges of her eyes. "What?" The word was ice-cold. Snappish. Bitter.

He froze and lifted his hand. In it was a green bottle. "Here's your pop."

She looked down. The cap was off. She wondered if he'd taken a drink. If she took it, would she be able to taste him on the rim? "No, thanks. I've changed my mind."

As she left, she was pretty certain she heard Mac murmur, "I see that."

His pain couldn't possibly be more than hers. But she couldn't tell him that. She'd already flubbed up once today, telling him about reading to a sister Morgana Carlyle—an only child—didn't have. All he had to do was read her bio to know she was a liar. Hopefully he'd never find out she was worse. A coward and a thief.

He'd been sympathetic and kind this morning. He hadn't judged her. But he would if he knew the truth. She had no doubt of that.

Mac knew he only had himself to blame for what happened. He'd forgotten that his brother-in-law was probably wandering around aimlessly without Lib to keep him busy. She'd mentioned Coop's breakfast meeting with Shane, but after that…naturally, the friendly, gregarious guy would drop by Gran's then seek out his buddy at the mine.

Crap. Mac wasn't good at this sort of thing. He and his sister shared a lot, but not stuff like this. He wasn't the warm, fuzzy, spill-your-guts type.

"I didn't come here to spy on you. You know that, right?"

"Yeah, I know."

Cooper let out a long, noisy sigh. "When Cal told me Morgana was with you, my first thought was you might pull the lights-off-in-the-mine-shaft thing. Morgie comes off all strong and fearless, but there's a part of her that's fragile and easily hurt. You might not have seen that because she's good at what she does."

"What do you mean?"

"She's an actress. Not like me. I can get into a part, but it doesn't consume me. I've had critics call me equally superficial—on-screen and off." His shoulders lifted and fell as if shrugging off the criticism. "But Morgana lives and breathes her current role. She puts a lot of herself into it, and sometimes all that giving doesn't leave much for anyone else, including herself."

The part she'd shared with Mac had been real. He was sure of it. "Is she... Does she do this often?"

Coop's eyes went wide. "Get involved romantically? God, no. I've never seen it happen. Even with us. I mean, we were done shooting when we started dating. I was trying to get over my failed first marriage and Mom was fending off rumors that I was suffering from clinical depression. Mom's the one who suggested I get out there and have some fun. She thought Morgana would look good on my arm."

He smiled. "She did. Does. But the best part was she got my sense of humor. And she's likeable. Loveable. I still care for her a lot. And I would be really upset if you...you know...hurt her."

Mac's contentiousness fled. He wanted to be mad at Coop for ruining the moment, but maybe Cooper had inadvertently saved him from a fate worse than embarrassment.

Eventually, he and Morgana would have had to admit that despite enjoying sex together, they had nothing in common. Not a damn thing. And she was leaving in a few days.

"Listen, Coop, I'm not going to bullshit you. Morgana and I got together because we're both single, healthy human beings who were attracted to each other and saw an opportunity. Just wait till your kid arrives, then you'll understand how rare these moments are."

That seemed to make Cooper think.

"We're grown-ups. We had the communicable-disease talk. She's not going to wind up pregnant. We're good."

Mac watched Coop's face—a very famous, open face that showed every emotion plain as a spreadsheet. Cooper wasn't convinced, but Mac had a feeling he wanted to be. So, he played his trump card. "I don't know how Morgana feels about this—you sort of interrupted our follow-up talk—but I'm not looking for anything long-term. I have *waaaay* too much on my plate, so to speak. A kid. A dog. My grandmother's health. A new business to get off the ground. Yep, this was just…what it is. Simple. Uncomplicated. That's all."

Coop nodded. "Uncomplicated is good."

"Right. And things might stay that way if you keep this to yourself."

His brother-in-law blanched. "Are you suggesting I lie to Libby?"

"Not exactly. Unless she looks at you at the dinner table today and says, 'Did my brother and your ex-wife have sex today?' I don't think there's any reason to call it a lie. Think of this as one more thing she wouldn't want to deal with. She's got enough on her mind with the baby and Gran's decline. Don't you agree?"

"Yes. I do. But…I'm a terrible liar, Mac. I'll try but I'm not promising anything. Okay?"

Mac had a feeling that was the best he was going to get. "Fine. Want a pop? I'm going to get dressed, then we'd better head home. The chick flick is probably over by now."

Back in his office, he removed the sheet and wrestled the futon into the upright position. He started to brush away the slight indent their bodies had left on the cover, but stopped to lay his palm flat for one quick second, recalling her warmth and responsiveness to his touch.

What I wouldn't give to redo those last moments together, he thought with a sigh. He wasn't sure what he would have said or done differently, but he would have liked her to know that she'd given him a gift he didn't take lightly. Hope. He refused to call what was in his heart love. But the part of him that had never expected to feel passion and fire was alive again, and he was grateful.

But he couldn't tell her how he felt without sounding like some kind of needy fool. Which was exactly what Misty had called him right before she stormed out of his life.

"You're not the man I thought you were, Mac. You were supposed to be rich and successful. I want more, Mac. I want a housekeeper—and a house that needs one because it's so big. I want to buy stuff without worrying about it breaking our budget. A gold miner is supposed to mine gold, Mac," she'd shouted at the top of her lungs. "You mine rock. Rock isn't worth squat. And I'm tired of living with dust and gravel in your pockets and mud on your shoes. If it weren't for Meggie, I'd think I was back on the farm."

She'd told him about farm life in great detail. She'd loved it as a child and hated it as a teen. When the house she'd grown up in burned to the ground, killing her parents, she'd thought she'd mourn them, but had, in truth, been glad to have that part of her life over.

He'd been blindly in love when she confessed her deep, dark secret. He thought he'd understood. He'd been conflicted, too, about staying in the family business when he really wanted to strike out on his own, go to college and see more of the world than a black hole and a wall of rock.

But he'd felt an obligation to his grandmother, his sister and the town of Sentinel Pass. Plus, he'd always felt a connection to the mine that had provided a living for his family for generations. He'd thought—convinced himself—that Misty just needed a family to feel that same sense of connection.

He'd made a terrible mistake in judgment. One he was never going to make again.

CHAPTER TEN

MAC FIGURED he'd spent twenty-four of the past twenty-nine or so hours since having sex with Morgana on edge, waiting for the proverbial other shoe to fall. He'd been on the *Sentinel Passtime* set most of the day because Shane was paying him as a consultant. Any questions about props, dialogue, stuff that had to do with mining, came to Mac. Too bad he'd rather have been anywhere else on the planet.

And on top of that, he'd needed to ask his sister to babysit. The mine wasn't a safe playground for children without adult supervision, and, unfortunately, Mac's ability to focus on his priorities went straight out the window whenever Morgana was around.

That was the worst part of having a conscience, he'd decided. It made breaking rules a complete waste of time because what joy you might have gotten from the moment was lost to recriminations and what-ifs.

Did she blame him for Coop discovering them? Mac had promised to keep her safe. Maybe that was why she'd taken off so abruptly and acted so cold. Or could her regret have stemmed from something else? They'd connected. He knew they had. And a part of him wanted to see where that connection might take them. But Morgana was probably three steps ahead of him. She would have already come to the conclusion that they had no future together. Bicoastal sounded about as appealing to him as being bipolar.

Morgana came from a much larger base. She was smart, privileged, worldly. She wouldn't make the mistake of getting emotionally entangled with someone like him. He knew that. But that didn't make him want her any less.

He'd watched from the sidelines every time she was part of the action. She'd played the role of Libby with more of an edge than he'd seen to date. The first scene of the day had involved Libby learning that Cooper had betrayed her trust by selling her story to Hollywood.

Thanks to Morgana's acting ability, Libby's hurt was all too evident. Mac had felt his big-brother protectiveness kick into high gear. Personally, he wanted to pound on Cooper—even though that actual exchange had happened months earlier.

He wasn't sure how actors kept fact from fiction straight in their minds. By the time Shane called, "Cut," Mac had felt emotionally wrung out.

He tried distracting his mind with paperwork between takes but found he couldn't sit at his desk without looking at the futon. Even escaping to the sanctuary of the mine had proved useless. In a tantrum befitting a four-year old, he'd kicked every single member of the Slocum family into the far corners of the shaft. And, then, felt not only guilty but foolish when he apologized. Out loud. Like some kind of crazy person.

Now, he had less than an hour to get the house ready for his sister's book club. He thanked his lucky stars that he'd found a local woman to clean for him once a week. Those few hours of a woman's touch kept him from feeling overwhelmed. Unfortunately, she came on Wednesdays. Two days from now. That meant he had to rush around picking up Megan's dolls, game pieces, clothes and clutter before fixing her a grilled cheese sandwich.

"Bella and Onie are friends now, Daddy," Megan said, waiting patiently on a stool at the counter adjacent to where he stood at the stove. The house was small and plain but well laid-out for entertaining.

Maybe if we'd done more entertaining, Misty wouldn't have— He stopped midthought. No. He was done with what-ifs. Misty made choices. He was done blaming himself for them.

"That's good, honey."

"Onie still bites her once in a while, but Bella's coat is thick and Onie's teeth are blunt so it doesn't hurt."

Mac held his palm above the skillet to test its heat then put the buttered bread in to sizzle. The smell made him hungry, but Jenna had promised to provide food for the meeting so he ignored the rumble in his belly. "How do you know the word *blunt?*"

"Libby told me. She opened Onida's mouth so I could touch her teeth. Onie didn't like that at all and Gran got upset. She said a bad word."

"Great-grandma cussed?"

Megan cocked her head and thought before answering. "She said, 'Screw you.'"

He tried to keep his expression serious and disapproving, but he remembered a time when his grandmother was known for her colorful comebacks. One of her favorites, "Don't tell me how to screw this cat, you don't even have hold of its tail" had become legendary in these parts. He hadn't seen Gran fired up or passionate about anything in months. "To Aunt Libby?"

Megan nodded seriously. "That's bad, huh?"

Mac nodded. "Yes. Gran must have been upset. Let's agree not to look at Onida's teeth any more, okay?"

"Okay. But after that, Onie didn't try to bite Bella any more. Can Bella watch *The Little Mermaid* with me?"

Coop had loaned them a portable DVD player to keep Megan occupied in her room while the Wine, Women and Words club met.

Mac still wasn't quite sure how he came to be host this evening. He sure as heck hadn't had time to finish reading the book, although thanks to Morgana, he had a general grasp of the story.

Nor did he know for certain why the group was getting together so soon. Were they trying to cram in a bunch of books before Libby and Jenna took off, as Jenna had suggested, or did they have some not-so-public agenda?

Libby had boasted that at the last meeting the members had successfully set up Kat and Jack to spend the week together. Mac had replied that they should change the name of the group to "The Busybodies." She hadn't been amused.

He hoped like hell they weren't coming here tonight to practice some kind of woman voodoo. Maybe invoke Kat's infamous *swoo*.

He'd once asked her if a case of bad *swoo* made a person immune. She'd pointed to Jordie—son number two from ex-husband number two—and let him draw his own conclusion.

"Plate in the dishwasher," he told Megan when she hopped off the stool, ready to dash away.

She didn't complain. She was a good little helper, most of the time. He did his best to teach her things that were traditionally considered part of the mom role. He only hoped he was doing them right.

A few minutes later, he let her teach him how to load the DVD into the player. "It's easy, Daddy. Uncle Cooper taught me." She adjusted the volume then set up the unit on her little white table and flopped into a Dora the Explorer covered-foam kid's chair. Bella curled up beside her, the picture of contentment.

"Enjoy," he said, kissing the top of her head. "I'll be in the living room if you need me."

He was halfway down the hall when the doorbell rang.

"Hi, Char. No Kat?" Mac remembered Libby saying the two friends usually car-pooled to meetings.

"Nope. She's still in Denver. Didn't Libby tell you what happened?"

She handed him the gnarled branch from a long-dead tree before stepping over the threshold. He recognized the infamous talking stick that his sister claimed kept peace and order during heated discussions. He hadn't expected it to feel so venerable and hefty.

"Jordie tripped and landed face-first on a rock," she said, dropping her cloth bag on the sofa. "Needed emergency dental work, so Kat drove him to Denver to see Jack."

She took a deep breath and looked around. Along with maroon-colored highlights in her tawny hair, she wore long turquoise-and-silver earrings that brushed the tops of her shoulders. Her entire outfit—peasant skirt, layered tanks adorned with a glittery gecko and beaded moccasins—probably came straight from the shelves of her store.

"Is he going to be okay?"

"Yeah. He sounds fine, although he still has a slight lisp," she added with a smile. "Kat and the boys are due back later tonight, but she has to drop off her dad's truck at the ranch."

Mac had hunted on Buck Garrity's land once or twice

when Buck's son, Cade—Kat's half brother—had been around. Last Mac heard Cade was living in Texas, breaking horses for a living.

"Poor Kat," he said, meaning it. "She can't catch a break. But I'm not surprised she drove all the way to Denver to see a dentist. She and Jack seemed pretty tight when he left town."

Char's grin confirmed his guess that despite the fact they had plenty of dentists in the Hills, Jack Treadwell was different.

"I guess that explains why the guy bought the old Smith house. He has a ready-made family to move into it."

"I guess," she said with a shrug. "I mean, Kat hasn't said for sure that she's in love with him. She's a little gun-shy, so to speak, but Jack's nothing like her first two mistakes."

Different was good. He hated to think he'd ever be drawn to the same kind of woman as Misty.

"Where do you want the talking stick?" he asked.

"Anywhere it won't fall and conk someone on the head," she answered. The look of mischief in her eye made him wonder if that had happened before.

He leaned it against the wall in the far corner of the room. He couldn't believe an old hunk of wood had any mystical power, but he was glad to let go of it just the same. "The weather's so nice, I thought we might eat outside. I found a couple of those candles that are supposed to keep the mosquitoes from carrying us off."

Char let out a snicker. "Sounds good to me. I've been inside a teepee all day." She lowered her voice. "You know, I wasn't all that gung-ho about the TV people coming, but, boy, can they spend money. I like them better every day."

Me, too. One, in particular.

"I heard they were filming at the mine today," she said,

poking about in her bag. He wondered what was in it. Food, he hoped. He'd never hosted a party where he didn't provide all the food and drink. This waiting around for stuff to show up went against his grain. "Was it totally freaky watching somebody play you?"

He glanced at the carved mantel clock that had been one of the few family possessions Misty had brought to their marriage. "I didn't see much. Shane had me doing stuff away from the action most of the time."

Char withdrew a small brown sack from her bag and walked to the counter where Mac had set out the six bottles of wine a delivery guy had dropped off that morning. No note, but he'd known they came from Morgana.

She set her little sack aside without comment, then picked up one of the bottles. "This looks good," she said after examining the label. "Can we open it first?"

"Sure," Mac said, joining her.

He gave her the corkscrew. He wasn't all that adept at opening wine bottles.

Returning to her earlier train of thought, she said, "Libby told me watching the filming was fun the first couple of days, but now she can't watch Morgana play her—no matter how good she is." The cork made a muffled popping sound as she pulled it out. "And she is good," she said, looking at him. "I caught a few minutes of filming the other day, and there were moments when she'd do some odd little Libby mannerism that made me do a double take—even though they don't really look alike."

Thank God for small miracles, he silently vowed. "Aren't we supposed to let this stuff breathe?" he asked when she reached for a glass.

She shrugged. "I'll blow on it if you want me to."

He gave her a look that would have made his sister laugh. It worked. Char laughed, too. Loudly enough that he almost missed the faint "Hello?" that came from the door he'd left open.

Morgana.

Mac's heart rate spiked and his momentary peace scattered like a flock of wrens in flight. He almost tripped over his feet spinning around to greet her. "Oh. Hi. Morgana. We were just talking about you." *Dumb.*

My God, she's a regular person tonight, he thought as he watched her walk into the room. He'd never seen her dressed in such casual clothes, slim-fitting jeans, flat sandals and a purple-and-yellow Mystery Spot T-shirt. Shane had given every cast and crew member one when they arrived in Sentinel Pass. This was the first time Mac had seen Morgana don hers.

"We…?" He had a momentary sense that she was just as flustered and ill-at-ease as he was…until she spotted Char. Then, suddenly, the Morgana he'd held in his arms became the Morgana everyone saw on-screen. The transformation was subtle, but startling. "Oh. Hi. It's Char, right? We met the other day but didn't get a chance to talk. Such a beautiful evening. The Black Hills really is a lovely place. You're so lucky to live here year-round."

Char chortled. "Come back in December and we'll talk."

Morgana tipped her head as if acknowledging Char's point, but under her breath, Mac swore he heard her say, "I wish I could."

But that made no sense, so he did the polite thing and offered her a glass of wine.

"Um, sure. One glass. I still have some lines to pin down tonight."

"Red or white?"

"Whatever you're having."

Char poured her a glass then carried it to her. "Thank you."

She tilted the glass toward both Char and him in a sort of toast. "Cheers."

Mac took a drink but the small sip seemed to stay lodged in his throat. He had to lift his chin and work at swallowing. A slip that Char seemed to notice.

"Mac and I were talking about the filming," Char said. "How come Libby's and Coop's names stayed the same? There are other characters based on real people, right?"

Morgana looked at him for the briefest of seconds. "Since Cooper and Libby are married and Coop's coproducing the show, he can't very well sue himself. Changing the names of the secondary characters gives a writer more latitude, plus it protects the innocent—we, the actors— from being sued."

Char laughed. "So Mac isn't Mac?"

Shane had assured Mac months ago that his private life was not fodder for the screen.

"Right," Morgana confirmed. "Libby has an on-screen brother, but his name is Zack."

"Which rhymes with Mac," Char pointed out.

"And Zack is a miner, but that's the only real similarity. Zane, the actor playing the part, has taken him a whole different route. Zack's the local playboy Lothario. A sort of love 'em and leave 'em heartbreaker."

Char's eyes went wide and she looked at Mac. "Really? Talk about creative license. Are you okay with that?"

"Why wouldn't I be? That's definitely not me. I'm the leavee, not the leaver, remember?"

He took a large gulp of wine. He hated that his bitterness slipped out at the most inopportune times. One quick glance at Morgana told him she felt sorry for him. Damn.

"Miss Char," a child squealed with joy. "Princess Morgana." Megan dashed into the room but stopped short when she saw Morgana. "Where's your pretty dress?"

Morgana touched her jeans, which fit her as if they'd been sewn to her specific curves and shape…and probably had. "Um…"

"I bet it's at the cleaners, honey." Mac set his glass on the mantel and held out his arms to her. "Besides, even princesses have off-duty time. Morgana's here to talk about books with Aunt Lib and her friends."

"And you, Daddy," Megan said, vaulting into his arms. She wrapped her arms around his neck and squeezed tight. "You're his friend, too, aren't you, Princess Morgana?"

Morgan felt as if the eyes of the world were on her, when in fact only three relative strangers awaited her answer. "Yes, sweetheart, I am. And yours, too."

Your friend…and your aunt.

The few sips of wine she'd swallowed sloshed around noisily in her belly like an old-fashioned washing machine—the kind her aunt used to have. She pressed her hand to her side, as inconspicuously as possible.

She'd been a mess all day—edgy and emotional. She didn't know what was wrong with her…unless the truth was making her sick. She'd lived on a diet of lies for so long that yesterday's force-feeding of reality might have been more than she could take.

Lies. Lies came easy. But little kids deserved better. "You do know I'm not a real princess, right? I have a job that lets me dress up and wear pretty clothes, but that's not who I am. I'm just me."

She snuck a peek at Mac, who was looking at her with a funny squint. Had she said something wrong? Given something away? No. She and Misty had been as different as two siblings could be. People had remarked about their differences often growing up. And their aunt and uncle never let the subject rest.

"Sunshine and storm. That's the two of you. Why can't you be more like your sister?" her aunt used to complain to Morgan.

Because one of them had to cause a ruckus, Morgan remembered thinking. Somebody had to pay for what happened to ruin their happy life, and Morgan wasn't going to let the world forget it. Misty could play nice, but not her. She wasn't happy and she didn't care who knew it.

"Morgana?"

Morgan blinked, realizing she'd lost track of the conversation. Damn. She'd done the same thing on camera that morning. Shane's surprise had in no way matched Morgan's mortification. She was a pro. She wasn't some foolish girl daydreaming about the hunky guy she'd made love with the day before.

"I'm sorry. What was that?"

"Char said it isn't like Libby to be late. Too many years spent punching the postal clock, you know. Have you talked to Coop today?"

About yesterday? God, no. She'd gone out of her way to avoid her ex-husband all day. "No," she said. "I haven't seen him since our scene together. But Cooper is notoriously late." *Except when he shows up unexpectedly. Then, he's too early.*

Char walked to the counter to refill her glass. "This really is good wine, Mac. Where'd you buy it?"

"I didn't. Morgana sent it over. I'm not exactly a connoisseur, you know." He shook his head in a way that reminded Morgan how much she'd liked running her fingers through his hair. It needed cutting, but she couldn't complain about its thick, dynamic texture.

The three of them talked about wines—California and imports—for a few minutes longer. Char mentioned meeting the owner of a local winery and promised to send a bottle home with Morgan. A nice gesture. Morgan was touched, but the word *home* produced the strangest twinge in her midsection.

She was saved from examining her reaction too closely by the arrival of Libby and Cooper and Jenna and Shane. The foursome had apparently walked together from Libby's house.

"Hi, everyone," Libby hailed, cruising in without knocking. Such a sisterly act made Morgan smile. For a minute. Until she remembered that she'd never have that kind of relationship with her sister.

"Sorry we're late. Coop had a call from his neighbor in Malibu. Rollie's been looking after the beach house for us."

With just a few hand gestures, she directed Cooper and Shane to set down the pizza boxes they carried while Jenna delivered the huge wooden bowl she held in both hands to the center of the table.

"Jenna and I deliberated about what kind of food they might serve at the Jitterbug Lounge," Libby said, producing a wad of paper plates from the plastic grocery bag hanging from the opposite wrist. "We finally went for easy. Are we eating inside or out, McDuff?"

Mac rolled his eyes at the nickname. "Out. I hosed off the chairs and tables this morning. They should be dry. I even dug out the mosquito candles. Hope they're still good."

"Perfect," Jenna said. "I'm starved."

Mac opened a second bottle of wine. "There's apple juice in the fridge, Lib."

His sister, who was busy talking to Megan, gave him a big smile. "Thanks. You're sweet. Megan's going to show me her movie. I'll be right back."

Morgan listened and observed as everyone went about the business of filling their plates. She could honestly say she'd never been a part of this type of group—a diverse mix of friends who liked each other. Most of the people she'd call close acquaintances were in the entertainment business, and work—or the lack of it—was their common bond. She couldn't help but feel a bit wistful.

Once everyone was sitting, all seven squeezed around an oval, glass-topped patio table, Libby, who had returned alone—"Meggie said she already ate and she'd rather watch Ariel"—told them about some ruckus in Malibu. "Rollie said the neighbors are all up in arms. There's nothing we can do from this end, but doesn't your agent have a place near Coop's, Morgana?"

Morgan swallowed the bite she'd been chewing. "I believe so. I've only been there once."

Cooper washed down his pizza with a large gulp of wine—the thirty-dollar-bottle variety—then wiped his mouth with his napkin. "What's his name again? William Hyde Park-Smythe or something?"

Morgan frowned. "It's William Hughes. He dropped the second name when he emigrated to the U.S. Why do you always give me such a hard time about him? He's not the jerk who never paid my taxes. William is a straight shooter. He's good to me."

Coop flashed one of his trademark smiles. "I don't know

why I don't like him. Maybe because he's better-looking than me. Or because he has that really cool accent. I need an accent."

"No, you don't," his wife said. "Morgana, do you think we could call Mr. Hughes to find out what's really happening? Rollie—God love him—is a sharp cookie but he's got the social graces of…well, of Mac."

Mac's eyebrows gathered in a stormy fashion.

Before he could reply in his own defense, Morgan said, "As opposed to Cooper? Who came here under false pretenses and turned everyone's life upside down."

"Hey," Coop protested. "If it wasn't for me, you two never would have met. Let alone—"

Mac slammed his fist against the glass, making everyone's goblet jostle. "Point taken, Coop. But the fact remains that you're here. We have a television show in the making. And nobody ever said I was Mr. Congeniality. Just ask my late wife."

Morgan glanced around the table. Everyone showed varying degrees of surprise and confusion.

"I didn't mean that you're antisocial, Mac. But you're not the most diplomatic when you're defending your own," Libby said supportively. "And thank God you stood up to Misty where Megan was concerned." She shuddered visibly. To Morgan, she said, "We don't know what's going on back there. Rollie tends to jump around when he's excited. You need a road map to follow his points, but we think some developer wants to put up a hotel and the locals are against the idea."

Morgan didn't feel any affinity toward Coop's house. He'd bought it after they split up, but she was willing to help if she could. "William isn't home at the moment, but I'd be happy to give you his number."

Her agent had called her that morning from New York. "I just dotted the last *i* and crossed the last *t* on the FreshFace contract. This is a great deal for you, Morgana. The initial retainer will not only get the IRS off your back, but the visibility from the print ads will be something you can bank on for years. Let me repeat, years. So, don't do anything between now and the signing that will jeopardize that, okay?"

You mean like sleeping with my dead sister's husband? she'd almost asked.

"So, when do we discuss the book?" she said with false brightness. False to her ears, at least.

"Well," Char said, "we usually begin the discussion while we're eating. When Libby started the group she made a rule that there was no personal talk until the book talk was done." She grinned. "You broke your own rule, Lib."

Libby snorted. "There's a lot of that going around."

Morgan looked down to hide her blush. *Please don't let that comment mean Cooper told Libby about what happened at the mine,* she silently prayed. She glanced at Mac. The instant his gaze met hers her heart set up a ruckus so loud she was certain everyone else at the table could hear it.

Her throat closed and her palms turned damp and tingly. She shifted uneasily in the molded plastic chair. This desire she felt for him was wrong on so many levels, but she knew—deep in some hidden part of her soul—that she wanted to make love with him again before she left Sentinel Pass. Even with the truth about his life staring her straight in the face. Even knowing that Misty was her sister and Megan her niece, she wanted him.

She didn't want to think about what kind of person that made her.

CHAPTER ELEVEN

"HOW'D BELLA DO with the other dogs at obedience school the other day?" Libby asked Megan, who had joined the party a few minutes earlier.

The group was slowly migrating from the patio to the living room—forced indoors by the arrival of a horde of citronella-impervious mosquitoes.

"Bella didn't bark or growl once," Megan boasted. "Not like some of those dogs. They were mean. Even meaner than Onie."

Mac shifted the empty plate he was carrying to his left hand and gently tousled his daughter's hair. It needed washing, he realized. Damn. A task that must have slipped his mind last night. Not surprising given everything else he had to think about. Like Morgana.

"I'll run the water for your bath, sweets. Give everybody a hug and tell them good-night."

"But, Daddy, I want the princess to read to me."

"I'll read to you after your bath, Megan," Libby volunteered.

"No. I want Morgana to."

Megan dashed to the other side of the room where Morgana was standing and grabbed her hand. His sister seemed justifiably hurt.

Morgana started to say something but Char, who was carrying a tower of used paper plates, scuttled between them. "I'm not surprised Bella is so calm and noncombative," she said. "She strikes me as an old soul."

Mac choked. "Dog reincarnation? Come on. You don't believe that."

Char dumped her load then moved to the sink to wash her hands. "What I believe is certain animals—like certain people—come into our lives for a reason. Kids know this at a gut level. I heard Megan tell Libby that Bella was at the animal shelter waiting for her. They bonded instantly."

"Megan's four."

"I'm almost five, Daddy."

Char dried her hands then walked to where Morgana and Megan were standing. She touched Megan's head the way people who don't have children tend to do. "I think we all should be more open to the gifts that come our way. Luca was just days away from being put down when Jenna found him, right, Jen?"

Jenna, who had been sharing a whispered conversation with Shane, stepped out of his arms and turned to look at them. "Huh?"

Libby clapped her hands. "Where's the talking stick? We're totally off topic."

Cooper spotted it leaning in the corner and herded the group to the sofa and armchairs set around a Craftsman-style coffee table. Mac had put out a couple of folding chairs, too. "Go ahead and get started," he told them. "I'm going to stick Meggie in the bath."

He picked up his daughter and started to leave when a tentative voice asked, "May I join you? Just for a minute. Megan wanted me to see her room."

His mind said no, but his heart was beating too hard to hear clearly. "Sure."

Mac didn't harbor any illusion that she'd be impressed by his home's conventional three-bedroom, two-bath floor plan. He was just thankful he'd left the door to the spare bedroom, which was part office, part junk room, closed. Megan's room wasn't bad. Pure little-girl fantasy. Pinks, purples, butterflies and princess stuff. Messy, but in a good way.

Megan was obviously thrilled by the chance to show off her prize possessions. She wiggled free of Mac's arms and pirouetted around, pointing out the obvious. "And this is a DVD player. It's Uncle Cooper's, but he let me borrow it so I wouldn't bug the book people. Do you want to stay and watch the movie with me until I fall asleep? It's *The Little Mermaid*."

Morgana gave her a hug. "I'd love to stay, but I promised your aunt I'd talk about the book. Maybe another time."

Another time. Mac knew that was a lie. He'd overheard some of the staffers discussing various stars' departure dates. He'd missed the exact hour of Morgana's flight, but he gathered it was sooner rather than later. It irked him when adults made empty promises to little kids.

"Bath time, Meggie love. You can start by brushing your teeth."

Megan skipped across the hall to the bathroom and closed the door. Privacy at age four. He was doomed.

"She's an amazing child. So bright and articulate. Her vocabulary is something else," Morgana said. "Earlier, while you were refilling wineglasses, she told me you were an exceptional father. That's the word she used."

He smiled but didn't say anything. Mostly, he hoped she'd leave so he didn't have to keep fighting the temptation to pull her into his arms and kiss her.

"Was her mother... Did she work with Megan a lot? Read to her and stuff?"

Mac heard a funny edge to her voice. Wistful? Sad? He didn't know. "You mean like homeschooling? No. Misty started out gung-ho, but she sorta lost interest as Megan got older. Not just in motherhood, but in everything. Me...our marriage, our life."

He couldn't believe the personal stuff coming out of his mouth. Hell, he hadn't even talked about Misty's unconfirmed depression—unconfirmed because Misty refused to acknowledge the problem—to Libby. Discussing Misty's mental health behind her back would have felt disloyal, but here he was spilling his guts.

Morgana turned to leave. "I'd better get back to the others."

Mac was confused. He hated to be confused. He reached out and grabbed her arm. She didn't play coy, she met him halfway. He poured every ounce of frustration he'd felt all day into his kiss. Fast. Furious. Shattering.

The second he heard the click of the bathroom door, he broke off the kiss and stepped into the hallway, blocking Megan's view of Morgana. "Bath time," he said.

Morgan used the opportunity to slip past him, but she knew her hair and lipstick were a mess. Megan might not be able to guess what Morgan and her father had been doing, but the adults in the living room surely would.

Her only recourse was to escape into the room a couple of feet to her right. Mac's room. A lamp had been left burning beside the queen-size bed. The room was neat and tidy, simply decorated. Too simple. There were no womanly touches. It was as if he'd stripped the place bare of anything his late wife might have used to put her stamp on the place.

She hurried around the bed and stepped into the bathroom. Small, compact. About the size of her walk-in closet back home. The overhead light seemed piercingly bright. She wet a tissue then dabbed and fluffed until she looked normal. Whatever that was.

She turned off the switch and started back the way she'd come, but a framed photo atop a shoulder-high dresser made her stop. Husband and wife in happier times. A baby on the way. Misty had short, spiky blond hair in this photo. She looked a lot like Morgan did when she wasn't playing a postmaster in Sentinel Pass.

"That was the summer before Megan was born," Mac said, suddenly standing beside her. "We'd just bought this house from my grandmother. Misty had been holding out for something bigger and fancier on a few acres. But we couldn't afford it."

"She was a blonde."

He nodded. The serious man of few words was back. "She was never happy with her hair. She switched color and styles more often than Char changes the streaks in her hair. Only Misty never went pink. I will say that."

"Hey, are you guys coming back or what?" Libby asked, popping her head around the doorway.

"Right away. Just checking on Meggie," Mac said.

"She's fine. I was going to use the bathroom but she said she'd prefer if I used yours." She rolled her eyes. "I really hope I'm ready for motherhood."

Mac snickered softly and touched her shoulder supportively. "You will be. Should I make coffee?"

Libby shook her head. "No. But I put on some water for tea. Char brought chocolate for dessert."

Morgan took another quick look at the photo then moved aside so Libby could pass. She had to quit torturing herself. True, Morgan had never made any effort to get in touch with her sister, but sisterhood was a two-way street, right? It wasn't as if Morgan hid under a rock all these years. Her face hadn't changed that much, even if her name was different. Misty hadn't made an attempt to contact her, either.

But did any of that matter? What she needed to be concerned about now was making sure neither Mac nor Megan paid for her mistakes a second time.

She walked straight to the kitchen and emptied the dregs of the last open bottle into a glass. She could feel Shane's gaze on her but she polished off the wine anyway. To hell with her lines. She'd wing it. She was a professional—whatever that meant.

Once everyone was seated, Jenna opened the discussion by asking, "So, Lib, what made you pick this book?"

"First of all, I like the author. I've read a couple of her previous books. She writes with humor and realism. Her characters are people I could meet on the street." She looked at Cooper. "Well, the kind of people I used to meet."

"Not actors, you mean," Morgan said, forgetting to soften her cynical tone.

Jenna and Shane exchanged a look. Damn. She needed to watch it. Shane was far too astute for a woman with secrets to get sloppy around. On the set, she didn't have to worry because she was playing a character. Off-set, she was playing a character, too, but people weren't supposed to know that.

"Um...I guess so. But I don't mean that in a denigrating way. Your job is a lot more difficult than the average person could possibly imagine. I had no idea what goes into making a TV show until I met Cooper. It's exciting being a part of it—even on the outside looking in. I'm sorry I haven't been around more, but with Gran..." Her voice faltered, but she brightened, adding, "I meant to thank you for reading to her the other day. Calvin said she loved your voice. It made her calm."

"I'm glad."

"Come back again. Anytime."

"She can't. She's leaving. Right, Morgana?" asked Mac, who was perched on a folding chair in close proximity to the hallway, where he could keep one ear open for Megan.

Morgan found his tone faintly accusatory. She lifted her chin and met his gaze. He had no right. She'd never promised anything. Neither had he. "Yes. That's me. Here today. Gone tomorrow."

The awkward pause that followed seemed to make everyone uncomfortable until Char held up the bag she'd brought with her. "Chocolate, anyone?"

The conversation quickly returned to the book, but Morgan had a hard time staying focused. She wanted to make a good impression. She'd even stayed up late the night before rereading her copy. But after all that had happened—making love with Mac, then finding out her estranged sister was dead—the fictional couple's problems seemed...um...fictional, compared to hers.

She mostly kept her opinions to herself until Libby said something that caught her attention. "Marriage can't be static. New challenges—like the arrival of children—are bound to change your dynamic."

"Unless your dynamic was never meant to have children." Morgan felt everyone's eyes turn her way, but she continued. "Even fairly decent people who manage to stay together for years out of love or whatever passes for love in some people's lives might find their marriage in jeopardy if you suddenly dumped a kid, or, God forbid, two, into the mix."

Libby lifted the talking stick, paused a moment then passed it to Morgan. "Are you talking about the hero's grandparents? They certainly didn't *want* to raise their grandson, but they rose to the challenge after their son died. That's what families do, right? But he was only one boy. What do you mean a kid or two?"

Morgana was the spotlight girl; Morgan hated to be put on the spot. She could remember having to sit in the front pew in church each Sunday. She was positive everyone was looking at her, thinking, "Those poor little charity cases. What would have happened if Binnie and Nolan Burdock hadn't taken them in?"

"Morgie?"

Morgan started. She'd done it again. Spaced out.

"Sorry. What?"

"Libby asked about your grandparents. How come you didn't turn to family when you left home?"

"I never knew my grandparents." The truth, but was it the right truth for the woman she was or the woman she was pretending to be? Suddenly, she couldn't remember.

Char looked confused. "I thought you were a fifth-generation toilet paper heiress or something."

"Paper, petroleum and pens," Morgan said from rote. An alliteration that had given her great satisfaction when she first came up with it.

She felt everyone staring at her. Curious. Questioning. She reverted to habit by creating a diversion. "I heard Libby say she thought you'd get a lot out of this book, Mac. Is that because your marriage was coming apart before your wife died? Maybe you could give us an insider perspective on a marriage-in-jeopardy story."

Several soft gasps filled the silence. Mac removed the cheap plastic reading glasses perched on the end of his nose and stuck them in his shirt pocket. Morgan hadn't seen them before, but she loved the professorial air they gave him.

He set aside the book Char had handed him earlier and said, "I haven't finished the book yet, but for the record, my marriage wasn't in jeopardy, as you say, it was over."

Morgan blushed. She hadn't expected such frankness.

"Did you fight a lot?"

"No. We never fought—until our last, very public shouting match in the cul-de-sac out front." He looked at her. "How 'bout you and Coop? Lots of fireworks when you were together?"

Touché. She couldn't help but smile. She looked to the couple holding hands on the sofa. "Not at all. Cooper hates confrontations. Right, Libby? That's one of the reasons we divorced. I thought he should fire his manager because she was robbing him blind. He refused to consider it."

Coop put his arm around his wife. "She was my mother. You can't fire your mother."

Publicly, Morgan had told people that Lena Lindstrom was the thorn that pricked their marital balloon of happiness. In truth, Lena scared Morgan. On the day Morgan and Coop returned from their honeymoon, Lena had spelled out the rules. "I know more about you than you want made public, *Morgan,*" Lena had said meaningfully. "So, if you want to keep things that way, you'll keep your fingers out of my pie."

Morgan had been shocked—and intimidated. That was the problem with a giant secret, it made you vulnerable. Lena never told Coop, though. Morgan was sure of that. He was too honest and guileless not to say something.

"Well, somehow, I can't picture your mother reflecting on her life the way the grandfather in the story did—even if she'd had time before she approached the pearly gates. Everyone has regrets. Lena wasn't the type to admit hers."

"What are yours?" Mac asked.

"I'm not on my deathbed."

"If you were."

She swallowed hard. "By leaving home the way I did, I might have hurt someone. As a kid, you never think about the impact your actions might have on other people. I thought by leaving I was helping this person, but now I'm not so sure."

"What happened to make you question your belief?" Jenna asked. Leave it to the writer to look to motivation.

"I've heard some things about this person that don't sound like the person I knew." *Please don't ask for specifics.* She felt the sweat tickling under her arms. To her surprise, her relief came from an unlikely source.

"I know what you mean," Char said. "I just heard a rumor about an old friend of mine. I haven't seen him in years, but he lives on the reservation, so his name has come up from time to time. All good. Now, they say he's gone off the deep end. Booze. Maybe drugs. Lost his family, his job, everything. I can't believe it's the same person."

Morgan smiled at her gratefully. "I'm sorry to hear that. Are you in contact with him?"

Char's eyes went wide. "Oh, hell, no. He's… No. That's all I'm going to say."

Morgan spotted the look between Jenna and Libby—surprise. The men looked perplexed and vaguely uneasy. But before anyone could say more, Megan emerged from the hallway, partially wrapped in a towel, but mostly dripping wet. "Daddy, I called and called. My fingers are turning into plums."

"Prunes," he corrected, rushing to scoop her up.

Bella stood there, too, a look of concern on her canine face.

Mac used the free end of the towel to wipe Megan's face, then he kissed her nose. A simple, careless gesture that made Morgan's heart constrict so fiercely she had to cross her arms to keep from crying out. A memory she'd completely repressed surfaced for an instant. Her father. Holding her like that. Fresh and clean from a bath, the smell of Ivory soap so strong she nearly swooned from it. He'd kissed her, then tickled her under her skinny little arm. She'd felt safe and loved and…happy. Yes, she'd known happiness then.

And she'd felt those feelings again more recently. In Mac's arms at the mine. Safe. Loved. Happy.

She was in love with Mac.

She sat up straight and folded her hands purposefully in her lap. Once she had her emotions under control she looked around—and saw Libby staring at her. Smart, intuitive Libby.

For an actress, Morgan was doing a really lousy job of remaining detached.

The group continued talking about the book after Mac left to put Megan to bed, then Cooper stretched elaborately and stood. "Is it bedtime for me, too?"

"Definitely," Libby said, holding out a hand. "It's been a long day. Do you want to walk home with us, Morgana?"

"Thanks, but I think I'll clean up a little so Mac doesn't have to in the morning. I have a flashlight on my key ring."

She said her goodbyes to Jenna and Shane. She guessed that Shane wanted to say something about her performance that morning, but she beat him to it. "I was a little off today. Stayed up too late reading this book so I could impress your fiancée's friends. Sorry."

He nodded. "I'd like it better if we have the old Morgana back on the set tomorrow."

"Done." *I hope.*

Char came to Morgan as soon as she'd packed up her leftover chocolate. "This was a fun meeting. I'm glad you were here," she said. "You're an okay duck. Not quite as odd as Coop."

Morgan snickered softly. "You have no idea how much that means to me."

Cooper, who was lounging by the door waiting for Libby to say good-night to Megan, overheard and protested. "Hey. I'm not strange. I'm just not from around here."

Char pointed at Morgan. "Neither is she, but she fits in twice as well as you. Maybe that means Morgana's a better actor."

The two took their discussion outside as Coop walked Char to her car. Morgan couldn't help but smile. Coop was a chameleon, too. He was simply more honest.

"Good night, then," Libby said, retrieving the talking stick that Coop had left leaning against the wall. "Thanks for coming on such short notice."

"Thanks for inviting me."

Libby paused at the door. Morgan wondered if this was

going to be the don't-break-my-brother's-heart lecture. Instead, Libby gave Morgan a quick hug. "Thanks again for reading to Gran. And…I think you're a good influence on Mac, too. He seems a little less angry at the world. After what Misty did to him, I didn't think I'd ever be able to say that. You're a good person, Morgana."

Morgan was stunned, to say the least, but she somehow managed a smile. A small one.

"A good person," she muttered under her breath as she got to work washing the dishes—the one chore she'd enjoyed on the farm because it was clean and fresh smelling. "No, Libby. I'm not. You have no idea what a lousy person I really am. None whatsoever."

She tidied the living room. Then, feeling a little bit like Goldilocks, she tried both armchairs before settling on the couch. She told herself she only wanted to talk to him. Achieve a sense of closure that Cooper had robbed them of when he showed up at the mine.

But her late night of reading caught up with her and, again like Goldilocks, she dozed off.

CHAPTER TWELVE

MAC EASED OFF THE BED, taking care not to awaken the sleeping child. He stretched to ease the kink in his neck. Megan's bed was too small, the mattress too firm for his taste. He'd had to add a rubberized pad after Misty died because Megan had started having "accidents"—even though she'd been potty trained for a year or better.

"Keep a good eye on her," he told Bella, gently patting the dog's head.

The animal answered with a deep sigh.

He paused in the doorway and looked at the image of the large dog curled up at the foot of his daughter's bed. If anyone would have told him a year ago that he'd be a single dad with an indoor dog and a little girl who was afraid of the dark, he would have called them crazy. And add a famous, heartthrob brother-in-law and new business in the mix and he'd have laughed himself silly.

He blew out a weary breath and closed the door. He still had the kitchen to clean up and a few bills to pay before he turned in for the night. Maybe he'd even catch a few minutes of TV. Shane had mentioned that the promos for *Sentinel Passtime* were starting to run.

He paused to kick off the cheap flip-flops he'd picked up at the grocery store and set them inside his bedroom door. He closed his eyes and inhaled deeply. Was her scent still present? Was he losing his mind?

With a firm shake of his head, he headed down the hallway toward the living room. He wasn't surprised to see the lights still on. He'd hated not being a better host, but his daughter came first. She always would. At least Libby had been here to make his excuses.

He looked toward the kitchen expecting to see pizza cartons and wine bottles sitting out, but the place was as neat as when his cleaning lady visited.

"Thanks, Lib," he murmured, padding softly to the refrigerator. He popped open a can of beer and took a long, refreshing gulp. Wine was okay, but not nearly as satisfying as a cold brew.

He skirted a plastic garbage bag sitting on the floor beside the counter and walked into the living room. He was midgulp when he spotted the figure asleep on his couch. His sputtering cough was loud enough to wake her. Unfortunately. Because for a second there, he'd felt as though he could have spent the rest of his life watching Morgana sleep.

"Oh, hi," she said, pushing into an upright position. She blinked and rubbed her nose the exact same way Megan did every morning. "I didn't mean to doze off."

He took another chug of beer to ease the lump in his throat. He didn't know why she was still here. Probably because of what happened between them at the mine. "No problem. I assumed you walked home with Libby and Coop."

She brushed her bangs out of her eyes and tucked the longer strands behind her ears. "I told them I'd clean up."

"Don't you have people to do that?"

She chuckled wryly. "Not with me. Besides, you got

roped into this because of me. Washing dishes was the least I could do."

He stepped closer, but opted for the chair instead of the spot beside her—where he would have preferred to sit. So he could accidentally brush against her shoulder and lean in close enough to smell her perfume. But he wasn't that big a masochist. She was leaving in a few days. Going back to a world he didn't have any desire to know better—or introduce to his daughter.

She fiddled with the hem of her T-shirt. No one else could make it look like a fashion statement. He had a feeling Morgana didn't even realize that's what she did.

But something wasn't right. Despite her poised posture and outward confidence, he could tell she was nervous. He knew because she very subtly ran the edge of the fabric back and forth under her fingernail.

"I thought we should talk. About what happened."

He nodded. "Okay."

When she looked at him, he saw real emotion. He'd seen lust and satiation, but those came with sex. Here was something else. Worry? Doubt? Fear?

What did she have to be afraid of? The closest he'd ever come to striking a woman was when Misty told him there was another man in her life and she was leaving him. But even then, despite feeling emasculated and hurt, he'd kept a lid on his anger—until she said she was taking Megan. Then he'd lost it—verbally. Every neighbor in the cul-de-sac had been able to give the police a play-by-play recap of their fight. But they also testified that he never raised a hand to her.

"What happened happened. You're leaving. I'm staying here. I don't plan on getting pissed off, if that's what you're worried about. But I'm not gonna apologize, either. I liked being with you too much to lie about it."

"I liked being with you, too."

He could tell she meant it. Hope mingled with testosterone. "You wanna spend the night?"

She nodded. "Yes. But I can't."

"Why? Because of Coop?"

She sucked in her top lip and looked away. After what felt like a full minute, she shook her head. "No. Because of Misty."

Not the answer he'd been expecting. In fact, that excuse was so far down the list of possibilities it hadn't even crossed his radar. "Misty? You think I'm still mourning and what happened between us was my way of replacing her with you? Or some stupid bullsh—"

"No. I think a part of you will mourn her—what could have been between you—forever. But given the circumstances as I understand them, you're justifiably hurt and angry and done mourning."

He nodded. "Damn right. Then, what's she got to do with you and me?"

Her smile was almost tragic. He put his beer can on the table and sat forward. "What's going on, Morgana?"

She scrunched up her face in a way he'd never seen then she let out a long sigh. "You can start by calling me Morgan. That's my given name. Morgan Leanne James."

"Morgana Carlyle is a stage name. So? A lot of TV people have stage names."

Her delicate eyebrows rose and fell. "What was your wife's maiden name?"

"Burdock. Why?"

She sat back as if he'd struck her. "They adopted her. Oh, my God, that makes sense. No wonder…"

"*They?* They who? What makes sense?"

She folded her legs under her. "Mac, what I'm going to tell you is history. Ancient history that I'd prefer stayed buried in some tomb with the Da Vinci code, but I realize you're under no obligation to honor my wishes. You may be angry enough to call the *National Enquirer* yourself. I wouldn't blame you, but please believe me, I didn't know."

"Didn't know what? Your name?"

"I didn't know Misty's name. Her maiden name. I tried to ask Libby but she was feeling flustered at the time and couldn't remember. Why would she? She said your wife never liked to talk about her childhood."

Mac still had no idea where this was going but he was starting to get a bad feeling in his stomach. "She said her parents were older. She was an only child. When they died, she inherited everything, but apparently the farm had been mortgaged to the hilt. That's why she was working in a campground when we met."

"Her *adoptive* parents were older. They had a small, not terribly prosperous farm near Valentine, Nebraska. Nolan and Binnie Burdock were childless until Misty's birth parents were killed in a car accident. Binnie was Misty's maternal aunt."

She delivered this new version of his wife's background with such calm authority he was tempted to believe her. But he didn't. How could she know things he didn't know when he'd been married to the woman?

"Is this some kind of game actors do to screw with the regular people?"

"No."

"Then how do you know this?"

"Because Misty was my sister. I was seven when she was born. Our parents were busy, successful people. I don't think I really knew what Dad did for a living, but we lived in three beautiful homes that I can remember. Chicago. Washington, D.C. And Ann Arbor, Michigan.

"Misty and I had a perfect, privileged life until our parents died. Then we were sent to live in the middle of godforsaken Nowhere, Nebraska. For the first two years I was there, I prayed every night to die so I could be with our parents. But I didn't die. I became a slave to the farm. I was never mistreated or abused, but everything I valued— clothes, shopping, books, reading, theater, art, travel, time—ceased to be. I could never conform to the life that was expected of me. So, I ran away."

She looked at her hands. "I was too young to take Misty with me. Honestly? I don't think I expected to make it. I was sure they'd find me and bring me back, but they didn't. I never saw Misty or my aunt and uncle again."

Mac tried to process this bizarre revelation but his brain couldn't. "You and Misty don't look anything alike. You're skinny. She was a little plump. And you're shorter than her. And her hair—"

"You said she dyed her hair. My hair has been every color imaginable—except maybe Char's." She tried to smile. "People never thought we looked alike. I once over-heard my uncle say he thought my mother had some other lover when she was in Paris. That's where our parents met. Mom was attending the Sorbonne. Dad was hitchhiking through Europe. She ran off with him, and they got married in Greece."

A tingle of panic shot up his spine. Until that moment,

he'd been convinced this was some kind of hoax. But he'd heard that story before. He honestly hadn't believed it because Misty's parents—the poor Nebraska farmers his wife had talked about on rare occasions—didn't seem the type to explore Europe. "Misty never mentioned having a sister. Not once."

"I'm not surprised. You know the adage about divide and conquer? That's what they did. Misty helped in the house and garden. I was expected to work with Nolan in the barn and the fields.

"Me," she said with a sour laugh. "A spoiled kid who never even had to make her own bed."

Like the persona she'd created—Morgana Carlyle.

"Misty rode the bus to school. Uncle Nolan drove me so I had time to finish my chores. She made friends. I was a loner who didn't want to fit in. I made no attempt to change. In fact, I resented Misty for adapting so easily. By letting go of our past, she was admitting our parents were dead and everything they'd wanted for us was gone, too. By the time I left, I hated her almost as much as I hated everyone else."

"So, you think she cut you out of her life after you left?"

She nodded. "Yes. I wrote her a couple of times and gave her a post office box number where she could contact me in L.A., but I never heard from her. I figured Aunt and Uncle had a lot to do with that. And, frankly, I don't blame them. I was a terrible brat. Surly and mad at the world. I made everyone's life miserable, including my own," she said with a dry chuckle.

"You have no idea how many times I was sent to bed without supper." She pressed a hand to her flat belly. "Some in the media have suggested that I suffer from an eating disorder, but I think food became one more part of the power struggle for me. If I didn't let myself feel hunger, their punishment had no power over me."

Mac's heart broke for her—for the child she'd been. What if he'd been in that car with Misty? Someone else would be raising Megan. Libby, no doubt. Libby would do her best, of course. She loved Megan. But Libby's priorities and values—especially since she'd married Cooper— were different from Mac's. Megan's life wouldn't have been the same.

Megan. *Holy—*

"You're telling me you're Megan's aunt."

She nodded. Tenuously, but still, she was as good as staking a claim. He wasn't sure what to think about that, but he was pretty damn sure he didn't like the idea.

"You don't really expect me to believe this, do you? You're a goddamn movie star. You live in freakin' Hollywood. You were married to my brother-in-law and now you're telling me you were also sister to my late wife. And I'm supposed to believe this is one big coincidence? Bullshit." It felt good to cuss, but not good at all to see the look of hurt on her face.

"What did you think was going to happen, Morgana…excuse me, Morgan? And why tell me your real name? Oh, I get it. Because this story doesn't jibe in the least with the story about your life. The other *real* story."

Her gaze focused on the floor, then she stood. "I don't know why I told you. I guess I felt compelled to be honest because of what happened between us. I don't usually let myself get that close that fast, but—"

"It would have been impossible to get any closer. And it wasn't all that fast. You and I were swapping swoo from the first moment we met. It was only a matter of time and circumstance before we hooked up—as they say."

He wasn't usually this blunt, but his daughter was involved here. "And since we're on the subject, I'd appreciate it if you'd keep that fact to yourself. I still have to live here after you leave. And you are leaving. That's what you do, right?"

The last was a low blow. Not his style. But he was as close to panic as he'd been the night Misty left him. He wasn't going to mess up Megan's life by opening the door to a stranger claiming a connection.

"Just for conversation's sake, do you have any proof of what you just told me?"

She shook her head. "None."

If he hadn't been so freaked out, he would have felt sorry for her. But he couldn't let down his guard. Not till he knew what she wanted.

Neither spoke for a minute then Morgana—Morgan, he corrected—took a deep breath and slowly let it out. He watched her change before his eyes. Her expression regained some of its usual sparkle—the vibrancy just didn't go very deep. And that distance he first noticed about her was back in place.

She looked at him as if he were a cab driver or a doorman. "I should be getting back to my cottage. Early wake-up call."

She turned to leave. Each movement studied and controlled, her posture rigid. He couldn't see a single telltale sign of her pain, but he felt it.

"Morgana, I'm sorry."

She turned slightly. "For what? You're right about that swoo." She smiled coquettishly. "I heard Shane and Jenna talking about the subject before I even arrived in Sentinel Pass. I consider myself lucky to have experienced it." He doubted that. "And you're right about my life, too. Things are finally coming together for me. Once I sign the contract for my cosmetics endorsement, I'll be able to get out from under a rather ponderous and unpleasant tax burden left behind by my former agent."

He'd heard some hints about her financial problems but this was the first time she'd actually spelled out the source of the issue.

"If I could ask one favor of you..." She paused. "If you could bring yourself to forget everything I just told you, I would appreciate it immensely. Maybe...maybe I heard the name Misty and simply imagined the connection. It's not like I ever saw my sister as an adult, right? How could I identify her from a photo so many years later?" She shook her head. "I mean, seriously. The chance that your late wife and I were related would have to be astronomical. Let's mark this down to me being a crazy, woo-woo Californian."

Right. Even though you and Misty both had an Aunt Binnie and Uncle Nolan. But that argument only held water if she wasn't lying. *Why would she lie?*

He didn't have an answer for that.

She tried to smile, but she wasn't that good an actress. A second later she fled through the door and down the path. And even though every instinct he possessed told him to go after her, Megan's dog barked at the sound of the door closing. Megan's cry followed a moment later. He had no choice but to stay. Megan was his one and only concern.

CHAPTER THIRTEEN

"JESUS, MARY AND ROBERT, what did you do last night, girlfriend?"

Morgan slumped a little lower in the makeup chair, hoping to avoid the intense scrutiny of makeup artist BreeE. That was her professional name. "One word. Two capital letters. Don't ask," was what she told all first-time clients.

Morgan had arrived on the set a good twenty minutes early, hoping to talk Shane into letting her leave after filming. She'd been prepared to beg, but he'd taken one look at her and pointed toward the trailer she and Jenna's mother were sharing. "I don't even want to know. Just go. If we need a blue screen to make you look human, I'm taking it out of your check."

Blue screen. She didn't look that bad. Did she? She looked up and caught her reflection in the mirror. Her peachy skin tone looked sallow thanks to the grayish-purple bags under her eyes.

"Insomnia," she muttered, rubbing them fiercely to avoid BreeE's skeptical look.

BreeE, who was fiftysomething with a dozen or so kids back in California, claimed to be "half-Black, half-Filipino and half-Jewish."

"Insomnia? The kind that comes in a bottle? Looks more like a hangover to me."

Morgan sighed. She wished she'd thought to take one of the extra bottles of wine from Mac's. That might have helped her unwind, even a little. "I had two glasses of wine at Libby's book club. Trust me. No alcohol or drugs." She'd dug through every nook and cranny in her cosmetics bag and couldn't find a single sleeping aid.

She leaned forward and reached for the black-and-chrome insulated cup sitting on the brightly lit makeup table. She took a small sip. Black. Not her favorite, but this morning even the thought of creamer had made her stomach heave.

"That good, huh?" BreeE asked sarcastically at Morgan's wince as the acidic stuff hit her empty belly. BreeE hovered, a sponge coated in what she called base paint ready to apply to Morgan's face. Normally, Morgan didn't mind this part of her day. She could let her thoughts drift in and out of BreeE's cheerful chatter. On the mornings that Jenna's mother, Bess, was in the adjacent chair, things really got lively.

Bess was a delightful, opinionated woman with a great sense of theater. Morgan loved listening to her stories about working in small productions in the Black Hills. Bess was also a loving mother. More than once, Morgan had fallen into a trance picturing Bess as her birth mother might have been if she'd lived.

"Where's Bess?" she asked BreeE, who seemed to know more about what was going on than Shane did.

"Left this morning. Apparently her boyfriend got himself thrown in jail for vandalizing somebody's property." She chortled in a nasally way. "Okay. *Boyfriend* just doesn't work when the guy is like eighty. Her old-dude friend."

Was this the infamous Rollie mentioned in last night's discussion? Cooper and Libby had forgotten to get William's number from her. Not that that would have made any difference, apparently.

"Did she have to bail him out?"

BreeE shook her head. "Naw. The police didn't keep him. I heard he's richer than Midas and has friends in high places, but all the commotion gave him heart palpitations and Bess is the only one who can get him to see a doctor. Apparently the guy is crazy about her."

Morgan was happy for Bess, but sad, too. Why did everyone she knew find true love without the slightest bit of trouble while she couldn't even manage to have sex twice with the same man? She was pathetic.

Why didn't I lie to Mac? Why did I have to bring up all that stupid old junk?

All she would have had to do was push the truth deep down in that small pit where she kept all the other unwelcome memories and she could have spent the night in Mac's arms. He would have made love to her. Made her feel whole and fulfilled and happy—for a few hours.

Maybe Mac was the bridge to a more authentic kind of life. Not the one she'd known in Nebraska, but the one her mother and father had been in the process of building for her before they died. She'd never find out thanks to her newly developed conscience, which everyone knew had no place in her world.

She must have let out a small cry because BreeE paused in her application of blush. "You okay, hon? Maybe you picked up a little bug? Whatcha eat for dinner?"

"Pizza." Three or four bites.

BreeE put her hands on her substantial hips. "Oh, well,

there you go. Nothing messes with sleep like indigestion." She pronounced the word with a long *i*. In-die-gestion. "How 'bout you have a little yogurt before I put on your lipstick?"

"Later, thanks. I think Shane's ready for me."

As if on cue, a knock sounded from outside.

BreeE yanked open the door with such force the whole place shook. "She's done, but she needs to eat somethin' fir— Oh, it's you. Come on in. I'm gonna get her a cinnamon roll. Screw yogurt. Don't let her escape till I get back."

Morgan would have been amused if she wasn't so tired. In fact, she couldn't even work up a smile to greet her costar.

"What's wrong with yogurt?" Cooper asked, obviously confused. He let BreeE get by then turned to look at Morgan. "Holy garbanzo beans. You look like hell—even with makeup. What happened? You and Mac? Oh, crap, Libby said we shouldn't have left you there, but I thought after the way you two were acting at the mine… Oh, damn, I'm sorry, Morgie. Did I blow it?"

Morgan shook her head as he collapsed in typical Cooper anguish in Bess's chair. "No. This isn't about Mac. I'm fine. I just couldn't sleep. I started thinking about my tax bill and whether or not my new contract would cover the principal as well as the interest. You know how I worry about money."

She could tell he'd bought her lie. "Well, that's true. You and Mom were alike in that way. I never really understood how someone with your background would care that much about every penny, but Mom said it was a case of the haves worrying about not having. Was she right?"

Morgan refused to agree with her late ex-mother-in-law strictly on principle. "Maybe I'm trying to prove something to my family, Cooper. Did you ever think about that?"

He frowned. "I thought you didn't have anything to do with them anymore. Morgie, what's going on? You don't seem like yourself."

She snickered softly. "For that to be true you would have to know the real me."

The words slipped out without her meaning to say them aloud. Luckily, the only one listening was Cooper.

Before he could ask her to explain, she jumped to her feet. Unfortunately, she got up too fast, leaving her equilibrium somewhere in left field. She reached for the back of the chair and missed.

"Morgana," Cooper cried, coming to her aid. He caught her before she went down. "Holy moly, are you drunk? Sick? Oh my God, you're not pregnant, are you?"

"No. No, Coop. I'm not," she said as forcefully as possible, but she still felt woozy.

"You like kids, don't you? The reason I ask is because Libby wanted to know why you and I didn't have one and I couldn't tell her. I don't even remember talking about the possibility."

Feeling steadier, she pushed away from him. "Tell her your mother managed to keep you so busy you were never home long enough to fool around."

He cocked his head, then smiled. "Oh, yeah, that's right. I was doing that play in London. God, I hated the weather. And the food."

"And I was doing that pilot in Hawaii."

He chuckled. "What did we call it? *Not-So-Lost?*"

She smiled. "They got the plane crash right, but none

of the freaky stuff that viewers like so much. It was bound to fail. Unlike *Sentinel PassTime,* knock on wood."

His friendly, puppy-dog innocence helped calm her scattered nerves, but she still felt light-headed.

"You always were superstitious. Or was that T-Fancy?"

Saltines might help settle my stomach, she thought, looking around. Bess was one of those constant eaters. "Neither," she answered absently. "It was your mother."

"Oh, yeah. That makes sense. Are you ready to go?"

He opened the door and stepped down, holding out a hand to help her. The morning air was crisp and dewy. It was almost cool enough to make her think of autumn—the season she missed most in southern California.

BreeE came toward them, a small plastic tray in hand. "Oh, good. You're still here. I got one of everything. The maple bars are to die for." She smacked her lips in an exaggerated way that made Morgan think of Misty. She didn't know why, but the tiny shard of memory ripped through her midsection, taking away any chance that even a bite of food would stay in her stomach.

"Thanks," she said, taking an ooey-gooey, sugary-smelling rectangle. The slick wrapper BreeE used to hand it to her gave Morgan a creepy feeling that sent a wave of gooseflesh up her arms. She couldn't repress the shiver that followed.

BreeE, who was wearing a cap-sleeve black smock over a red T-shirt and jeans, shoved the tray into Cooper's hands and said, "Hang on. I'll get you a sweater."

The door of the trailer slammed behind her and Morgan dropped her doughnut. "Oh," she groaned. "Darn."

When she bent over to pick it up, a wave of blackness swept through her body. She shook her head and tried to take a deep breath, but her extremities felt cold and disconnected and then…there was nothing. Just blackness.

Forty minutes later, the calls began to come in earnest. First, Libby. Sweet. Concerned. Then, a woman who said she was the production company's publicist. Like Morgan would fall for that. Next was William, her agent.

"Morgana. I heard you passed out on the set. What's going on? You're never sick. Tell me you're not sick."

"I'm not sick."

"Pregnant?"

"Absolutely not."

"And this isn't a matter of the old eating disorder rumor becoming fact?"

"No. No. No. Even though that's probably what everybody thinks. I had a damn sweet roll in my hand but didn't get a chance to take a bite because I blacked out." Almost the truth. "I don't know why. Probably lack of sleep. No big deal, William. I promise."

She read concern in his silence. "What do you want me to say for damage control?"

"That I've been pouring myself into a project I've come to love and stretched myself too thin."

Much better than the truth. That I'm a fake and a fraud and a terrible person and probably partly to blame for why my only sister is dead.

"I could say something about a combination of late nights, the altitude—it's, like, seven thousand feet there, right?— and a stomach flu combined to create a perfect storm."

Morgan managed a laugh. "Some of the peaks around here might be that tall, but it's not like I was rock climbing, William. Stick to the facts. It's not altitude sickness. I'm just tired."

"Fine. I'll make up something innocuous and add that you appreciate your fans' concern…yada yada."

She closed her eyes, wearier than she'd ever felt. "I know you'll make me look good. Thank you, William. For everything you do for me."

Another pause. "Okay, who is this? What did you do with Morgana?"

She laughed—because she knew he was teasing. Theirs was a professional, but she liked to think friendly, relationship. "Stop. I'm not that bad. Am I?"

"A tad self-involved, but far less than most of my clients. You're a sweetheart. I tell everyone that."

She didn't believe him, but she didn't care enough to argue. "I have to go, William. Shane had the medic look me over. He said I was suffering from low blood sugar and dehydration. I have to drink a whole glass of orange juice and eat something that looks like a meal they'd serve you in prison before I can get back on the set."

"Low blood sugar and dehydration? Well, why didn't you say so in the first place? Those are diagnoses people understand. So, you're scheduled to be back here on what…Saturday?"

"Um…I think so."

Shane had mentioned something about a wrap-up party. And Cooper had jumped in wanting to make it an early birthday party for Libby. Although it made no sense and flew in the face of her need for self-preservation, Morgan was tempted to stick around for it. Just one extra day. Maybe two.

"Morgana?"

She realized she'd missed William's question. "What?"

"Am I to understand you're considering staying? Why,

for God's sake?" His worry brought out the English accent he tried to keep hidden.

Another person with secrets. Maybe that was why they got along so well.

"Do I need to remind you that your product endorsement might evaporate at even the smallest hint of scandal?"

Her finances were at a pivotal place. The money from the show would keep her afloat, but she really needed that endorsement contract to make the IRS monkey on her back go away. Until that check was in the bank she couldn't afford to fall apart.

"No, you don't. But…I haven't gotten to see Mt. Rushmore yet. It's a national treasure, William. You're British. You wouldn't understand." Then she added a quick, "Ciao." And hung up.

He wasn't the only one who didn't understand what was going on in her head. Neither did she.

MAC LOVED working on the backhoe. His wasn't a fancy new one with an enclosed cab and all sorts of gizmos, but it was big, powerful and when he was sitting in the nicely cushioned seat with his hands firmly gripping the levers that worked the bucket, he felt in charge. Digging, shoveling, dumping…all acts he did with finesse. He was so skilled, in fact, he almost could convince himself that he had a similar handle on his life.

An illusion, of course, but the demands of the big machine kept his brain too busy to think of all the things beyond his control—like Morgana's secret. The one he told himself he easily could have gone the rest of his life without knowing.

Morgana. No, her name was Morgan. Would he ever get that right? Did he care?

That was the worst part. He could tell himself he didn't give a flying fig but in truth he cared way more than he should have considering who she was.

His freaking sister-in-law. Good lord, if the media got hold of that he'd have to move. The people of Sentinel Pass could only take so much disruption of what they perceived as the correct order of things. Women didn't leave their husbands then drive their cars off the road. If that did happen, then someone was to blame. And the most likely person to blame was the husband who, shortly before she died, had been seen yelling at her and pulling their daughter out of her arms.

He'd understood why he'd fallen under suspicion by the police, but he'd never really forgiven his friends and neighbors—the people he helped protect when he put on his firefighter gear—for doubting him. He tried, but... Maybe things would have been different if Gran had been able to stand up for him. Libby had tried, but she wasn't Gran.

And once his grandmother was gone...honestly...he just didn't know.

A movement at the edge of his peripheral vision chopped into his thoughts. A person. A woman. His heart rate spiked for a second. He thought it was Morgana, but, no, it was the woman she spent her days impersonating—his sister. Another bizarre complication that made him want to throw up.

He lowered the bucket, tipping it outward to dig into the ground slightly. Just enough to add an extra brake if the tires slipped. Once the engine was turned off, he removed his protective earphones and safety glasses. He shifted sideways, looping one leg over the seat. "Hey, Lib, what's up?"

With the motor stilled, the usual morning sounds started

to come back to him. A few cars down on Main Street. *Is that where the crew is filming today?* he wondered. Was Morgan on camera? Exchanging quips and bright innuendoes with Cooper? Her ex. His brother-in-law.

His groan melded into the racket a congress of crows was making in a stand of pines that bordered the back of Mrs. Smith's—correction, Jack Treadwell's—property. Mac had finally memorized the guy's name after seeing it on a check that had shown up in the mail that morning.

Libby started toward him, taking care not to trip over the clumps of dirt the backhoe had left in her path. When she glanced up, he could see that she wasn't smiling. In fact, she looked so serious his gut immediately clenched as if someone had reached inside and tightened a fist around his innards.

He hopped off the tractor and hurried to meet her halfway. "Whatever it is, it's not good."

She swallowed before answering. "Cal is calling the hospice this morning. He thinks it's time. I don't want it to be time, Mac. I need her too much. We all need her."

Gran. Damn. He'd taken his eye off the ball and let his attraction for Morgana get in the way of his obligation to his family. He cursed soundly and wrapped his arms around his sister. He let her cry, fighting back tears of his own.

He'd known this day was coming. Sooner, rather than later. The treasured grandmother he'd relied on for so many years had been slipping away for months. The fact that she'd lived a dynamic life that spanned nearly nine decades wasn't comfort enough.

They stood in the sun, Libby's halting sniffles the only sound. Agony, regret twisted through his gut like a poisonous snake. "I was just thinking about her," he said, hanging his head in shame. "About how things might have been different after Misty died if Gran had been her old self. God, am I the most stupid, selfish person on the planet? As if it was Gran's fault I screwed up my life."

He drove one fist into the opposite palm. "Misty hated it here, you know. She was jealous of the mine and my relationship with you and Gran. But I told her we couldn't move. The mine was still making enough to pay its taxes. If I walked away, we'd lose it. And you and Gran…the town…everyone was counting on me." *I picked everyone else over her.* "So, she left. And she died. And now Gran's dying. I failed her, too."

Libby wiped her eyes. "No, Mac, that's not true. Gran always called you our rock. That's not something you should feel ashamed of. And what's happening now… Cal says we have to believe that this is Gran's path. There's nothing we can do to change that."

He ran his hand across his brow. "It's too soon, Lib. It hasn't even been a year yet."

He knew she understood what he meant. "I know. I feel the same. If she leaves now, she'll never meet my b-baby."

Tears coursed down her cheeks as she put a hand on her belly.

Mac placed his hand over hers. "She'll know, Lib. Gran will always be a part of our lives. I'm not worried about that. I just don't want to let go."

He comforted her a second time, then, when her tears seemed to lessen, he put an arm around her shoulders and walked her back to her car. "Come on. Cal's gonna need us. We'll be with her in shifts. She'll never be alone—even if there's a hospice person there."

"Where's Meggie?"

"I dropped her off at day care. Barb called last night to say she was back from her granddaughter's."

He helped her into the passenger side, then got behind the wheel. "Don't want our expectant mother to run down some innocent pedestrian because she can't see through her tears," he told her.

Libby's chin lifted. "I saw some suspicious moisture in your eyes, too, McDufus."

He gave her a brotherly tap on the shoulder. "Put on your seat belt. We're not taking any chances. Things are screwed up enough as it is."

She looked at him questioningly, but thankfully she didn't ask. His problems just got relegated to the back burner. Morgan would be long gone by the time he got through this crisis.

Of that, he was sure.

CHAPTER FOURTEEN

"MAC? GOT A MINUTE?"

At the sound of Cooper's voice, Mac looked up from the open book in his hands. The Bible. Calvin had handed it to him the moment the doctor arrived. Not Gran's regular doctor but one who worked with the area hospice service. Mac, Cal and Libby had had a crash course in the process of dying ever since Calvin called in the cavalry that morning.

Mac had chosen not to be part of the medical evaluation. Gran deserved some privacy, he thought, even at the end of her life.

"Sure." He closed the book. He couldn't say what page he'd been reading. The words hadn't really made sense.

Coop sat down across from him. They were in the sunroom—Gran's favorite spot. Onida was curled up on the love seat beside him. Calvin had handed her to Libby when she and Mac first arrived because the dog had seemed wound up. Onie was the reason Mac had opted to leave Bella in the garage instead of bringing her along.

He'd driven back to his house to shower and change clothes out of respect for his grandmother. She'd never liked him tracking through her house in dusty boots.

"So...do they really think this is the end?"

"No one will say how long, but it doesn't look good."

"My poor Lib," Coop said sadly.

Mac looked at the man who was his brother-in-law and breathed a silent sigh of relief. Coop would be here for Libby, no matter what—an emotional obligation Mac had honored ever since his mother passed away.

"Take care of your sister," she'd said to him one day a few months before she died.

He'd been a child with no understanding of death. But the gravity of her tone had impressed him. "I will," he'd replied. He'd never faltered. Never left Sentinel Pass, except for a short stint at trade school, where he'd learned to work on motors and handle heavy machinery.

He might never have done that if his grandmother hadn't pushed him out of his safe little nest. "You need to see a little more of the world, grandson," Mary had insisted. "Meet new people."

He'd been on a weekend bike trip with some college pals when he met Misty.

Misty. A pretty, complicated, broken thing he'd brought home to make whole. But she'd kept secrets to the very end. Maybe they'd become the truth to her—the same way Morgan's had.

"Coop, do you know much about Morgan…Morgana's past?"

"You mean her family?"

Mac nodded.

Mac could tell the question made Coop uncomfortable. He cleared his throat—twice—and looked at the floor. "Well…I know what her bio says, but…um…it's not uncommon for people in our business to re-create themselves, you know. What did she tell you?"

Mac went with his gut. "The truth."

Coop looked surprised. "Really? Wow. She must really care for you a lot. She never told me the truth. Ever. And we were married."

Mac frowned. "But you know about her family?"

"Sorta. My mother had her investigated. I told Mom that Morgie's life before we met had no bearing on our marriage, but Mom dumped this file on my lap and wouldn't take no for an answer." He smiled sheepishly. "Mom was…strong-willed. Like Lib, only not as nice."

"Do you still have the file?"

He sat back as if struck. "Oh, hell no, I burned it in the fireplace before Morgie got home."

"You didn't read it?"

He frowned. "I'm not much of a reader. I caught a couple of high points. Her real name. Morgan, not Morgana. I forget what her last name was.

"And I saw her age." He brightened. "She didn't lie about that. A lot of people do." He thought a moment then shrugged. "I'm as curious as the next guy, but I figured she'd tell me if she wanted me to know. How can you hope to make a successful marriage if you don't trust each other?"

Isn't that the truth?

Coop let out a long, sad sigh. "She never told me and we divorced a month or so later. What does that tell you?"

It told Mac he had no idea what to think. She'd told *him* the truth and not Cooper.

"You're not going to out her, are you? I mean, the way she looked this morning tells me your relationship is on the skids, and sometimes people say things they don't really mean when they're mad."

Mac didn't deny that things between him and Morgan

were on the rocks. He glanced at the little dog asleep beside him. "I'm not that petty, Coop. Besides, who would I tell?"

"The gossip lady. I forget her name. Libby points her out all the time and says 'Don't say that around…Mar…va.' That's it," he cried triumphantly. "Marva the Mouth. I told Shane we should use a character like her in the story and he did. Sorta. We made her a him and he doubles as a mail carrier. Men can gossip, too, you know."

Mac knew. Marva hadn't been the only one speculating over coffee whether or not he had had a hand in Misty's death. The whispers and stares had driven him underground—deep into the Little Poke. He would have stayed there if it hadn't been for Megan. But the gossip had really rocked his sense of self. It wasn't easy going from the town's golden boy to a murder suspect overnight. His grandmother had remained philosophical. "This, too, shall pass," Gran had advised.

He told himself he stuck it out for Megan's sake. This was the only home she'd ever known and she still had Gran and Libby. But once Gran was gone—and Libby and Coop were back in Malibu—he and Megan would be alone. In a town that had changed for him well before Hollywood arrived.

"Do you like living in California?"

Cooper shrugged. "I like the beach, but in all honesty, I like Sentinel Pass better. I can be me here."

The answer surprised Mac. "Who are you in Malibu?"

Coop's blond head shook back and forth. "You don't want to know me. Your sister says I turn into a helium-balloon version of myself. If she weren't there to hold on to my string, I'd fly up into the stratosphere and pop." His hands made an exploding gesture. "Hey, speaking of stratosphere, isn't there a place around here where they set some kind of record with a hot air balloon? Shane and I wanna see it before we leave."

"Stratosphere Bowl. When are you leaving?" *When is Morgan leaving?* he really wanted to ask.

"Most of the crew is taking off tomorrow. Shane's sticking around through the weekend. Jenna isn't going back until after the Mystery Spot closes. I think Morgie was trying to change her ticket to leave tonight. But I could be wrong. Her agent was pretty upset about her passing out on the set today."

Mac started, which made Onida yip. "Morgan fainted?"

"Just for a few seconds. Maybe a minute. Low blood sugar or dehydration or something. She's fine. We finished all our scenes. She's a professional. But William—her agent," he said mockingly even though Mac had been privy to the conversation the night before and knew who the man was, "is afraid her new product endorsement gig might get pulled if they think she has health issues. Apparently, they were a little worried about her reputed eating disorder from the beginning."

"She doesn't have an eating disorder."

"I know, but when she's worried she doesn't eat and when she doesn't eat she gets woozy. And one thing I do know about Morgie is she's always worried about money."

Mac could understand why now. "Aren't you going to make a boatload of money with this show?"

Coop brightened. "We sure as heck hope so. At the moment, the numbers look promising, but you never know."

He launched into a convoluted explanation of residuals and market shares. Mac tuned him out. Was Morgan really leaving? He'd wanted her to, but he didn't like the way they'd ended things. Unpleasant. Not quite as bad as when Misty left, but still, not good.

Maybe he should offer an olive branch. Ask her to help out with Megan while he and Libby were preoccupied. Everyone—all of Libby's book club friends—would want to help, but… He needed to think about this. The question he really needed to ask himself was whether or not he wanted Morgan to be a part of Megan's life.

He picked up the Bible again. *What,* he asked himself, *would Gran do?*

"MAY I HELP?"

Morgan wasn't sure where she got the nerve to ask. She'd noticed Libby's friends, Char, Jenna and Kat, standing together near the caterer's tent. She'd never been a part of that kind of clique and usually felt far too intimidated to approach one, but Char and Jenna had been kind and welcoming at the book club meeting, so she wandered closer. Close enough to hear that Libby's and Mac's grandmother had taken a turn for the worst.

"I think we have meals covered," Jenna said, double-checking with Char and Kat.

"Mostly," Char said, "Mac was worried about Bella. We were discussing whether to take turns checking on her or arranging for her to stay in a kennel."

"Where is she now?" Morgan asked.

"In the garage. She has food and water, but I'm sure she's not very happy. And Megan isn't going to like the idea of being separated from her."

Morgan agreed. "I was just headed back to the guest-house to pack. I can let Bella out and even take her for a walk. What about Megan? Is she with Mac and Libby?"

Kat scowled. "No. She's at the day care. I think she should come home with me. The boys would keep her too busy to worry about Gran."

Char put a hand on her friend's arm. "Kat, the last thing you need at the moment is a toddler. Take a breath. You're going to be the next person to pass out." She looked at Morgan tellingly. Morgan didn't know why she was surprised to learn everyone knew about her fainting spell that morning. Small towns were no different than a closed set.

"Besides," Jenna said, "didn't you just say you needed to take the boys shopping for back-to-school clothes? Between Jordie's trauma and your student teaching, you have your hands full. Let Char and me handle this."

Kat frowned stubbornly. "But—"

"Libby's going to need us a lot more when Gran passes," Char said. "Right now, we have to think about Megan. How do you tell a four-year-old that her beloved great-grandmother isn't going to be around anymore?"

"The same way someone told her about her mother, I suppose," Morgan said, more to herself than anyone else.

"What's that supposed to mean?" Kat snapped, her tone defensive.

Morgan's heart rate sped up. "I—I was trying to imagine how hard it must have been for Mac. And now to have to go through this again so soon after his wife's death…it just seems unfair."

Kat's demeanor changed instantly. Morgan could practically see straight into her heart. "Oh. You're right. It sucks. I'm sorry I jumped on you. I've been emotionally deranged lately. Swoo overload."

Swoo. That word again. She couldn't admit that she and Mac had discussed it in reference to their own sweet, hot sex, so she plied her acting skills. "Swoo? Where have I heard that? Oh, I know, your mother's character uses it in dialogue," she said to Jenna.

"I know. I stole it from Kat. It's her mother's word. Kat says if the show is a success, she's going to set up a Web site called Got swoo dot com and sell T-shirts."

The three friends chatted a few minutes longer about what swoo was and wasn't. Morgan didn't listen. She knew what it was—a Mack truck that left her sideswiped on the edge of some emotional highway.

She was about to say something to bring them back on topic when Jenna's cell phone rang. She listened a moment then said, "Yeah. She's right here. She already volunteered to do that." All three women turned to look at her. "Okay. I'll tell her. Let us know if anything changes. Bye."

She slipped it back in her pocket. "That was Mac. He'd like you to pick up Megan. The day care place is on your way. I'll give you directions. Apparently, he just talked to Meggie on the phone and she's upset about Bella being in the garage. Mac can't leave because the hospice doc is still there and they're waiting to talk to him."

Was this a test? One she was sure to fail? "Of course. No problem."

"Wait," Kat said. "I have a problem with this. She's a stranger. We're practically family. Why is she picking up Megan?"

Jenna looked at Morgan. Her fair complexion colored with a pretty blush FreshFace Cosmetics would have loved to replicate. "Well…um…nobody's said for sure, but Mac and Morgana…um…seem to have…um…"

"I'm Megan's aunt."

"Uh?" Char croaked. "You mean you're playing Megan's aunt."

Morgan shook her head. "No. I *am* Megan's aunt. At least, I'm ninety-nine percent sure Misty was my sister." She saw their looks of shock but continued before anyone could ask for details. "Our parents were killed in a car accident when I was twelve. Our maternal aunt and uncle became our guardians. They moved us to a farm in Nebraska. It wasn't the life I thought I was entitled to, so I ran away. Misty adapted better."

"But I read your bio," Char protested. "Only child. Wealthy parents. Blue blood and silver spoon. What's all that? A lie?"

"It's the history I envisioned for myself. Much closer to the life I would have led if our parents had lived."

"You're Misty's sister?" Kat asked, shaking her head. "You didn't know she was married to Mac? Or that she was dead? Oh God, that sucks. That totally sucks. Does Mac know?" Kat smacked her forehead with her palm. "Of course he knows. That's why he asked you to pick Megan up. Does she know?"

Morgan shook her head. "No. And…and Mac and I haven't had a chance to talk about my relationship with her. So, I don't plan to tell her. She's been through enough. And now, her great-grandmother is passing. I don't think Libby knows, either. I only told Mac the truth last night and he's…he's an honorable man. He doesn't gossip."

Morgan listened as the women discussed the situation. Each expressed similar degrees of shock, sympathy and concern. Kat's antipathy had vanished. Morgan could see she really did have a big heart that only grew armor when it was defending someone she loved.

"I should go. Bella probably really needs a walk."

As she turned to leave, she spotted a person sitting on a stool behind the serving table a few feet away. An older woman who looked vaguely familiar. She hadn't been there when Morgan first joined the book club friends.

Recognition hit her with a dose of cold dread. This was the woman someone had called "The Mouth." Mention had been made of her connections with the gossip magazines that were on every newsstand.

"Oh, no," she murmured under her breath. A knot formed in the pit of her stomach and a cold sweat broke out under her arms. She knew nothing good would come of this information getting leaked to the press. She could probably kiss her endorsement agreement goodbye. Uncle Sam would take her house and most of what she made on *Sentinel Passtime*. The publicity might even hurt the show. Shane might be forced to fire her to save face. She could almost see the headlines: TV Postmaster Linked to Dead Sister/Sister-In-Law's Husband/Brother. She might never work again.

Her fingertips started to tingle from hyperventilating. Then, suddenly, she pictured Mac and Libby sitting at the bedside of their beloved grandmother. She couldn't stop the juggernaut aimed at her life, but she could do something to help the people who needed her right now. She kept walking—and even managed one of her well-practiced paparazzi smiles for the woman who followed her every move.

She stopped off at her trailer long enough to grab her purse and change shoes, then she hurried along Main Street. She thought about calling William to warn him about what was about to hit the fan, but she didn't. Mac had given her a generous gift—one last chance to spend time with her niece. She wasn't going to blow it worrying about things she couldn't change. There would be plenty of time for that when she was back in California.

CHAPTER FIFTEEN

MORGAN AND HER WARDS, Megan and Bella, were about half a block from the McGannon home when a low rumble drew Morgan's attention skyward. Their walk had been so captivating, Morgan hadn't even noticed the purplish-gray clouds tumbling over the ridge of hills behind Sentinel Pass. "Uh-oh. I think that might be thunder."

Megan cocked her head to listen. A second clatter echoed deep in the clouds. "I think it might be elephants."

Elephants? Only in the mind of a four-year-old. Morgan grinned and blinked back tears. *Oh, Misty. Your daughter is amazing.* The pressure on her chest was so intense it could have been from one of Megan's elephants sitting there. "We'd better hurry home. Don't want one of them to step on Bella."

Megan petted the dog's head. "Bella doesn't like storms. They scare her."

Morgan reached down and offered her hand. Together they raced to the house. Breathless and laughing, they arrived in time to catch the phone.

"Hello? McGannon residence."

"Is everything okay? You sound out of breath."

Mac. Serious. Worried. Sad. She hoped he wasn't calling to tell her the worst. "We were racing the rain."

"It's raining? I haven't even looked outside."

"We felt a couple of drops, but Megan was too fast for them. How's…um… Is…?" She didn't know what to say.

"Gran's hanging in there. We're not sure if she still hears us, but she doesn't seem to be in pain. We're taking turns being with her. Coop just took Libby home to rest. I was hoping you might be able to stay with Megan a while longer. Um…maybe even overnight."

"Of course. I'd be happy to. Megan's day-care provider gave me the lowdown on Megan's routine. She said she kept her a couple of times when you were busy." With the police, the woman had added in a tone that bothered Morgan. She didn't know why people were always so quick to focus on the negative. "Megan and I already came up with a plan in case you couldn't come home. Supper, bubble bath, book reading and bed. Does that sound okay?"

"And brush teeth. She forgets."

"Got it." To Megan, she made a teeth-brushing gesture. Megan turned and did the same to Bella.

God, I love this little girl. And her father, a tiny voice added. Morgan ignored it.

"Make yourself at home. The sheets on my bed are clean. Just be sure to leave Meggie's door ajar. She was having nightmares pretty regularly before we got Bella. The storm might trigger one."

"Will do. But the couch is fine for me. I'm not that fussy…despite the fact my ex-mother-in-law called me a diva. Which, as my aunt would have said, was a case of the pot calling the kettle black," she said, a little shocked by the ease at which the truth rolled off her tongue.

Mac's pause seemed significant, introspective, then he told her, "If you're in my room, you're more likely to hear

Meggie. And, trust me, the couch isn't that comfortable." Said like a man who'd slept there on occasion. "No reason for both of us to be awake all night. Coop told me you fainted this morning. Something about a rough night."

Thanks, Coop. At least Mac had no way of knowing that she'd been thinking about him all night. "I am a little wiped out," she admitted. "I plan to turn in the minute Megan falls asleep."

"Take the bed. Please. That way when I do come home I can slip in without waking you."

She was so tempted to say, "You could crawl into bed with me." But she didn't.

Good. Maybe she was finally developing some self-control. "Fine. Whatever works best for you. I'm here so you can focus on your grandmother."

Before he hung up, he told her how his grandmother had reached up and touched his cheek an hour or so earlier. "It felt like she was saying goodbye," he admitted, his voice raw with emotion. Morgan almost lost it.

"I—I just hope for Cal's sake she doesn't linger too long," he said. "It's hard watching your loved one fade away and not being able to do anything to stop it."

After that, nothing else seemed important, so she handed the phone to Megan to tell her daddy good-night.

The evening passed too quickly, with Morgan trying to memorize every sweet, funny, tender little moment. Like Megan wearing a crown of bubbles, just as Misty once had. Back then, the two sisters had shared a tub every other night— even though Morgan was older and felt she deserved more privacy. And the bubbles were a product of Joy dishwashing liquid. No sweet-smelling, kid-friendly bubble bath that came from a plastic bottle shaped like a Sesame Street character.

The books Megan picked to read were nothing familiar to Morgan. The brilliant colors on large, shiny pages told sweet, clever stories that held a life lesson or two. She'd been too old for bedtime stories by the time she'd moved to Nebraska. Usually, she and Misty would slide into their respective single beds beneath line-dried scratchy cotton sheets and whisper back and forth to each other until their aunt scolded them.

Their second-floor bedroom had been cold in the winter and hot in the summer. The lone window, a tall, narrow, double-hung unit, was situated between the two beds with a small nightstand beneath it. If she closed her eyes, Morgan could almost picture the eerie shadows the moonlight cast through the old-fashioned lace curtains.

Megan seemed content to follow her nighttime routine without any fuss. She asked several times about Gran and her daddy. Morgan avoided any mention of the word *death* and firmly assured her Mac would be home before she awoke in the morning. Morgan prayed for everyone's sake that was true.

"Good night, sweet girl."

"Good night. Morgana?" At some point that afternoon, she'd stopped calling Morgan princess.

"Yes?"

"Is my great-gran going to heaven to be with my mother?"

Oh, dear.

Morgan rested one hip on the mattress. Bella inched closer and laid her nose on Morgan's lap. "I think she is. Probably soon."

Megan's lips pulled together in a pout. "I hate it when people leave without saying goodbye."

The sentiment was so adult Morgan didn't know how to

respond. She swallowed the lump in her throat. "Sometimes, they don't have any choice. It just works out that way."

Megan thought a moment. Then she yawned and closed her eyes. "I hear money."

"Money?"

She rolled to her side, scratching her nose with her small fist. "Mommy told me rain is money in the bank. Ours isn't, but that's what she said."

A memory hit Morgan as if it were yesterday. "Pray for rain," Uncle Nolan said, pausing at the wire fence that kept deer and bunnies out of the garden where his wife and nieces were working. "Every drop is like money in the bank."

"Then hopefully it will rain all night and in the morning we'll all be rich," Morgan said, striving for lightness. She leaned over and kissed Megan's forehead, then she petted the dog and left. Her heart was pounding and tears burned in her eyes. She'd never felt more conflicted—even when she first ran away from home.

I hate it when people leave without saying goodbye. The way Morgan had left her sister. The way she planned to leave tomorrow.

Guilt made the bile in her mostly empty stomach rise. She swallowed hard and walked into the living room. She flopped onto the couch and grabbed a throw pillow. She squeezed it to her belly as tight as possible. She'd made so many mistakes in her life. She had to make damn sure this wasn't another one.

Should she try to be a part of her niece's life? Would Mac object? He'd feel conflicted, she was sure. Especially given the feelings that existed between them. Feelings that wouldn't stay in the safe little box where she wanted them to remain. Her boxes were overlapping and breaking open.

A mess. That's what her life was at the moment. A strange, unhappy mess.

The one good thing to come of this was Megan.

"I have a niece," Morgan said, sitting up. An amazing, smart, funny, cool kid.

But Megan's life was pretty full. She had a wonderful father and extended family. She certainly didn't need someone like Morgan showing up to confuse matters.

"Your mommy was my sister, but I left her because I was a self-centered little twit who only cared about my own happiness. And now I'd like to be part of your life. And maybe your daddy's…in a long-distance, totally impossible way. Unless I've messed up my career so badly I wind up being blackballed in Hollywood and have to flip burgers for the rest of my life."

She tossed the pillow aside and jumped to her feet. This wouldn't work. She had to go home and do everything in her power to salvage her reputation. Besides, she couldn't drop into Megan's life the same way she'd dropped out of Misty's all those years ago. And she couldn't pretend she didn't have feelings for Megan's father. Even in Hollyweird people frowned on one helping oneself to one's dead sister's husband and child. That was wrong. Wrong. Wrong.

She paced to the windows and watched the rain cut a diagonal swath through the double spotlight mounted on the side of the garage. Rain is money in the bank, Misty had said. Morgan supposed it wasn't surprising that Misty had held on to a philosophy so closely related to the land. In Morgan's world, the adage went: *image* is money in the bank.

Morgan had spent years cultivating an image that didn't fit in this small house in the heartland of the country. She didn't fit. She never had. Leaving may or may not have been the right thing to do where Misty was concerned. She'd never know. But it was the right thing to do for Mac and Megan. They both deserved better than her.

She wandered through the house, restless and tense, but the long day was catching up with her. Against her better judgment, she walked into Mac's room. Misty's photo was gone. She didn't know what that meant, if anything. But she was too tired to think anymore.

She sank onto the pretty green-and-gold-and-cream comforter and pulled up the edge, rolling over like a bug in a cocoon. Within seconds she was asleep.

She awoke at the sound of the front door opening. Mac's bedside alarm clock read two o'clock. A strange time to come home, she thought. Unless his grandmother had passed away and there wasn't any reason for him to stay at Cal's.

The thought made her sit up. She was still debating about whether or not to go into the living room when he came to the doorway. She'd left the bedside lamp on—more for her sake than Megan's.

"You're supposed to be asleep."

"I was. I heard you come in."

"Oops. Sorry."

She shrugged. "Is your grandmother…?"

"She's resting peacefully. The hospice nurse gave her something. Not morphine. Just something to help ease her breathing and make her relax. Libby showed up a few minutes ago, so I left."

"Cooper let her out of the house in this storm?"

His left eyebrow shot up. "You must not know Lib very well. She's a bit strong-willed. But she's not reckless. Besides, the storm blew itself out around midnight."

Morgan cocked her head. Sure enough, there wasn't

any sound of rain driving against the windows. "Oh. Did you check on Megan?"

He walked to his closet and bent down to unlace his boots. "Sound asleep. I should have gotten a dog months ago. The two looked so peaceful there."

Wow. A guy who admits when he's wrong. A rarity. "I should go, then."

He stopped unbuttoning his shirt. "I...um...I'd rather you didn't. I mean, if anything happens with Gran, Libby has strict orders to call and I'll have to take off. I don't want to wake up Megan to take her with me."

That made sense. "Of course. What was I thinking?"

"It's too late to think. Go back to sleep. I'm gonna brush my teeth then crash on the sofa," he said before ducking into the bathroom.

She put a hand to her hair. She was a mess. So far from sexy she didn't have to worry about something starting between them. What had happened at the mine was a fluke that would never be repeated now that she knew the truth about Misty. But that didn't mean they weren't entitled to a little peace and comfort. Human compassion.

He came out wearing baggy gray basketball shorts and a plain white T-shirt. He looked every bit as tired and emotionally beat-up as she felt.

"Mac, we're grown-ups with too much on our plates to mess around right now. Why don't you join me?" She leaned over and patted his side of the bed. "Sleepover buddies. That's all."

Mac looked at her and swallowed. She'd never looked more real. More vulnerable. He wanted to spend the night beside her more than anything he could remember wanting in months. Maybe years. But he knew what she was offering. Friendship. Companionship. No sex.

Under normal conditions he wouldn't have been able to be in the same room with her and not want her, but watching his grandmother struggle for every breath for the past hour had been pure torture. "Are you sure?"

She gave a wry chuckle. "I'll try to keep from attacking you in your sleep, but I gotta tell you I have a weak spot for guys in basketball shorts."

He knew she was kidding, but there was something in her eyes that looked so lost and wounded, he couldn't say no. None of this could be easy for her, he realized.

He pulled a comforter from the shelf in the closet and carried it to the bed. A few seconds later he was lying beside her. In bed with another woman.

The thought should have freaked him out but it didn't. Morgan didn't feel like another woman. She belonged here. He couldn't say why and he was too tired to think any more, so he rolled on his side to face away from her.

Neither spoke for a few minutes. Mac wondered if she could drop back to sleep that easily. He was envious.

Then, in a soft whisper, she asked, "Do the doctors think it will be long?"

A wave of sadness swept over him. "I read all the pamphlets the hospice people gave Cal. It could be hours. Or days. Gran was a strong-willed woman but her body is tired. I just wish we'd had more time with her." He swallowed against the tightness in his throat. "I wanted to take her on a cruise to Alaska. We talked about it before Megan was born, then there never seemed to be enough time. Or money."

He squeezed his eyes tight to keep back the tears and

focused on the one thing that brought anger, not pain. "Money," he repeated. "I hate that word."

He heard her sigh, then she said, "I've been on two cruises for different promotions. They're not cheap, even if you have a lot of things comped."

Her kindness made him smile, but he knew she didn't understand what he'd meant. "I'm not broke, Morgan. At one time, I had a pretty healthy savings account thanks to settlement from a class action suit filed on behalf of my mother and other workers who developed cancer because of their company's bad safety measures. Gran made sure Lib and I both got half. Lib planned to use her share to pay off Cooper when their whole baby-by-contract thing went ballistic. I never touched mine. A fact that drove Misty crazy. The money became a huge point of contention in our marriage."

"Why?"

He thought a moment, wondering how to explain the biggest problem in their married life without making Misty seem greedy and avaricious. "She hated living on a budget, with car payments and mortgages, while all this money sat in our savings account earning some paltry interest."

"Is that why she was leaving you?"

"Partly. Misty said she'd rather be flat broke than have money she couldn't spend. What she didn't understand was my dad called it blood money. Using the money for myself would have felt as though I benefited from my mother's death. It creeped me out."

Morgan inhaled deeply and sighed. "I can understand why you felt that way even though part of the reason I ran away from home was because I thought my aunt and uncle had stolen my inheritance. In hindsight, I don't think there was much money to begin with, but try telling that to a teenager with a chip on her shoulder."

"Misty had some strange ideas about money. She'd pinch pennies like we were going broke then suddenly splurge on an expensive house plant or new set of knives or a fancy suit she had no intention of wearing. She emptied our savings account the day she died."

"What happened to the money?"

He shook his head. "Nobody knows. The bank puts the withdrawal just a few hours before our big fight. She took it in cash, big bills. There's no record of her opening another account in town. When I came home from work, she told me the money wasn't doing me any good, so she planned to use it to start fresh with someone else."

Anticipating her next question—the one that came to everyone's mind when they learned about Misty's wreck— he told her, "This area doesn't have a CSI team like the one on TV, but the cops couldn't find any evidence of burned money in the car."

She didn't say anything for a few minutes, then she whispered softly, "I can understand how the money would become an issue for her."

He rolled over to look at her. "What do you mean?"

She was lying on her back, her eyes trained on the ceiling. "We were poor little orphans. That's what Uncle Nolan called us." Her brow was lined, her expression intense. "You have no idea how much I hated him for saying that. For Misty's sake more than my own. She was just a little kid. How did that make her feel?"

"I bet it made you both feel dependent. Just how he wanted you to feel."

She looked at him as if the thought had never occurred

to her. "Maybe that justified his spending whatever was left of our inheritance. All I know is if you live a life of penury, money takes on false value. You imbue it with the power to give you safety, security, love and success. The more money you have the better you feel about yourself."

"Wow. That's pretty insightful."

She glanced at him, a wry smile playing on her lips. "I played a psychiatrist once."

"Oh."

She brushed something—sleep, probably—from her eyes then told him, "Megan asked if your grandmother was going to heaven to be with Misty."

He and Libby had talked about how to tell Megan. He'd hoped he might have a little while longer to figure out what to say, but his empathic, observant little girl had beaten him to the punch. "Did she seem upset? Confused? Sad?"

"Not really. A little worried, maybe. How did she handle her mother's death?"

His gut clenched. He hated thinking about those horrible, surreal days after the accident. "Pretty well, I guess. She reverted back to pre-potty-trained times for a while and didn't talk much for the first few months. I thought about calling a child psychiatrist, but, honestly, I had so much on my plate I didn't know if I was coming or going."

"The loss of a spouse is the number one trauma, isn't it?"

"Probably, but then add a murder investigation to the stress. When it came out that we'd been fighting and there were witnesses to prove it, her accident became a big question mark and I looked guilty as hell."

"Well, of course you would. I watch *Law and Order*. We all know it's always the husband."

Her tone was light and teasing. It actually made him

smile. It beat sympathy. Sympathy made you feel like a loser. "Yeah, well, I had a four-year-old alibi plus my sister to vouch for the fact my truck wouldn't start. To tell you the truth, the foul play theory was easier to swallow than hearing Misty might have done it on purpose."

"Suicide?"

He realized too late he'd said too much. This was her sister he was talking about. "It was one cop's opinion that the skid marks would have been longer if she'd tried to pull out of it. Maybe he thought he was doing me a favor by telling me, but I actually felt worse. I mean, what kind of husband doesn't know his wife's bipolar?"

"She was diagnosed?"

"No. But I've done a bunch of reading. She started having mood swings after Megan was born. She was a good mother, but she didn't seem happy or fulfilled. I suggested a job, but she couldn't find one that fit her needs. The only thing she enjoyed was working in her garden, which became a sort of obsession with her. Then, out of the blue, she got a letter about her high school reunion. One of the organizers was an old boyfriend. They reconnected online."

He looked at Morgan. "Does that sound like a woman who would kill herself?"

She shook her head.

"She told me she planned to make a new life with him. I called her bluff. Dangled the keys in front of her and said, 'Fine. Go. But you're not taking our daughter.' That's when everything went to hell."

"How could she just walk away?" Her tone sounded incredulous.

"I don't know. That's why I read those articles on depression." Hoping a physiological explanation might let him off the hook. Better Misty was sick than he was a lousy husband, right?

"Did she ever see a therapist?"

He made a *pffing* sound. "She went ballistic the one time I suggested it. We tried attending church. She walked out in the middle of worship one morning. Told me she couldn't respect a God who was stupidly cruel. We never went back."

He wished he knew why she'd changed, but he didn't. All he knew was what she'd told him at the end. That he was boring, too busy with the mine and his "other" family. He'd never understood the jealousy Misty seemed to harbor toward Gran and Libby. And the mine. Especially the mine.

"Do you think her problems were tied to her past?"

"I don't know. Libby and I were orphaned at a young age, too."

She heaved a sigh. "But at least you had each other. And Misty lost not one but two sets of parents. That's gotta suck big-time."

He hadn't known that, of course. Maybe that was the key, but it didn't lighten his burden of guilt. He'd still failed her. She'd never told him the whole truth about her past. She'd kept big, deep, dark secrets…and he'd let her. *So much for being Sentinel Pass's go-to guy,* he thought ruefully.

"I remember pinching Misty as hard as I could after Mom and Dad died. Why? Because she didn't cry. She probably didn't understand what was happening. She wasn't that much older than Megan at the time, but I was furious at her. She seemed too complacent. I needed her to be as sad and miserable and angry as I was."

He suddenly remembered the first time he and Misty met. After striking up a conversation at the desk of the RV park, they'd wound up outside, sitting on a picnic table. She'd shared with him her recent loss.

"When I asked her about her family, she told me they died in a house fire while she was in Omaha one weekend. She seemed so…detached when she talked about it. As though she was talking about something that happened to someone else."

He closed his eyes, trying to picture the look on her face. "She said, 'They probably never knew what hit them.'"

"Those were her exact words?"

He opened his eyes. "Yeah. Why?"

He saw a small shiver pass through her. "That's what the police told us about our parents. A drunk driver broadsided them. They never knew what hit them."

Neither spoke for a minute, then Morgan rolled over to face away from him. "Too much talk about death. It's not good for sleep. I'm going to think about elephants instead."

His face scrunched up. Elephants? Megan loved elephants.

He rolled over, too. Toward Morgan, then he gathered her into his arms because he couldn't not. She stiffened for a second, then gave in with a sigh that was warmth and comfort and peace combined. The thing he'd been searching for all day. He closed his eyes and was gone. Just like that.

CHAPTER SIXTEEN

MORGAN OPENED HER EYES to light. And a small face very close to hers. Megan.

Before she could speak, Megan put her finger to her lips and let out a muffled shush sound.

She motioned for Morgan to follow her.

Morgan tried to get her bearings as she carefully folded back the covers. She was still wearing the same clothes she'd had on yesterday. She remembered falling asleep in Mac's arms. At some point in the night they must have each rolled in different directions because he was still asleep, his back to her, his breathing heavy and even.

She eased off the bed and looked around for her shoes. Right beside the bed where she'd left them. She picked them up and tiptoed barefoot into the hallway, carefully closing the door behind her. Her toes curled against the chill. "Good morning, Megan. What's up?"

Megan pointed to Bella, who looked at Morgan expectantly, her tail swishing back and forth on the carpet. "Bella has to go potty and Daddy says I'm not supposed to unlock the door for anybody. Even Bella."

Her earnest answer made Morgan's heart swell in her chest. She gave the little girl a quick hug, then took her hand. "He's right, of course, so let's let her out together."

She ignored the coating on her teeth and the need to use the restroom herself. First things first. She dropped her shoes and shoved her feet into them. Since Mac had left Bella confined the day before, she assumed he didn't want the dog running around the neighborhood, so she went to the patio door. She hadn't been in the home's backyard since the evening of their book club.

A chill in the air made her wish she had socks, too. In the area of the patio that was still shaded, the concrete gave off a cold, damp feeling. There were little puddles left over from the rain, but the air smelled fresh and clean. She took a deep breath and let it out. "Wow. What a beautiful morning. Look how blue the sky is."

Megan looked up. "'Cept for that one elephant. He must have got left behind."

Morgan scrutinized the fluffy jumble of clouds until she saw the image Megan was pointing at. "Good eyes, Meggie. That's awesome." It took all of her willpower not to pull her niece into her arms and hold her tight forever.

Megan yawned, then looked around for her dog. "Uh-oh. Bella's gonna get in trouble. Daddy doesn't like her to dig—'specially in Mommy's garden."

Morgan started toward the animal, calling her name. "Bella, come. Here, girl. Stop that. Oh dear, look at your feet. They're all muddy."

Megan shook her finger sternly. "Bad Bella." The dog stopped digging and looked at her mistress, head cocked as if she'd heard the word before and couldn't quite believe Megan had used it.

Morgan reached out and petted the dog. "It's okay, Bella. A nice big pile of dirt, softened by the rain—what dog could resist? Mac will understand."

Megan still looked worried. "But this is where Mommy was growing my future."

"Pardon?"

Megan's lips pressed together, her brow knitted. "It's a secret. I'm not supposed to say." She gave the dog a sour look. "We might be in trouble now."

Tears formed in her eyes. Big, crystalline tears that shimmered in the morning light. Morgan could sense her distress. She went down on her knees, the wet grass soaking through her jeans, and gathered her into her arms. "Megan, sweetheart, it's okay. Bella can dig here. There's nothing growing."

"Uh-uh," Megan insisted, hiccuping slightly. "It is, too. See?"

Morgan looked at the overturned pile of reddish clay a little closer and spotted something black. A hunk of plastic, she assumed. Maybe Misty used it to keep weeds out. Or was it? She squinted against the sunlight. No, that wasn't a sheet of plastic, it was a bag.

Her sister buried a black plastic bag? Why? A buzz of anticipation blossomed in her chest. *It can't be.* She looked at Megan. "Do you know what that is?"

Still sniffling, Megan nodded. "I was supposed to be watching *Noggin,* but I looked out the window, and Mommy saw me. She said I couldn't tell Daddy. That he had to learn a lesson about what was important or this would never grow. Mommy said it was my future."

Oh my God. Her sister had taken the money and hid it as a way to shake up Mac and make him reevaluate his priorities. Morgan didn't know what that meant, exactly, but it seemed to confirm in Morgan's mind at least that Misty hadn't driven off intending to commit suicide.

She looked at Megan and brushed back a lock of hair from her face. "You are such an amazing girl. You kept your mommy's secret all this time, but I think it's okay to tell your daddy, now. He definitely knows what's important. You are. And Bella. Shall we go wash her feet, then have breakfast while we wait for him to wake up?"

Megan looked at the garden a moment. "Okay. Can we have booberry toaster waffles?" She said *booberry* on purpose, the way a ghost would. A happy ghost.

"Sure."

They were each on their second one when the phone rang. Morgan picked it up but didn't say anything when she heard Libby's voice—and Mac's. He'd answered on the extension. She hung up without hesitation, her appetite gone.

Mac joined them five minutes later. Fully dressed. Hair neatly combed. "That was Lib. I have to go," he said to her. He swept his daughter into his arms. "Can you go pack a few things—some books and toys to take to Jenna's? She's invited you and Bella to come over for a playdate with Luca."

Megan's eyes went wide with joy—for a minute. Then her smile faltered and she looked at Morgan. "Bella's feet are still wet."

Mac, who had set his daughter down to get a cup of coffee, shrugged. "They'll dry."

Morgan walked to her and put a hand on her shoulder. "Go ahead and get your things, sweetie. I'll tell him, if that's okay with you."

Megan's relief was obvious. "Come, Bella. We need to look pretty for your boyfriend."

Once she'd left the room, Morgan turned and faced Mac, who was watching her closely. "What's going on?"

She motioned with her finger. "I'll show you."

"What am I looking at?" he asked a minute later. They were standing a few feet from the garden. Weeds, a few volunteers, including a bedraggled, viney tomato plant sans fruit, didn't make for much of a view.

"Bella was digging this morning. Megan got upset because this was her mother's garden. Misty's most special place." She took a step closer and toed the corner of the black lump. "Megan saw her mother bury something before she died. Something Misty didn't want you to know about. She told Megan it was her future and that you weren't supposed to know about it until you had your priorities straight."

He tossed the remaining bit of coffee in his mug with a violent snap of the wrist then dropped the cup on the grass. "You think this is…?" He didn't finish the question. He stepped toward her, his face contorted in anguish. "If she buried the money then she planned to come back. After she taught me some kind of lesson?" He swore.

"Why the hell couldn't she just talk to me?" he cried, raking his hand through his still-damp hair. "This is crazy. I could have sold the place and never known it was here. I just don't get it."

"She didn't plan to die, Mac."

He didn't appear to hear her. He was too busy wrestling with the corner of the wet, slippery garbage bag. Despite a manly tug, the clay held tight to its prize—until he kicked at the dirt with the heel of his boot. Clods of soil flew, and with the next pull the bundle popped free. He staggered back, shaking the sack to loosen the dirt.

Mindless of the mess, he plopped the dusty, muddy bag on the outdoor table and brutally ripped it apart. Sealed bundles of bills, the kind issued by a bank, tumbled about—too many for Morgan to count.

"She went to a lot of trouble to make sure the money stayed clean and dry," she observed.

He shook his head. "One shovel. That's all it would have taken to destroy the bags. Think what a rototiller would have done. Or my backhoe."

Morgan hadn't thought about that.

He was right. This was a poor plan. The strategy of a desperate person. Someone who wasn't thinking clearly. She couldn't help but wonder what went wrong for Misty.

Mac stared at the bundles as if he couldn't believe they were real. She had no idea how much money there was, but it had to be a lot. He didn't touch a single wad. He just stood there, staring.

Aware that time was passing and Megan had been told to hurry, Morgan cleared her throat and said, "I don't think Megan knew what was in the bag. Her mother told her she was growing her future. It could have been magic beans for all she knew. She was barely four at the time, right?"

He nodded, but she could tell he was struggling to make sense of this development. She tried to keep his focus on the immediate problem—his daughter. "Megan was pretty upset with Bella for digging this morning. I've never heard her scold the dog before. You won't say anything that makes her feel worse, will you?"

He looked at her, his expression wrought with confusion and pain. "I don't know how any of us could feel worse than we already do." He shook his head. "That call was from Libby. Gran had an okay night but…it won't be long. She's struggling to breathe. Jenna said your agent has been trying to reach you. Something about the two of you flying to New York for an emergency meeting. Shane's got you booked on a flight out in two hours. That's why Jenna is taking Megan."

Morgan wasn't surprised that William went through Shane. She'd turned off her phone, and William didn't have this number. He wasn't the kind of agent to pretend everything was going to be okay when it wasn't. Things were bad where her contract was concerned.

"What are you going to do with the money?" she asked, thinking she might have time to deliver it to his bank for him.

He shrugged. "You take it."

Her jaw dropped. "What? No."

He snatched up a fistful of bundles and shoved them into her hands. "Take it. All of it. My dad was right. This is blood money. First, my mother's, and now, Misty's. I don't ever want to see it again. You can burn it for all I care."

"Mac, please. You're not thinking straight. This is a lot of money. You can't give it away."

"I just did."

He turned to leave.

Her hands were shaking so badly she had to set the cold, surprisingly heavy bundles down. "Mac, wait. We need to talk."

He froze. "Where have I heard those words before?" He pivoted, his face a dark, brooding slate that didn't tell her anything. "Is this where you break the news that you're hooking up with an old boyfriend? Oh, I get it. This agent of yours is more than an agent, right? He's dropping everything to meet you in New York because he's in love with you."

She understood. When in pain, strike out. Make sure everyone knows how miserable you are and why. "William is a friend. He cares about me—and about making money. And when one of his clients does something that jeopardizes a lucrative contract, he springs into action. He's flying to New York because I screwed up. Believe it or not, falling in love with my dead sister's husband isn't a surefire career move."

He stared at her a moment longer. Sadly, her confession of love didn't register even a blink. "You're leaving. Just like your sister."

The sound of a dog's bark came from inside the house. He turned to go, but hesitated. In a low, unnaturally rough voice, he said, "For reasons I can't begin to understand, Misty didn't take the money that meant so damn much to her. So, you take it. If Meggie and I screwed up your career, this will give you the cushion you need to fall back on. Take it and leave. Now, while I'm helping Megan get ready." His brown eyes were filled with pain. "Please, Morgan. I have to go say goodbye to my grandmother now. And help my daughter deal with another loss. That's all I want to think about."

And I don't need you here to make life more complicated. He didn't say the words, but she knew that's what he was thinking.

Morgan drew upon her not inconsiderable skills to keep from falling apart in front of him. She pushed away her need to hold him, comfort him, be with him through this horrible loss…and maybe longer. That kind of future wasn't what he wanted. And she didn't blame him.

The James girls really did a number on him. *First, Misty. Now, me.*

She spotted her big, ridiculously expensive designer purse inside the doorway. She grabbed it, then with as much dignity as she could muster, used her arm to sweep the money into the purse's open maw. When she looked up, Mac was gone.

As she hurried toward the front door, she heard a low

masculine murmur coming from Megan's room. It killed her not to say goodbye to her niece, but she'd survive. She always did.

Her left shoulder felt a good inch or two shorter from the weight of her purse as she trudged along the path to her little cabin. She had no idea money weighed so much. As she walked, she remembered a conversation she once had with her chiropractor.

"You and those damn grocery bags you call a purse. Why don't you carry a little one?" he'd asked.

"Maybe I'm hoping someone will fill it full of money," she'd answered with a laugh. "I want to be prepared."

Today, her dream had come true.

Lucky me, she thought, barely able to see the doorknob of her cabin through her tears. *Lucky me.*

MAC LOOKED at the tears streaming down his sister's face and knew he'd arrived too late. Coop had one arm around Libby's shoulders as the two stood beside his grandmother's bed. The bed Morgan had helped him set up only a few days earlier.

"She's gone."

Cal, who was sitting on the other side of the bed, hunched forward, one hand clasping Gran's, spoke. "Fifteen minutes ago. She just stopped breathing. No fuss. That's my Mary."

Mac stepped closer. Gran's eyes were closed. Her brow smooth. The last time he'd seen her, she'd been fighting for each breath. Now, she looked more like herself.

"'If you live, you die,' she used to say," Cal told them. "We talked about death a lot when she was still herself."

Mac knew exactly what he meant. That core element

that was his grandmother hadn't been around for a couple of weeks. Her spirit lingered—he'd felt it—but her mind had closed up shop. She'd simply been waiting for her body to get the message.

He made himself touch the shoulder of the tiny, shrunken figure who was no longer his grandmother. Not the woman who moved in and took over raising her grandchildren when her daughter-in-law got sick and died. That Gran had been indomitable, fearless and bullheaded. "Just like you," she used to tell Mac. "We're two peas in a pod, sonny boy."

"Oh, Gran," he whispered softly. "I'm gonna miss you so much." He bent over and kissed her cheek. Her skin was cool to the touch, and oddly deflated—as if someone had opened a valve and let her soul out.

Libby gave a small whimper. Mac turned and went to her. "This isn't what we want, but we don't have a say in it. Her body got tired. She's been ready for a while."

"I know, but—" Sobbing, she clung to him.

Mac fought his own tears as he comforted her. "She wouldn't want you to make yourself sick, Lib. You gotta think about the baby. Gran's second great-grandchild. She'd be shaking her finger at you right this minute saying, 'Don't tell me how to screw this cat.'"

Libby slugged him, but her cry changed to a partial laugh, too. She looked at Cal and the two completed the phrase together. "You don't even have hold of its tail."

Cooper looked a little shocked. The poor guy obviously didn't know what to make of such deathbed talk. Mac put a reassuring hand on his brother-in-law's shoulder. "Gran was one of a kind. Irreverent. Cut-to-the-chase. Right to the end. We were damn lucky to have her in our lives." He sniffed and brushed away a tear or two of his own then asked Libby, "What happens now?"

"Coroner's on his way. And the people from the mortuary," she said. "Cooper has a list of people to notify. Cal wanted us to wait until you got here."

Mac was grateful to have that onerous task delegated out of his hands. "When the coroner releases the body," Cal said, "we're going to need to bring a gurney back here. I'm not sure it'll be able to turn the corner. Guess I didn't design this place right after all. Who thinks about that kind of thing?" His voice broke.

Mac and Libby both went to the older man and hugged him.

"Don't worry, Cal. Gran can't weigh more than sixty pounds. I'll carry her out to the hearse."

Cal attempted to smile, but his already red eyes filled with tears. In a halting voice he said, "I—I need some time alone with her, okay? I'm gonna let Onie say goodbye. I don't think she's gonna last long without Mary."

Mac barely managed to swallow the lump in his throat. "Lib and I will be in the dayroom. Call if you need us."

They walked slowly, the reality of their loss sinking in with each step. In typical Gran fashion, their grandmother had prepared for this day with thoroughness and fore-thought. She'd handled the business of dying as she had the business of life, purposefully and with grace. Even her funeral was planned down to the last detail.

Mac helped Libby sit. She wasn't ungainly large with her pregnancy yet, but she seemed a little shaky. Mac understood. He'd felt the same way after he learned Misty was dead. Like pieces of him were missing and the holes made it hard to stand or move or think.

"Here. Drink. Terrible connection," Cooper said, rushing in with a glass of water in one hand and his phone wedged between his shoulder and ear. He left just as quickly.

Libby looked after him, a bemused smile on her lips. "He's been a mess all morning. Morgana's agent called before dawn. I guess he forgot about the time change. Wait…" She frowned. "It's earlier on the west coast. Oh, what do I know? I wasn't really paying attention. It just sounds serious. Poor Morgana."

"What about her?"

She took a sip, then looked at him over the glass. "She didn't tell you?"

"We had other things to talk about," he said, his tone surly even to his ears.

"More important than her career? Her future?"

"What are you talking about?"

She closed her eyes and sank down in the chair. "Men," she muttered, shaking her head. "I can't tell you all the details, but Coop says one of the scandal sheets got the scoop on Morgana's real past. Not the rich one she claimed."

He knew that. "So?"

"So, apparently any perceived flaw—real or imagined—puts her very lucrative product endorsement job at risk, and apparently her not-so-glamorous real life story is a doozie. Coop's word."

He imagined some people might find the sad tale titillating. He didn't. "Her birth parents died and she and her sister were adopted by their aunt and uncle, who were Nebraska farmers. What's wrong with that?"

Libby's jaw gaped a moment. "She told you that?"

"Yes."

"Wow. Kat was right. Morgana does love you. Jenna and

I were betting on lust. Char thought there might be some quirky fake-incest thing going on."

"Oh, please. The character she plays is a woman who has your job. She's not you."

Libby nodded. "I agree. The fact that you know that *and* are so quick to defend her tells me you love her, too. What are you going to do about that?"

"Nothing."

"Why?"

"Because…" He blew out a sigh. He could tell she didn't know the rest of the story. Her friends had probably kept silent knowing she had so much to deal with where Gran was concerned. "Libby, does the part about her growing up on a farm in Nebraska sound at all familiar to you?"

"No. Not really. I mean, Misty grew up on a f—" She stopped. "What are you saying?"

"Misty had an older sister who ran away from their adoptive family when Misty was a little girl."

Libby let out a strangled peep; her eyes went wide. "Misty never mentioned a sister."

"I know. And any family photos she might have had were lost in the fire that killed her parents. She didn't like to talk about the past. We never once visited her parents' graves. Anybody who might have come looking for her would have had a hard time connecting all the pieces."

"You're serious. Morgana is Misty's older sister."

"Morgan. That's her real name. Morgan James."

"But that wasn't Misty's maiden name. I can't remember what it was, but…"

He shrugged. "The aunt and uncle adopted her."

"Oh my God," she said putting her hand to her mouth.

"This is unreal. It wouldn't even happen in the movies. Does Cooper know?"

Mac threw out his hands. "She told Jenna and Kat and Char when they made a stink about her babysitting last night. I don't know who else knows or how the papers got wind of it. I can't see your friends telling anyone."

"No. Of course not. Oh dear. Poor Morgana—Morgan." Libby took another drink of water, but her hand was shaking so badly, Mac had to reach over and set the glass on the table. "This makes her Megan's aunt."

"I know."

"The press will have a field day with this. That squeaky-clean cosmetics company will probably dump her faster than it takes their waterproof mascara to dry."

He let his head fall back against the wall. "It's a strange coincidence that she wound up playing you—her late sister's sister-in-law—but it's not that big a deal."

Her brow crinkled in a way he hated. "Not unless they find out she's in love with you. My brother. Her estranged and recently deceased sister's husband. That kind of thing might even affect the show's ratings. Before long, you'll see Larry King pointing at Sentinel Pass like we're some kind of cult."

Mac hadn't thought of that. If the show ended and Sentinel Pass got a bad reputation, the bed-and-breakfast he and Cooper planned to build might never happen. "Maybe I should have held on to Mom's settlement money after all," he said more to himself than Libby. "Meggie and I might have to move."

"The money?" She reached out and grabbed his bare forearm. "You found the money?"

He nodded. "This morning. Misty buried it in her

garden. Megan knew it was there but Misty made her promise not to tell. Morgan thinks Megan pictured it growing like in *Jack and the Beanstalk* or something. Anyway, Bella dug it up."

"Where is it now? What do you mean you gave it away?"

He didn't say. She'd figure it out. "My head hurts. I wanna go sit in a dark mine for a while."

Libby didn't look as sympathetic as he thought she ought to. "Tough. We've got a funeral to get through. I know this is going to sound selfish, but I'm glad it was today and not later in the week. I was worried Gran was going to die on my birthday."

He looped his arm around his sister's shoulders and hugged her tight. "Gran never would do that to you. In a way, I think she planned this so when the baby comes you could focus all your attention on him—or her. Do you know which it is?"

She started to cry again, but she somehow managed to answer. "No. Not yet. How do you think Megan is going to take the news about Gran?"

Considering how upset she'd been about Morgan leaving without saying goodbye, he wasn't sure. Before he could reply, Coop appeared in the doorway and motioned for Mac to follow him. "Cal says they're ready to take her. Do you need my help?"

Mac didn't answer. He drew on that part of his miner's soul that knew how to see in the dark to help him get through this last task. He brushed past the people who had gathered in Cal's and Gran's bedroom—a couple of deputies, some hospice folk, the funeral director he'd met last week. He ignored them all and walked straight to the bed.

Cal, who was holding a squirming, unhappy Onida in his arms, nodded once. "Now."

Mac carefully wiggled his hands under his grand-mother's body, grateful to see someone had pulled the sheets around her like a swaddled baby.

There was a rigidness about her that didn't feel natural, but she was so tiny she actually fit quite nicely in his arms. As he turned, the sheet that someone had draped over her head fell away and he saw her face. He smiled at her and said softly, "It's just you and me, Gran. Time to go."

He walked slowly and carefully. He sensed that the others followed, a respectful distance back. His heart, which should have been thick with pain, was, in fact, beating hard and fast. He suddenly remembered a day in his youth when he and Gran had hiked into the forest to release an owl he'd rescued. The bird's wing had been grazed by a kid with a pellet rifle. During the weeks that Mac had nursed it back to health, his grandmother had reminded him that the bird was a wild thing, not a pet.

"You have to let him go free, Mac."

"But what if he gets hurt again and dies?"

"Then his body will feed other animals and insects and eventually disappear into the earth. Death is a good thing, dear. It happens to us all someday. You and I don't have a say in that."

She'd been at his side as the big bird flew away. She'd been with him to bid goodbye to his mother and father. She'd held his hand when Misty died. And now, it was his turn to step into the circle.

When he deposited her frail, empty body on the gurney beside the waiting hearse, he paused to brush a kiss on her forehead. Her spirit had flown, but he guessed a part of her was still nearby. "Tell Misty I'm sorry," he whispered softly.

Then he stood, took a deep, ragged breath and shook hands with the funeral director and his assistant. He hugged his brother-in-law and sister and Cal. He didn't cry. He couldn't. His grandmother had prepared him well. He was sorry to lose her, but as long as he was alive, she'd be with him in spirit.

"Cal, you should rest," he said, helping the old man into the house. They headed for the kitchen. Mac pulled out a chair at the table. "Did I hear Libby say your daughter was coming?"

Cal sat heavily and leaned forward to rest his elbows on one of the colorful place mats Megan had given Gran for Christmas last year. "Yep. The whole fam-damily, as your grandmother would have said. They'll stay with me until after the funeral, then try to talk me into moving in with one of them. But that isn't going to happen. Mary and I talked about this day. We're not exactly spring chickens, you know," he said with a small chuckle.

Mac poured them both a cup of coffee and joined Cal at the table. The others would be back soon, he figured. He swallowed a gulp of the strong, bitter brew. "Lib and I will take care of the funeral. Everything is planned. Heck, I think Jenna even helped Gran write an obituary a few months ago."

"Yep. Mary liked all her ducks in a row. I sorta hoped I'd go first. She would have done a better job of things where you kids are concerned, but we'll muddle through. I got the list of stuff she wants given away."

Mac had heard some mention of a master list. Mementos Gran hoped would remind her friends and family of her.

Like they needed any *thing* to do that. "You plan on staying here alone?"

Cal shook his head. "Naw. That would be foolish. I got a granddaughter a few years younger than you going through a rough patch. Two kids. Worthless ex-husband. The youngest child's got breathing problems. Bad air in that part of California. I figured I could turn the sunroom into a bedroom for her girls."

"Gran would like that."

He sighed. "Don't know how long it'll take. The older child's in school. I think the father's got some kind of hold on them—financial or emotional, I don't know. In the meantime, I gotta get the garden ready for winter."

Garden. The one thing Misty and Gran had had in common. Now, there were two things. They were both gone. So was Morgan. Not dead, thank God. But gone. Pushed away because he was too afraid to try again, risk living and loving one more time.

Suddenly, Mac's control started to crumble. He lowered his head to his arms. Cal—kindhearted soul that he was—patted Mac's shoulder. "There. There. She's in a better place."

Mac hoped—prayed—that both Gran and Misty had found peace. But where did that leave him?

Alone. And the one woman who saw him for what he really was—and loved him despite his flaws—stood to lose everything she'd spent her entire adult life working for if she came back to him.

CHAPTER SEVENTEEN

"HOW DOES IT FEEL to be a has-been at your age?"

Morgan gave her agent a dirty look, even though she knew he was kidding. "Not as lousy as you might think," she said, giving the question some serious thought.

They were in a cab that smelled well-used, euphemistically speaking. She'd never liked riding in cabs; they made her feel claustrophobic. But this time, she was too wiped out to care. A crash that left her hospitalized might be just the thing to take her mind off all the mistakes she'd made in her life.

She squinted at the driver's nameplate on the back of the seat and realized she couldn't even begin to guess what country he might have called home prior to coming to America. She was envious. Right now, she would have welcomed a name no one could spell, let alone recognize.

"Seriously, pet, how are you taking this? You're not suicidal, are you? I was thinking this kind of debacle calls for mass quantities of chocolate. Or wine. Or wine and chocolate."

She smiled, picturing the members of the Wine, Women and Words book club. "It still might. Maybe a few extra pounds could win them back," she joked. Not really. Her weight issues were only one small part behind the board's decision to back out of their contract. Or rather, enforce the archaic loophole that allowed them to renege if she said or did anything they felt shined an unflattering light on their company. "But don't think you have to babysit me, William. I'm not going to slit my wrists or anything," she said, sinking back in the lumpy seat. "I'm trying to be philosophical. The take-away from this has got to count for something, right?"

"Um…yes? What exactly are you taking away? Not that extraordinarily healthy bonus I'd worked out for you."

He had every right to be angry. He'd worked hard to put this agreement together. The print ads would have elevated her career to a new plane. Of course, he would have benefited financially, but nothing compared to what she would have gotten out of the deal.

The car slowed as they reached a bottleneck created by a construction crew working on the street—one of a gazillion such road hazards in New York City. The slower progress gave her time to study the queue of people waiting to buy discount theater tickets. She hadn't been to a play in years. Maybe she'd see one while she was here. She'd heard good things about *Jersey Boys* and *Wicked*.

William cleared his throat. "We were talking about your mental health after having pissed away a contract I worked my stylish tush off to obtain. Pardon the poorly structured sentence. My mind is still trying to make sense of your lack of emotion. You could, at least, give me the courtesy of sharing your thoughts."

She sighed heavily. "I could, but you wouldn't like them." She turned to look at him. "Honestly? I'm relieved. I know I shouldn't be. I know that all hell is about to break loose. That my name is going to be dragged through the public mud and all sorts of nasty lies and innuendos are going to appear as six-second sound bites. I'll officially be a laughingstock, and the IRS is going to own my sorry ass for the rest of my life. Unless they choose to throw me in jail—then it will belong to some butch lifer named Dolly."

"Dolly?"

"Maude? Dorinda? Allison? Who knows?"

He was too British to appear shocked, but whatever other mixed heritage he possessed made it hard for him to keep a straight face. "The possibilities are endless. But, seriously, that wasn't affected ennui in the FreshFace boardroom? You truly don't care about losing this job? Why?"

"You won't understand."

"Make me."

Maybe she owed him that much. He'd been a good friend as well as an excellent agent. "Because I'm in love. First time ever. With the worst possible choice in the entire universe. If he were to actually share my feelings and want me to be part of his life, the media would never let us forget the fact that he was married to my estranged sister before she died. And if, God forbid, we married, my beautiful, amazing niece would become my stepdaughter, and we both know I'd be a disaster of a mother."

She grinned at his look of complete and utter horror.

"I know nothing of the sort, but if you feel that strongly about the subject then stop."

"Stop what?"

"Stop being in love."

She laughed. "Just like that?" She snapped her fingers.

"Yes."

She threw up her hands. "Maybe you have that kind of self-discipline—is it a British thing? But I can't. Believe me, I tried. I knew our being together was a bad idea—even if I didn't know how bad—but we're talking megapowerful swoo. We were only together once, but Mac's so far into my heart I don't know where me leaves off and he begins."

"*Swoo*? What the bloody hell is that?" William looked repulsed in a way only a British man could. "Is it contagious?"

She reached out and gently touched the sleeve of his fine wool suit. "You should be so lucky. I'm serious, William. My future looks like dog do at the moment. If this toxic publicity begins to affect the show's numbers, Shane won't hesitate to replace me. I not only wouldn't blame him, I don't care. I've spent most of my life wishing someone loved me, but what I didn't know is that I couldn't be loved until I loved. Now, I do."

"The swoo did that to you?"

"Sorta."

"And that's a good thing? You feel good about it."

She frowned. "I'd feel better if Mac felt the same way, but it's complicated."

"Bugger."

"Pretty much."

The horns, sirens and crowd noise filtered in. They were close to the lovely boutique hotel near Penn Station that William favored. Morgan had stayed there several times on her own. She adored their pillow menu.

"Well, it's too early to tell about the numbers, but Shane did issue a statement declaring *Sentinel Passtime*'s unconditional support for you. You're lucky to have friends in high places."

She was lucky to have friends, period. Cooper wasn't returning her calls—probably because he was focusing on helping Libby get over her grandmother's death. Shane had given her five days to get back on the set. Mac…well, she'd sent flowers to the funeral and gifts to Megan and Bella, but she hadn't heard back from him. She doubted that she would. The family was in mourning. She wished desperately she could have been there.

But, as usual, she was on the outside looking in.

"We're almost here," William said, extracting his bill-fold from his pocket. "Oh, and I left that number you wanted on your phone. My friend's firm is the best in the business, but they're also ridiculously expensive."

"It's only money, William," she said, anticipating his elaborate cringe. "The important thing is to make sure there's a lot more of it when Megan is ready for college."

William scowled. "Are you sure you don't want to hold back a little bit to offset what you just lost? Even the best lawyer in the country might not be able to save your lovely tush from the tax cretins."

She took a deep breath. She'd been tempted. There'd been a time in her life when she could have rationalized a way to keep a share for herself. But not now. Love, she decided, had changed her. Money wasn't the answer. It simply paid the bills. Love made everything worthwhile.

"You're doing it again."

"What?"

"Smiling. It really pissed off the old suits in that meeting. They wanted to see you cry, but you smiled. That was almost worth what it cost us."

She waited until they were out of the cab before she stopped him and said, "William, I'm sorry for all the problems and high drama I've created. I wish I'd made you a nice chunk of change from that product endorsement, but I'm not sorry to have my past out in the open. From now on, I want to succeed or fail on my own merit, not on someone's perceived image of me. Are we clear on that?"

He tilted his head as if seeing her in a new light. "Yes, my girl, I believe we are." He took her arm. "Want a nightcap?" he asked as they passed by the door to the bar.

She shook her head. "Morgana Carlyle drank. Morgan James goes to bed early to write a long letter to her niece."

He looked a little crestfallen. "Morgan sounds like a total bore."

Morgan threw back her head and laughed. "She is, William. She truly is." Morgana needed everybody to love her. Morgan would be happy if one little girl, one dog and maybe, just maybe, one miner liked her that way.

IN THE SIX WEEKS since his grandmother's death, Mac had come to the conclusion that the dead may not be physically present but they sure as heck could pester your subconscious. Gran and Misty both had been on his mind a lot. Gran, a comforting presence who showed up in sweet little notes left in the odd book or memento she'd asked Cal to distribute. Misty, a less comforting presence who bugged his dreams and appeared regularly on TV. Well, a grainy black-and-white photo from her high school yearbook showed up. Luckily, none of the gossipy entertainment tell-all shows had a more recent shot.

As Libby had predicted, rumors spread like a fast-moving plague. Morgana's story made good copy; Morgan's even better.

Mac hadn't seen her—not in the flesh—since the day he gave her his money and asked her to leave. She'd sent a gorgeous spray of tulips that had to have cost a small fortune for Gran's funeral.

A few days later another box arrived. A bling-studded collar for Bella and a beautiful doll for Megan, along with a short note apologizing for leaving without saying goodbye. Naturally, Morgan had been too diplomatic to mention that he'd been a complete ass and basically had kicked her out.

He could remember doing that. But he couldn't remember why, exactly. Maybe the shock of finding the money along with the dread and emotional pain of knowing he was about to lose his grandmother had pushed him over the edge into some dark, miner's crevasse. He'd hung out there in the comforting black hole for several weeks—until his daughter and his sister dragged him back into the world of the living.

"Snap out of it or else," Libby had yelled at him one day. She'd stopped by to pick up Megan to attend Tag Linden's birthday party. Tag was the elder of Kat's two sons, and Mac couldn't imagine he was thrilled to have a four-year-old girl come to his party, but Libby had insisted father and daughter were both invited.

"It's going to be at Kat's father's ranch—you know, where the buffalo roam," she'd added, smiling playfully.

Mac was starting to resent the way she'd seemed to bounce back so handily from their loss, but before he could say so, she grabbed the sleeve of his shirt and pulled him aside so Megan, who was adding the finishing touches to Tag's homemade birthday card, couldn't hear. "Okay, that's it, McDroopy. Time's up. You've been this moody wounded grizzly ever since Gran died and I need you to shake it off. We all do."

"That's easy for you to say."

"Is it? Why? In case you haven't noticed—and I'm

pretty sure you haven't because you've had your head too far up your b—"

"Hey. I've been preoccupied. I get it."

She blew out a hiss of frustration. "No, you don't. If you did, you'd see that I'm a hormonal wreck and when my husband—my support system—went back to California to finish filming, I stayed behind to help you and Megan. If you were half the man our grandmother thought you were, you would have already been on a plane and gone to Morgan and offered to stand by her side during the hella-cious and totally unfair roasting she's gotten from the press. But, instead, you've succumbed to the maroon gloom that, as far as I'm concerned, killed our dad."

"A rock slide killed Dad."

She snorted. "Believe what you want. You always do."

That conversation had taken place three weeks earlier. His curiosity piqued, he'd turned on the television that evening while Megan was in her bath to see what his sister was talking about. Surely the big story that had been un-folding since news of Morgan's humble origins first leaked had faded into yesterday's fish wrap.

Wrong.

The male cover-model commentator had stood in front of a big-screen image of Morgan and Misty when they were little girls. Morgan might have been nine or ten; Misty was just a toddler. Sweet, adorable little girls on a minia-ture train. Candid, unposed. His heart had swelled with something other than pain for the first time in weeks.

Where on earth did they get that picture?

Then the commentator's words sank in. "As you see in this newspaper photo taken before her parents' untimely death, Morgan James—aka Morgana Carlyle—might look like a caring, loving older sister here, but this was before she ran off to Hollywood leaving her younger, orphaned sister with family relatives."

"Family relatives?" he'd muttered. "Are there any other kind?"

He'd had to jab his fist into the palm of his other hand to keep from hitting the jerk on the screen. He couldn't afford a new TV, but he really hated the man's smug, condescending tone. "Morgan James changed her name and spent the next fifteen years of her life making everyone believe she was someone she wasn't."

"Bull crap. She's not a phony. She really is that person. Both of those people." He shook his head. He knew what he meant, even if it didn't make any sense. Any more sense than talking to a TV.

That odd, unlikely epiphany had prompted him to take stock of his life, his mistakes and his faith in the future. One thing he decided was he needed to tie up some loose ends from the past so he could move on. A decision that brought him and Megan to Valentine, Nebraska.

"You're sure you're okay with this? It isn't the same as a birthday party with your friends," he said, looking at his daughter in the rearview mirror. "This could have waited for another few weeks."

"No. This is good. Mommy would like it," she said, drawing the big bouquet of cut flowers to her nose. He'd let her pick out whatever she wanted at the local florist shop. To his surprise, she'd chosen mums and bright, happy Gerber daisies over roses.

He looked to his right. The compact metal box containing Misty's ashes was held in place by the seat belt. The funeral director who'd handled Gran's service had been happy to help. He'd contacted the right people in Valentine and located the graves of Misty's adoptive parents. He'd helped Mac purchase an adjacent lot and arrange for delivery of a new headstone with a small vault where they could inter Misty's ashes. His late wife would have a final resting place. He and Megan were taking her home.

"Can we go see where Mommy lived after we're done at the cemetery?"

"We can try. I only have an address. No directions."

When he'd suggested burying her mother, Megan had pondered the idea for several days before she agreed it was a good idea—as long as they could bring Bella, too.

"How's the dog doing? Does she still have water? It hasn't spilled all over the place, has it?" he asked. Not that he really cared. His truck could survive a little water, but fussing over Bella and the flowers seemed to keep Megan's mind off the length of their trip.

"She's good. Aren't you, Bella?"

A loud woof made him jump slightly. The dog rarely barked. He couldn't turn around to see what she was barking at because they'd arrived at the cemetery. He pulled into a parking place and turned off the engine.

"What was that about, Miss Bella? You never bark."

The dog leaned across the opening between them and licked his face. Which made Megan laugh. "She loves you, Daddy."

"Lucky me."

And oddly enough, he meant it. His life was pretty good at the moment, despite the sadness of having lost his grandmother. Gran would have been the last person to want anyone to mourn too long. She'd buried three husbands, a son and daughter-in-law and too many friends to count. She knew that the sad made the joy all the more precious.

He thought about all the changes in his world as he helped Megan out of her booster seat. *Sentinel Passtime* was getting a big viewer share—or whatever Coop called it. Shane was ecstatic. According to Libby, the network had picked up the show for another two years.

That meant there was plenty of money to start building the B & B near the mine. Libby had nixed the idea of using her home. "Coop and I are always going to be a part of Sentinal Pass—even if we don't live here year-round. End of discussion." Actual construction wouldn't start until spring, but Mac had plenty of paperwork to do in the meantime.

Kat's fiancé, Jack Treadwell, was almost ready to move into the old Smith place. He'd tossed Mac a bunch of work that had helped fill the gap left by Gran's death. And Morgan's departure.

"Can I leave Bella's leash off, Daddy?"

Mac looked around. The cemetery wasn't huge, but there were several cars in the parking lot and he didn't want the dog to disturb anyone who might be visiting a dead loved one. "No, honey, this is a public place. There's probably a leash law. Besides, we don't know where we're going. Bella's smart. She can lead us."

Megan looked impressed by his logic. "Okay. Here, Daddy, you carry the flowers."

"I'd be happy to. Give me a minute to—" He'd been about to say "—get your mother." Dang, he was losing it.

He tucked the canister containing Misty's cremains—a word that gave him the willies—under his arm, then picked up the vase again. Before starting off in the direction of the caretaker's cottage, where he'd been told he'd find a map with the lot numbers clearly marked, he paused to scan the area one more time.

He'd known it was a long shot when he sent the e-mail. Coop had assured him it was her current address, but there'd been no reply. Not that he expected one. Morgan didn't owe him—or Misty—squat. In fact, he owed her more than she could possibly know. She had every right never to want to see him again. But a guy could hope.

Maybe it was wrong to be thinking about another woman on the day you were burying your late wife's ashes, but nothing about his situation made sense. He could admit that now. Maybe if he and Morgan ever saw each other again, they'd even laugh about the irony. Someday.

He was halfway to the caretaker's cottage—Megan and Bella a foot behind him—when Bella suddenly veered sharply to the right.

"This way, Daddy," Megan said, eagerly following her dog.

"Um, wait…girls, hold up… Let's double-check the number first. Bella." The word came out louder and sharper than he'd intended. Both dog and little girl froze. He noticed that a woman with short hair and a ball cap standing in front of a headstone a few yards off looked at him, too.

Damn. He hadn't meant to shout.

He abandoned his original plan and hurried toward them. "Sorry. I wasn't yelling. I just didn't want you to get too far ahead of me."

"But you said Bella could lead the way, Daddy."

True. He had. He took a deep breath. The brisk edge of autumn was tinged with a hint of smoke. Did people still burn leaves, like they did when he was a kid? He reached down and scratched Bella's ear. "Sorry I doubted you, girl. Lead on."

The sunlight glinted off the rhinestones in the dog's collar as the pair trotted happily between the neat rows. He followed a bit more carefully. He didn't want to do a header and spill his flowers or the ashes.

Because he was concentrating on his steps and not looking ahead, he would have overshot his destination if not for the adult cough that made him pause. He looked up. Their path had taken them straight to the woman he'd seen from a distance.

Up close he realized the short brown pageboy was a wig and the ball cap bore the *Sentinel Passtime* logo. When she removed her oversize sunglasses, his mouth dropped open and he blinked in surprise. She looked so very different. Not just the hair color, but her face was fuller. She'd put on a few pounds—and they looked great on her.

"Morgan."

Bella barked a happy greeting that blended with Megan's cry of joy. "Princess Morgana, you're here."

Mac realized that part of the reason he hadn't recognized her was her outfit—a dull gray fleece jogging suit topped with a heavy cream-colored cable-knit hooded sweater. No jewelry. No makeup. She almost blended in with the headstone.

Which had been her intent, he realized a second later. She was hiding out from the people who had made her life a living hell for the past month or so.

"You came," Mac said. He clutched the box and the flowers a little harder to keep from reaching out and pulling her into his arms. God, he'd missed her. He wasn't sure he even knew how much until this moment. "I wasn't sure you got my e-mail."

"My e-mail got hacked. Again. I've been offline for a while, but William has a way of checking for me. He calls with anything important. I should have let you know I was coming, but I didn't want to risk the media finding out. That would have made things…ugly."

"Libby told me things have been pretty bad—with the press. You lost the makeup contract."

She nodded but didn't elaborate. Instead, she went down on one knee to give first Megan, then Bella, another big squeeze. "It's so good to see you two. I've missed you both so much."

Megan reached out and touched her wig. "You look different. Are you still a princess?"

Morgan glanced up at Mac. He saw both sadness and irony in her look. "Not so much. I'm just me. And my real name is Morgan, not Morgana."

"Oh." Megan thought a moment then asked, "How come you didn't come back?"

"I had grown-up things to take care of, sweetheart. I'm sorry I didn't get to say goodbye, though. Did you like the presents I sent? Bella's collar looks pretty on her. I knew it would."

Megan, who obviously forgave any slight with the ease of a four-year-old, brought Morgan up to speed on the important issues in her life. "My great-gran died. She's in heaven with my mommy. We put her body in the ground. The big her. Mommy's just a little her," she said, using her hands to illustrate the difference. "Right, Daddy?"

He moved his shoulder to indicate the box in question. Morgan stood and walked up to him. "May I?" she asked, cocking her head to see the engraved plate on the top of the box.

He turned it so she could read the words.

When she leaned in, he was able to make out her scent. How could he have forgotten how wonderful she smelled? Like cinnamon and vanilla and something too delicious for words.

"Is this the right spot?" he asked, stepping away from her. He needed to stay focused on his purpose for being here. Once Misty was buried, they'd sit down and talk about what had happened between them. He circled around the low, highly polished marble headstone.

"Yes. The marker is beautiful. It made me cry, but in a good way. Thank you."

Mac swallowed the lump in his throat as he studied the memorial he'd ordered and paid for but hadn't seen before now. His mouth went dry and there was a heavy weight on his chest. He allowed Morgan to relieve him of the box so he could set the vase of flowers in the brass holder built into the monument. "Come here, honey, I'll show you your mommy's name."

Megan flew into his arms. Together, they traced the words, reading out loud, "Misty James Burdock McGannon. Daughter. Sister. Wife. Mother. Loved and missed, forever."

Megan pointed to an image sealed in the stone. "And there's her picture. Isn't she pretty?" Megan looked from the oval photo to Morgan and back. "She looks a little like you."

Morgan knew it was time. She'd have liked to discuss the matter with Megan's father first, but before she could open her mouth to speak, Mac said, "There's a reason for that, honey. Your mommy and Morgan were sisters."

"Really?"

Morgan was encouraged by his kind and forthright tone. She sat cross-legged on the chilly grass, the box in her lap. If she stopped to think how strange it was to be here, the three of them and Misty…

"It is what it is," a voice from her past said. Her aunt hadn't been a deep thinker, but Binnie Burdock was a kind woman who had tried to ease her older niece's pain to the best of her ability. Unfortunately, Binnie's oft-quoted philosophy had never made sense to Morgan. Until now.

There was no changing the past. They had to deal with the present they'd been given.

She ran her fingers over the nameplate on the box that contained her sister's ashes. "Your mommy was my baby sister. I was seven when she was born. She was so cute and sweet. I loved her very much, but when we got older, our mommy and daddy died and we went to live on a farm with our aunt and uncle." She looked at the simple, austere headstone a few feet away. "They didn't have any children of their own. Your mommy made them very happy. She became their little girl, but I was older and I missed my mom and dad too much to let myself love them back. After a while, I went somewhere else to live. Your mommy and I didn't see each other again."

"Did you forget about her?"

Morgan shook her head. "No, honey. Never. But I was ashamed of the way I left. I didn't think they'd forgive me, and I didn't know how to ask. I guess I figured that eventually your mom would contact me if she wanted a relationship. After all, I was on TV—even if I had changed my last name." Over the past few weeks, she'd given serious thought to her motivation. She'd always assumed money was behind her decision to pursue acting as a career, but maybe there was more to it. "I don't know why she didn't try to reach me. Maybe she was angry because I left. Or maybe she was so young, she forgot about me. It makes me sad to think so."

"She didn't forget," Mac said, dropping into a squat beside his daughter.

"How do you know?"

He looked at Megan and smiled. "When the doctor told us we were having a baby girl, Misty said, 'I want to name her Morgan.' I'd never heard that name for a girl. We went back and forth until we compromised on Megan. I thought it was an alliterative M-thing, but after meeting you, I figured it out. She didn't forget."

Morgan's throat was too tight to speak but she managed to smile through her tears. "Thank you," she mouthed.

"My birthday's in four days. I'm gonna be five," Megan said proudly.

"I know. I have a present for you in the car."

"Will you come to my party? Auntie Libby and Uncle Cooper are coming back. And Kat and Jenna and the boys. And Char. She's bringing balloons. She always picks really neat ones."

Morgan looked at Mac. "I-I'd like to come. If your daddy thinks I should."

Megan shrugged as if that was no problem whatsoever. She seemed pretty confident that Mac would welcome Morgan with open arms. Morgan wasn't as sure. He'd hinted that he wasn't mad at her anymore in the e-mail he'd sent inviting her today. But they still had to talk, clear the air. She needed to spell out exactly what she'd done with his blood money.

At some point, she had to tell him the truth—that she

loved him. But, even if he felt the same toward her, would he ever let himself trust another James girl?

She didn't know. And, sadly, nothing in her experience to date had given her reason to think that love alone was enough to overcome the roadblocks life threw in your way.

CHAPTER EIGHTEEN

MORGAN PULLED ASIDE the heavy drapes and peeked outside. Nothing stirred. No one was pacing back and forth trying to build up enough nerve to knock on her door. Her rental car was right where she left it after their impromptu funeral, dwarfed by Mac's giant truck.

Mac had followed Morgan to the chain motel on the outskirts of town. He'd carried their bags to their rooms, which were side by side, but not connected. Then, she'd joined father and daughter and dog for a drive down memory lane and a filling, if somewhat uncomfortable, meal at a local restaurant.

Later, back at the motel, Mac had whispered something about talking "after Megan falls asleep." Morgan had paced within the confines of the small room, finally giving in to the temptation to put her ear to the wall to eavesdrop on Mac and Megan. She couldn't hear anything over the muffled murmur of the TV.

She tried to make herself study her new *Sentinel Passtime* script, but the words blurred and were soon replaced by memories she'd have preferred to avoid. So many images had popped into her head when they'd visited the farm. The house was gone, of course. And the barn and outbuildings had either been torn down or moved. The only thing that remained was the shelter belt of lilacs and elms where Morgan had loved to escape to when she needed to hide out. Misty had always known where to look for her when their aunt and uncle couldn't find her.

"Why do you run away all the time?" Misty had asked one day when Morgan failed to come directly to the house after getting off the school bus.

Knowing Uncle Nolan had been waiting for her help with some disgusting job she didn't want to do, Morgan had taken a book she'd checked out of the library and disappeared into the shelter belt.

"Because this isn't where I'm supposed to be," Morgan had shouted in reply to her sister's question. She knew it wasn't Misty's fault that she'd adapted to their changed circumstances better than Morgan had. Misty was younger and eager to please. But that didn't make Morgan resent her only sibling any less. "You don't remember Mom and Dad the way I do. If you did, you wouldn't be so nice and sweet and agreeable to these people who are stuck in some ridiculous time warp on the cusp of modern industrialization."

Misty hadn't understood. Neither had Morgan, really. But Morgan knew for certain this wasn't the life she wanted. And she wasn't about to hang around hoping things would improve. They wouldn't. Her aunt and uncle weren't capable of change, she'd decided. If they had been, they wouldn't be content to eke out a living in the middle of nowhere.

That had been the day she made up her mind to leave. From that point on, every dime she made, every penny she found on the ground, every chance she had to learn about life outside of Nebraska, she stored away. And when she figured she had enough to get to California, she'd left.

Returning to the bed where she'd tossed the pages of the script aside, she sat again. She scrubbed her hands up and down across her eyes, determined to stay focused on the present until she had a chance to talk things out with Mac.

Over the past few weeks, she'd changed her mind about disappearing from Mac's and Megan's lives. If he told her to leave and never come back, she'd do that, but only until Megan was eighteen. Which, of course, was what Morgan should have done with Misty.

"Why didn't I?" she murmured under her breath.

If she had, Misty might never have married Mac. Megan might not have been born. So, no, despite the way everything turned out, some good had come from Morgan not being involved in her sister's life.

A soft knock on the outer door. She jumped to her feet, causing the script to slide to the floor. She quickly picked it up and stuffed it into the large leather purse sitting beside the room's only guest chair.

"Hi," she said, opening the door. "Is she asleep?"

"Yes." He held up a small white plastic baby monitor. "Misty used it all the time when Meggie was napping and she wanted to work in her garden."

Little blue lights rose and fell in a gentle arc with the sounds of the night or Megan's breathing. Morgan didn't know which. Another one of those mommy things she'd never had the chance to learn about. The thought made her sad, but she faked a smile and motioned him in.

"I have something for you," he said after setting the monitor on top of the TV. "Megan made this and wanted me to send it to you, but I told her we'd try to deliver it personally."

He fished a small, folded piece of paper out of his shirt

pocket. He was wearing the same cotton twill button-up shirt he'd had on earlier. The dark khaki green looked good on him. She'd wanted to compliment him but hadn't wanted to get too personal.

"What is it?"

"A drawing she did for the grief counselor I took her to. I was afraid that Gran's passing and your leaving might trigger some memories of her mother's death."

"Really? Wow. I'm impressed. Lately, I've been asking myself if my life would have turned out differently if someone had thought to get me and Misty some counseling." She shook her head. "I mean, I was so angry for so long. I made everyone's life miserable. And poor Misty had to suck it up and be good for both of us. No wonder we were so messed up."

He walked to her and took her into his arms. "You're the reason I took Megan to therapy. It never occurred to me after Misty's accident. I was too caught up in my own pain to realize Megan might not be able to articulate what she was feeling. After your experiences—and Misty's inability to talk about her feelings—I suddenly got it." He pulled back enough to look into her eyes. "Thank you."

She buried her chin against his chest. The material of his shirt was softer than it looked. She closed her eyes and inhaled. His wonderful, masculine smell filled all the empty spots she'd carried with her for too long.

They stayed like that, just holding each other for a good minute, at least, then Morgan made herself push back. "What did he say? The counselor?"

"She. A very nice lady with a long string of abbreviations after her name. The funeral director who handled

Gran's ceremony and helped with Misty's arrangements gave me her name.

"Megan saw her three times. This—" he handed her the paper "—came out of the last meeting. The psychologist said it's where a four-almost-five-year-old who has been through what Megan's been through should be, grief-wise."

Morgan carefully unfolded the vanilla-colored construction paper. Several crayon stick figures were scattered about, with three grouped together. The largest figure—the father, she assumed—was in the middle of the group. His six- and seven-fingered hands were touching the other two main figures. A little girl and a woman. They both wore bright yellow crowns.

Looking over her shoulder, Mac pointed to the larger crowned figure. "Princess Morgan, of course. Megan told the therapist that if you would marry her daddy then she'd become a princess, too. Because, and I quote, 'that's how it works.'"

Morgan blinked. "She thinks we're going to get married? Why would she assume that?"

"Probably…because I told her so."

Before she could think of any kind of reply, he drew her attention back to the paper. "The other people are important, too. Bella—note the five legs. Megan said one is supposed to be a tail. It's hard to erase crayon." Morgan smiled. "And these two at the edge of the paper are Misty and Gran."

Morgan traced the bolder of the two with her finger. "Are they in heaven?"

"I don't know. The therapist said Megan seemed comfortable with her mother and great-grandmother living in another place, like heaven, keeping busy with their flowers and gardens while she was still here on earth."

Mac could almost recall the woman's exact words. "Your daughter has a surprisingly healthy grasp on the concept of death. She seems to intuitively understand that although her mother and great-grandmother won't be alive anymore, their memories will live on in her and the people who love them. People like you and your future wife...the princess."

Before he could tell her he wasn't marrying anybody, she'd added, "When Megan first mentioned this woman, I was afraid we were going be needing quite a few more sessions." She chuckled dryly.

"What she didn't tell you is Morgan isn't a real princess. She's just beautiful. And...her aunt."

"I figured that out on my own. I watch TV," she said, her tone not one bit scandalized or sanctimonious.

"You don't have a problem with that?"

"Well, I don't know the woman, so I really can't advise you, but one of my degrees is in anthropology. And I can tell you it's not unusual for a male in a tribe to take his deceased wife's sister as a second spouse. You used to see it a lot, even in the eighteen hundreds and early twentieth century."

Morgan cleared her throat and he realized she'd said something and was waiting for an answer. "Sorry. I was remembering what the head doctor said."

"I've been zoning out a lot, too, lately. William calls it 'Miner time,'" she said with a little wince. "Unfortunately, Shane picked up on that, and he and Cooper have been giving me a hard time about you."

Mac tried not to smile. "My sister and the book club girls haven't let up on me, either, if it's any consolation. Kat even enlisted the aid of her fiancé, Jack. The guy's nice enough, but a little out there. He told me about this dream... Never mind. He's crazy in love with Kat and they're planning a December wedding. He just wants everyone to be as happy as he is."

"Jenna mentioned the wedding. That's wonderful. Kat's a really nice person. I'm glad things worked out."

He took the drawing from her and set it on the table. Then he put his hands on either side of her shoulders and made her look at him. "Are things going to work out for us?"

"I don't know. I love you, Mac. I honestly didn't know what all the fuss was about until I met you. But there are so many reasons why we shouldn't be together."

I love you, Mac. She'd said it. He wanted to focus strictly on that, but he couldn't. Not till he knew for sure what he was up against. "Name one."

"Megan."

"She thinks you're the perfect mother—half princess, half aunt. What could be better?"

Morgan blinked. "I'm so far from perfect, it isn't even funny."

"According to the psychologist, Megan is highly intuitive and equally well-grounded. I'm taking that to mean she can see the real you—the side you don't show on camera or to anyone else—and she knows you'd love her just as much as her mother did." *Maybe more.* Because toward the end of her life, Misty had turned inward. Megan became a chore, not the wonder she'd been before. "You're the least self-absorbed actor I've ever met. That's partly why I love you."

She smiled at that. "You do? Really? You've never said so. Are you sure?"

He took her hand and pulled her to the bed so they both could sit. He wanted to make love with her, of course, but they needed to get everything out in the open first if they had any chance of making it as a couple.

"When I was a kid, I collected broken things. A cat that got picked up by a hawk. A three-legged dog. An owl with a damaged wing. I thought I outgrew the need to fix things, but then I met Misty. A beautiful young woman who reminded me of a baby bird that had fallen out of the nest and didn't know what to do next."

"I don't dare ask what I am."

"That's just it. I never saw you as broken. You're this picture-perfect woman who has it all together. Every once in a while I'd glimpse some tiny flaw, but you're such an accomplished actress, you made them look like facets in a diamond. It wasn't until you left that I could see they were actually hardened tears of pain. And then I couldn't fix anything because you were too far away and my life was falling apart. Again."

"Picture-perfect," she said, her smile rueful. "Tell that to the cosmetics company who threatened to sue me for breach of contract because my published bio was a fake."

He shook his head. "I'd like to drive my backhoe through the lobby of their fancy New York offices," he said with a barely contained growl. "So what if you weren't some trust-fund baby with more money than sense? Everything you have you earned. You don't have a damn thing to apologize for, Morgan. To them or to your sister. She could have contacted you and didn't. Relationships are a two-way street. She did the same thing with me and our marriage. When I was too busy working two jobs to shower her with the kind of attention she needed, she'd spend the entire night sulking."

He sighed. "That gets old real fast, and I just quit playing the game. What happened next was a sad twist of fate. And none of it is our fault."

He started to reach into his pocket for the ring he'd brought with him when a soft whimper came across the monitor.

"Megan?"

"Bella. I forgot to let her out." He made a face. "Even fathers with five years' experience can blow it sometimes."

She blinked as if she'd never thought of that. "Let me," she said, standing. She put out her hand for the card key. "I'll be right back."

Morgan was glad for the break. Her mind was reeling from Mac's revelations. He loved her. Megan wanted her to be her mother. There'd been something there that almost sounded like a proposal. She didn't know what to think. Happiness wasn't supposed to be this easy…was it?

She walked the few feet to the room next door. She'd left her sweater in her room and the night's chill made gooseflesh erupt on her bare arms. Her fingers shook when she tried to fit the card in the opening, but the green light appeared on her second try.

She opened the door and softly called, "Bella. Come here, girl."

The dog greeted her with tail-wagging joy.

"Good girl. Come on. Let's go outside and do your business."

Bella backed up, instead of rushing out, as Morgan expected. Confused, she walked in another step and looked around, worried that something might be wrong with Megan. No, the child was sprawled on her back in the middle of the bed, mouth slightly open, her chest rising and falling beneath the covers. "What's wrong, girl? Mac said you needed to go outside."

Bella whimpered slightly, then she trotted to the far side of the room where an open suitcase sat. She nosed around a moment, then ran back, a box of some kind in her mouth.

Morgan took it from her. A jeweler's box. Swallowing, she looked around to locate the base unit of the baby monitor. "Mac," she softly called. "You better come here. I think your dog might be psychic." *I hope. Unless this isn't what I think it is.*

Mac appeared within a heartbeat, his expression fraught with concern. He, too, looked at Megan first, then, realizing all was well, turned his gaze to Morgan. "Did you forget something when you came to my room? Or did you change your mind and forget to tell Bella?"

His woolly eyebrows that she loved so much made an up-and-down motion until he noticed what the dog had in her mouth. "Oh," he exclaimed softly. He smiled and bent low to praise Bella. "What a good dog you are. Megan was right, you are our guardian angel. Thank you."

He took the box from her mouth, pulled out the tail of his shirt to wipe off any dog slobber and then grabbed Morgan's hand. "Next door. Fewer witnesses if you turn me down and break my heart."

Like that's going to happen. Excitement and joy were crowding out her ability to think, let alone breathe.

Once they were back in her room, he made her sit on the end of the bed, then he dropped to one knee. "I know this is going to seem sudden—especially after the way we left things in Sentinel Pass, but I know Gran would have been the first to tap me on the shoulder and say, 'Life is short. Live it with joy.'"

He took a deep breath. "That's what you are to me, Morgan. Joy and hope and limitless possibility. You're the surprise gold in a mine I thought was long tapped out. If you agree to marry me, I promise to do my level best not to forget how much I love you and how much I need you to keep me from getting lost in the dark."

Her heart was pounding so hard she could barely hear her own voice. She looked from the black velvet box to his eyes and prayed that her answer was the right one—for him and Megan. "I love you the way I think my parents loved each other. And even though I hated them for dying, I now understand they were lucky to go together. That's a gift you've given me, Mac. Being away from you and Meggie these past few weeks has been bad enough. I couldn't imagine a lifetime without you both."

His smile grew into something beautiful and shimmering.

"It may be completely selfish given all the stuff people will say about us—and Misty—but I love you, Mac. I have to marry you."

He cocked his head slightly. "Have to or want to?"

"Both. They're one and the same. I can't go back to my old life. Money was my only goal because I thought it was a substitute for love. It isn't. I know that now."

Money.

"I almost forgot. In my bag is the paperwork for a new account I opened for Megan. Crazy as this sounds, the morning after I lost the FreshFace account, I hired the best, most expensive tax firm in New York. They not only worked out a deal with the IRS that's going to let me keep my house, their investment branch set up a killer trust fund for Megan. In thirteen years, she ought to have enough to go to any college in the country."

"College money," he said. "Not blood money. I like that. Gran would like that, too. Thank you."

He kissed her and she felt as liberated and happy as she could ever remember feeling. She'd done good, for Megan and for Misty.

She broke off the kiss before it led too far down the path of no return. "Um…about that ring?"

He threw back his head and laughed. Something she liked so much she was going to make it her goal to make him laugh more.

"The gold in the band came from the Little Poke," he told her. "My father had it made for my mother. They couldn't afford a big diamond, but Gran's second husband was very generous and pretty successful. He bought her a fancy ring she never particularly liked so after he passed away, she put the ring in the safe and forgot about it.

"When she died, she left me both rings and suggested I put the diamond in my mother's band and give it to the woman I love."

"Oh, that's so sweet."

"And prophetic, as my sister said."

Morgan shook her head. "Why? Surely your grandmother hoped you'd marry again."

"It's not that. It's her words. She wrote that the ring would be 'worthy of a princess.'"

With that he opened the box and took out the ring. Morgan had to wipe away her tears with her free hand as he slipped it on her finger. The diamond was pretty, but it was the rich luster of the wide gold band that really stole the show. She knew how much blood, sweat and tears had gone into producing it. There was no ring like it in the world. And he was giving it to her.

"I'm not a princess, Mac."

"You are to me. And Megan. Will you marry us, Morgan?"

"Yes," she answered. What else she could say? After the strange and convoluted efforts of Fate, Misty, Bella, Gran—whoever had brought the two of them together—how could she say no?

"Yes. Forever, yes."

The little blue lights on the monitor cascaded and fell like a tiny explosion of pyrotechnics. She had no idea why. It wasn't as if Megan or Bella could hear them.

But somewhere, somehow, the people who loved them were celebrating. Of that she was certain.

* * * * *

Don't miss the next book in Debra Salonen's series
SPOTLIGHT ON SENTINEL PASS!
*Coming in September 2009 from
Harlequin Superromance.*

In honor of our 60th anniversary,
Harlequin® American Romance® is celebrating
by featuring an all-American male each month,
all year long with
MEN MADE IN AMERICA!
This June, we'll be featuring American men living
in the West.

Here's a sneak preview of
THE CHIEF RANGER by Rebecca Winters.

Chief Ranger Vance Rossiter has to confront the sister
of a man who died while under Vance's watch...
and also confront his attraction to her.

"Chief Ranger Rossiter?" The sight of the woman who'd stepped inside Vance's office brought him to his feet. "I'm Rachel Darrow. Your secretary said I should come right in."

"Please," he said, walking around his desk to shake her hand. At a glance he estimated she was in her midtwenties. Her feminine curves did wonders for the pale blue T-shirt and jeans she was wearing. "Ranger Jarvis informed me there's a young boy with you."

The unfriendly expression in her beautiful green eyes caught him off guard. "Yes," was her clipped reply. "When we arrived in Yosemite the ranger told me I couldn't go anywhere in the park until I talked to you first."

"That's right."

"Knowing you wanted this meeting to be private, he offered to show my nephew around Headquarters."

So this woman was the victim's sister…. "What's his name?"

"Nicky."

The boy who haunted Vance's dreams now had a name. "How old is he?"

"He turned six three weeks ago. Were you the man in charge when my brother and sister-in-law were killed?"

"Yes. To tell you I'm sorry for what happened couldn't begin to convey my feelings."

The woman's gaze didn't flicker. "I won't even try to describe mine. Just tell me one thing. Was their accident preventable?"

"Yes," he answered without hesitation.

"In other words, the people working under you fell asleep on your watch and two lives were snuffed out as a result."

Hearing it put like that, he had to set the record straight. "My staff had nothing to do with it. I, myself, could have prevented the loss of life."

Ms. Darrow's expression hardened. "So you admit culpability."

"Yes. I take full blame."

A look of pain crossed over her features. "You can just stand there and admit it?" Her cry echoed that of his own tortured soul.

"Yes." He sucked in his breath.

"I work for a cruise line. Aboard ship, it's the captain's responsibility to maintain rigid safety regulations. If a disaster like that had happened while he was in charge he would have been relieved of his command and never given another ship again."

Rachel Darrow couldn't know she was preaching to the converted. "If you've come to the park with the intention of bringing a lawsuit against me for negligence, maybe you should." It would only be what he deserved.

"Maybe I will."

In the next instant, she wheeled around and hurried out of his office. Vance could have gone after her, but it would cause a scene, something he was loath to do for a variety of reasons. In the first place, he needed to cool down before he approached her again.

The discovery of the Darrows' frozen bodies had affected every ranger in the park. A little boy had been orphaned—a boy whose aunt was all he had left.

* * * * *

*Will Rachel allow Vance to explain—
and will she let him into her heart?
Find out in
THE CHIEF RANGER.
Available June 2009 from
Harlequin® American Romance®.*

HARLEQUIN

60

YEARS

of pure reading pleasure

We'll be spotlighting a different series every month throughout 2009 to celebrate our 60th anniversary.

Look for Harlequin® American Romance® in June!

Join us for a year-long celebration of the rugged American male! From cops to cowboys— Men Made in America has the hero you've been dreaming about!

MEN
Made in America

American ★ Romance

Look for

The Chief Ranger

by Rebecca Winters, on sale in June!

Escape Around the World

Dream destinations, whirlwind weddings!

Honeymoon with the Boss

by

JESSICA HART

Top tycoon Tom Maddison is used to calling the shots—until his convenient marriage falls through. But rather than waste his honeymoon, he'll take his boardroom to the beach and bring his oh-so-sensible secretary Imogen on a tropical business trip! But will Tom finally see the sexy woman that prudent Imogen truly is?

Available in June wherever books are sold.

REQUEST YOUR FREE BOOKS!

2 FREE NOVELS PLUS 2 FREE GIFTS!

HARLEQUIN®

Super Romance®

Exciting, emotional, unexpected!

YES! Please send me 2 FREE Harlequin® Superromance® novels and my 2 FREE gifts (gifts are worth about $10). After receiving them, if I don't wish to receive any more books, I can return the shipping statement marked "cancel." If I don't cancel, I will receive 6 brand-new novels every month and be billed just $4.69 per book in the U.S. or $5.24 per book in Canada. That's a savings of close to 15% off the cover price! It's quite a bargain! Shipping and handling is just 50¢ per book*. I understand that accepting the 2 free books and gifts places me under no obligation to buy anything. I can always return a shipment and cancel at any time. Even if I never buy another book from Harlequin, the two free books and gifts are mine to keep forever.

135 HDN EYLG   336 HDN EYLS

Name	(PLEASE PRINT)	
Address		Apt. #
City	State/Prov.	Zip/Postal Code

Signature (if under 18, a parent or guardian must sign)

Mail to the **Harlequin Reader Service:**
IN U.S.A.: P.O. Box 1867, Buffalo, NY 14240-1867
IN CANADA: P.O. Box 609, Fort Erie, Ontario L2A 5X3

Not valid to current subscribers of Harlequin Superromance books.

**Are you a current subscriber of Harlequin Superromance books
and want to receive the larger-print edition?
Call 1-800-873-8635 today!**

* Terms and prices subject to change without notice. Prices do not include applicable taxes. Sales tax applicable in N.Y. Canadian residents will be charged applicable provincial taxes and GST. Offer not valid in Quebec. This offer is limited to one order per household. All orders subject to approval. Credit or debit balances in a customer's account(s) may be offset by any other outstanding balance owed by or to the customer. Please allow 4 to 6 weeks for delivery. Offer available while quantities last.

Your Privacy: Harlequin is committed to protecting your privacy. Our Privacy Policy is available online at www.eHarlequin.com or upon request from the Reader Service. From time to time we make our lists of customers available to reputable third parties who may have a product or service of interest to you. If you would prefer we not share your name and address, please check here. ☐

HSR09R

HARLEQUIN®

Super Romance®

COMING NEXT MONTH

Available June 9, 2009

#1566 A SMALL-TOWN HOMECOMING • Terry McLaughlin
Built to Last

The return of architect Tess Roussel to her hometown has put her on a collision course with John Jameson Quinn. The contractor has her reeling…his scandalous past overshadows everything. Tess wants to believe that the contractor is deserving of her professional admiration and her trust, but her love, too?

#1567 A HOLIDAY ROMANCE • Carrie Alexander

A summer holiday in the desert? What had Alice Potter been thinking? If it wasn't for resort manager Kyle Jarreau, her dream vacation would be a nightmare. But can they keep their fling a secret…? For Kyle's sake, they *have* to.

#1568 FROM FRIEND TO FATHER • Tracy Wolff

Reece Sandler never planned to raise his daughter with Sarah Martin. They were only friends when she agreed to be his surrogate. Now things have changed and they have to be parents—together. Fine. Easy. But only if Reece can control his attraction to Sarah.

#1569 BEST FOR THE BABY • Ann Evans
9 Months Later

Pregnant and alone, Alaina Tillman returns to Lake Harmony and Zack Davidson, her girlhood love. Yet as attracted as she is to him, life isn't just about the two of them anymore. She has to do what's best for her baby. Does that mean letting Zack in—or pushing him away?

#1570 NO ORDINARY COWBOY• Mary Sullivan
Home on the Ranch

A ranch is so not Amy Graves's scene. Still, she promised to help, so here she is. Funny thing is she starts to feel at home. And even funnier, she starts to fall for a cowboy—Hank Shelter. As she soon discovers, however, there's nothing ordinary about him.

#1571 ALL THAT LOVE IS • Ginger Chambers
Everlasting Love

Jillian Davis was prepared to walk away from her marriage. But when her husband, Brad, takes her on a shortcut, an accident nearly kills them. Now, with the SUV as their fragile shelter, Jillian's only hope lies with the man she was ready to leave behind forever….